SCREAM VENGEANCE

CHET CUNNINGHAM

Scream Vengeance
Paperback Edition

Dark Wolf Books
An Imprint of Wolfpack Publishing
701 S. Howard Ave. 106-324
Tampa, FL 33609

www.darkwolfbooks.com

Paperback ISBN 979-8-89567-616-5
eBook ISBN 979-8-89567-615-8

SCREAM VENGEANCE

1

DETECTIVE STACY DEFRAIN shook her head in anger and disbelief. A chilling wave swept over her as she stared at the lifeless body.

"This is totally weird," she said "It could have been a suicide if her hands weren't tied behind her back and her ankles not tied together with panty hose." Stacy was five ten, slender, with short brown hair, a tipped up nose, and flashing blue eyes. She wore tan slacks and a brown blouse with a matching jacket.

Three members of Detective Team One from San Diego PD Central had shot out of the building when they got the call at 9:18 a.m. A report had come from 911 that a woman was dead hanging from her kitchen ceiling fan in a house in the Linda Vista section of town. She was leaning over at a forty five degree angle held there by panty hose tied in a noose around her neck.

Team One Sergeant Cain Baker had taken it in the instant they stepped into the kitchen. The woman was fully clothed with shoes, green slacks, and a yellow blouse. A pair of panty hose had one half looped around the woman's neck in a noose and the other half tied to the motor of the ceiling fan above the blades.

"Somebody rigged this when the woman was standing under the fan," Sergeant Baker said. "Then she either fell or was pushed so the noose came tight and strangled her. She couldn't get back on her feet or someone prevented her from doing so." Cain scowled. He was thirty two and had been a cop for nine years but had never seen anything like this. He was six feet tall, well muscled, and kept trim and fit at 190 pounds.

"Wouldn't it take some time to strangle?" asked Detective Kevin Kirkpatrick. He was the newest team member, had a short compact body, a former boxer with a face formed and reformed by right crosses and left jabs. His eyes were dark green with flinty chips of brown.

"Depending how much of her air was cut off, it could take three to ten minutes." Sgt Baler said. "She'd pass out first then slowly strangle to death. Not a pretty picture."

Stacy looked at her small notebook. "Nine eleven said a neighbor next door called. She said one of the little daughters woke up and came into the kitchen about nine o'clock and found her mother this way. She's only seven. She ran next door to her friend. When Mrs. McLoughlin hurried over she found the six year old girl sitting at the kitchen table eating cereal and staring at her mother."

"Kevin, send uniforms both ways on both sides of the street asking what they saw or heard late last night or early this morning. Somebody must have heard something. A car starting or a dog barking. Anything." Kevin nodded and marched out the kitchen door.

Lieutenant Larry Anderson, SDPD's crime lab boss, slid into the kitchen past Stacy. He was six five, basketball at SDSU, but not good enough for the pros. He wore his usual light blue coveralls uniform. "They said it was strange. You hear about the little six year old eating cereal?" They said they had. "Well, about time I and my crew get to work. I'll bring in the photog first to get it on record."

Stacy and Cain took the hint and went back outside. The house was maybe fifty years old, in an established neighborhood in a not too moneyed section of cheaper tract homes. It needed a new coat of brown paint. The houses were not in as good repair as the better middle class sections of town. The lawns not as well kept up and few with sprinkler systems or lawn care help.

Stacy frowned making ridges on her forehead. "I just realized what was missing in the kitchen. There was no smell of death. No blood smell, no death smell,"

"You're repeating yourself, Stacy. But you're right. It is just a kitchen. Not even many food smells."

Stacy shook her head and grinned. "Now I know what it was. Cinnamon. There's a chance there is a fresh batch of cinnamon rolls in that kitchen. We can look later."

They stared at each other for a minute. Then Stacy looked at her notebook again.

"We have an ID on the woman from Mrs. McLoughlin, the next door neighbor," Stacy said. She had talked to her on the phone during the drive. "The vic is Judith Landcaster, about 28. Two daughters are

Jane and Susan. She said Judith was quiet and no trouble. Her kids went to a neighbor's house after school and summers her mother came and stayed with them. She said Judith told her that from time to time she had trouble paying her bills. She's a single mother. Divorced about four years ago. She got the house and he got the car. The house needs a new roof but Judith said she couldn't afford it."

A half dozen black and whites and unmarked police cars cluttered the curb. Cain saw the uniforms talking to people up and down the street.

He looked back at Stacy, the best interviewer on his team. "So, somebody ties up the victim under the fan, binds the noose around her throat, and the other end to the fan. Whoever did that had to be tall enough or stood on a chair."

"We should check for signs of forced entry," Stacy said. "I'll take the side windows and the back door." Cain checked the front door then the three front windows. No sign of any glass broken or windows jimmied.

Stacy came back shaking her head. "All clean," she said.

"Who was the first officer on the scene?" Cain asked.

Stacy found him and brought him back to Cain.

"I'm officer Mandel, Sergeant. Like I told the lieutenant, I got the call. This is my regular beat so I knew the street. I came in with my siren on, woke up the late sleepers, and found half a dozen civilians already on the front lawn. I shooed them home and took a look inside with the neighbor who called. Then I protected the scene and checked the doors and windows. No sign of forced entry I could see. About five minutes later three more units and Field Lieutenant Cox came."

"Thanks, Mandel put it in your report," Cain said. He turned to Stacy. "So far we've got zilch. Somebody came in the night. The woman was still dressed so it probably was before midnight. Kids sleeping. The victim must have known the killer and let that person into the house. Then quietly, without waking up the kids, the killer tied up the woman strung her up and pushed her over, strangling her."

"My bet is we have no fingerprints other than those of the residents," Stacy said.

Lt. Anderson came out shaking his head.

"This is getting stranger and stranger. We found residue on her lips and cheeks. She'd had tape put over her mouth, which kept things quiet. We went over the kitchen with a monster magnifier and couldn't find a thing not supposed to be there. No fibers, no dirt off a shoe, no prints. We don't even know who owned the panty hose. We checked in the woman's dresser and she evidently didn't wear them. Had one pair of knee highs and mostly panties."

"So you save the panty hose."

"We cut her down. The Assistant ME is in there now. He said he found no obvious wounds or bruises. Cain, I'm not going to be much help to you on this one."

"You'll find something," Cain said. "You always do. Maybe the panty hose will lead us somewhere."

Detective Kevin Kirkpatrick came up with a report on his uniform's survey.

"Damn near nothing, boss. One guy heard a car start up about two a.m. and drive away slowly. He was out watering his lawn at night so the sun wouldn't evaporate half of the water. He said the car was up four or five houses from him and went away from him, so he couldn't see the make, model or the color. He figured it was about two a.m. He got home from work at one, had a sandwich, and then went out to water. Said he had to keep down his damn water bill."

"That's it?" Cain asked.

"Yeah. One guy bitched about a neighbor next to him who rides his motorcycle in at three a.m. every day from his job and tries to make all the noise he can. I told him to file a complaint."

Stacy lifted her brows. "Hey, let me check for oil or tranny drips on the street. Might be something." She went out to the street, had two black and whites and a blue pastel moved, and then did a slow survey on the black top where a car might have been left by the killer when he went inside. Nothing new. In this neighborhood of many older cars there were drips galore, but none that could have been left last night. She told Cain.

"Yeah, figures." Cain stopped the AME on his way out of the house. He was new to Cain but had the little black doctor's bag they all carried.

"Hey Doc, any preliminary for us?"

The man stopped and looked up. He was a head shorter than Cain, took off his glasses, and rubbed his eyes. "Too damn early for me. I was on shift until two a.m. this morning. On this one, you guessed it. Preliminary is death by strangulation and it wasn't quick. The way the fabric was pressing against the windpipe I'd guess it took about fifteen minutes."

Cain frowned. "How much of that time would she have been unconscious?"

"A guess, but maybe ten minutes. You'll get a copy

of the autopsy report. The Lieutenant said we had to have it before two o'clock. Don't know what the damn rush is." He put on his glasses, walked out to a black sedan with San Diego County Medical Examiner emblem on the door, and drove away.

"What about the kids?" Stacy asked.

"Mrs. McLoughlin has them right now. She said she'll call their grandmother to come and get them."

"Okay, let's get to work. We need to interview in depth the neighbors who knew Mrs. Landcaster. If she has a best friend, where she worked, what she was like, boyfriends, etc. You know the routine. Stacy, you take Mrs. McLoughlin next door. I'll get the neighbor on the other side. Kevin, you work the two directly across the street. We're looking for anything and everything. Both of you have your tape recorders. Use them. We've got to find a starting place."

The detectives spent an hour with each of the neighbors, digging into what they knew, had heard, suspected, or wondered about Judith Landcaster. They met at eleven o'clock at the unmarked and headed back to the office.

"I didn't get much," Stacy said. "Money was short so that made a big impact. They almost never went out to eat. They had only the basic cable TV to cut the cost. No air conditioning. They used fans. Things like that. Definitely no boy friends. She didn't think Judith was a church person."

Once back in central in the Team One Room, they compared notes and recordings and came up with a composite.

Judith Ann Landcaster:

Age: 28
Work: Secretary at A&M Placement, a service that supplies nurses to jobs worldwide.
No church affiliation.
Daughters, Jane, 7 and Susan 6.
Divorced three years ago.
She got the house, he got the car. He's now out of state.
No men friends. Doesn't date.
About 5 feet 8 inches and l40 pounds.
Making payments on house mortgage.
Drives a six year old Honda.
Kids both in public school.
No wants or warrants, one traffic ticket.
Her parents live in suburban La Mesa.
No last will and testament. Was going to do one, didn't.
No forced entry into house.
Killer must have known Judith and was admitted.
No hobbies.
Went to High School in town.
Had a year at San Diego State pre-divorce. None since.
Her children were her whole life.

Stacy printed out the list in 24 point bold type and put it on their six by eight foot tack board.

The three stood and eyed the list.

"Now there is one of the driest holes I've ever seen," Cain said. "Not a single thing to hang our investigation on. No suspect, no potential suspects, no goddamn nothing."

"I'll call photography and get a death scene 8 x 10 to put up on the board," Stacy said.

"Anybody get her phone number?" Kevin asked.

"I'll check the SBC and get her phone records. Could be something there.'"

"I got her number from the neighbor," Cain said. "It's 858-417-3353."

"I'm on it," Kevin said and reached for his phone.

There were five desks in the Team One Room. Each had a four drawer gun metal filing cabinet, a metal desk, a chair, and the usual office stuff on top. Each had a lock drawer in the desk and the files could be locked as well. They seldom were. Fluorescents overhead bathed the twenty by twenty foot room in soft, bright light. Sergeant Baker's desk sat near the door a little apart from the others. He was the boss of the team and never worried about getting his hands dirty in the action. He slumped in his swivel chair and stared across the room at the list.

"We've got nothing," he said. He automatically rubbed his right knee. It had been bothering him since the last marathon and he was worried about getting in shape for the next one three months away. He should be doing at least five miles a day by now.

"I better go tell the Lieutenant. He's gonna be pissed."

Lt. Hopkins was the boss of Detective Teams One and Two out of Central. He seldom went into the field.

Before he left his desk, Cain's phone rang. He picked up.

"Cain here."

"Hey, we found some residual material on her cheeks that came from tape. We've been able to identify it. It's an unusual type of black tape that is most often used by computer repairmen and jewelers. I don't know if that helps any, but we have enough to ID it down to a specific roll if you find anything we can compare it to. Oh, this is Anderson."

"Know that pleasing voice of yours, Lieutenant. Thanks for that tidbit. We'll put it up on our evidence board."

He stood and was about to go out. "Oh, Stacy, see if you can track down the woman's mother and set up an appointment for an interview with her as soon as possible. Like this afternoon. Mrs. McLoughlin might know her number."

"I'm on it," Stacy said. "As soon as the lab guys are done out there, I want to go back and check out the refrigerator door for posted notes and any telephone books, or pads or letters that she might have left. I didn't notice a computer but she probably has one in her bedroom. Might be something there."

"Do it," Cain said. walked out the door, and down the hall toward Lt. Hopkin's office. He wasn't going to enjoy this visit.

2

TWYLA FARNHAM LIFTED her long eye lashes and stared hard at the girl on the witness stand. It was Superior Court in and for the City and County of San Diego, state of California. The charges against her client were assault and battery, and she was surprised the DA brought it to court. They had zilch. Now the victim of the assault was on the stand breaking down little by little. It was cross examination time.

"Miss Marston, you have just detailed a long relationship with the accused on a hand holding best friends basis," Twyla said. "There was no sex involved. Is that correct?"

"Yes, Walt was a good friend, until that night."

"Did you go with him voluntarily to the park?"

"Yes, we'd been there several times before after dark. I didn't think anything about it."

"That night, when you went to the park with Walt, were you a virgin?"

"What? I won't answer that." She turned to the judge. "Your honor do I have to...."

Judge Harriet Landowner simply frowned at the witness and nodded.

June Marston wilted a little. "Well, technically I guess I wasn't. But it was just one time and I was thirteen, and..."

"So you went to the park knowing very well that you would be vulnerable to sexual advances?"

"Yes, I guess."

"You guess."

June scowled, shook her head and ran her fingers through her long hair. "Yes, I knew he might try. I'd put him off before."

"Did you tell your best girl friend, Phyllis that same day that you were ready to have a hot sexy time in the park?"

"No, of course not. I never said anything...."

"Miss Marston, remember you're under oath. This is a court of law, not some little girl chit chat gossip club. Now, think about it. Didn't you tell Phyllis you hoped that you could get laid in the park that night?"

"He hit me, he scratched me, he pushed me down, and he tried to rape me."

"How hard did he try, Miss Marston? Isn't it true that you unbuttoned the fasteners on your blouse before he even touched you?"

"No. Well," she looked over at the judge. "Well, maybe a few buttons."

"Isn't it true that you took off your blouse and he was looking around scared somebody would see?"

"Well....maybe. He didn't seem worked up when I kissed him before that."

"How many times did you kiss him, Miss Marston?"

"Six or seven times."

"Was it more like fifteen or twenty times?"

"Oh, yes. All right. Maybe twenty."

"Miss Marston, isn't it true that the accused never hit you? That he did not assault and batter you? That in fact you were the aggressor and that you actually seduced him?"

"No." She shouted the word and turned red in the face and began to rock back and forth on the stand. She looked over at the judge who simply stared back at her.

"Isn't it true, Miss Marston that you had experienced sexual intercourse with several boys before that night in the park with Wade?"

June twisted on the stand. The rocking motion stopped and she looked over at the judge. The judge nodded at her.

"I guess that's right, two or three at least, but it wasn't all my idea. You know how insistent a fifteen year old boy with a boner can be."

A ripple of laughter slanted through the dozen spectators in the court room.

The judge rapped her gavel. "I'll have quiet in the court or the bailiff will remove everyone." .

"When did your last period end, Miss Marston?" Twyla asked.

"Judge, isn't that kind of private? I mean..."

"Answer the question, Miss Marston."

"Over two months ago."

"So you figure that you're pregnant?"

"I never miss my period. Regular as clockwork. Until last month."

"So you thought you were pregnant and you hadn't told your mother. Did you seduce Walt and then bring these assault and battery charges so it would come out that he also raped you?"

"I....I didn't know what to do. I needed a good excuse to tell my mother when I started to show."

"So you planned this in advance, and then told your mother he tried to rape you and hit you and pushed you down in the grass, and she filed the complaint against Walt."

"No, no, no." June stared hard at Twila. "Damn you lawyer. Damn you."

"Miss Marston, we'll have none of that street language in my court. Apologize to Miss Farnham."

"No. Hell no."

"Miss Marston, I'll ask you once more. Didn't you seduce the accused because you were afraid you were pregnant and wanted an excuse?"

Tears seeped from her eyes. June Marston wailed and tore at her hair with her hands. Then she calmed and looked at Twyla Farnham.

"Yes, I did, you fucking bitch. I hope you rot in hell."

The judge cleared her throat. "That will be enough from you Miss Marston. Not another word." She turned to Twyla. "Miss Farnham, do you wish to make a motion to the court?"

"I do your honor. I move that the charges against my client, Walt Windon, be dropped in light of the testimony just recorded."

"Motion granted the accused is free to go. Miss Marston, you will be charged with perjury, and with contempt of court. For the later you will spend the next ten days in Juvenile Hall and your parents will pay the tab. The district attorney will inform you of what other charges will be leveled against you. Next case."

TWYLA GOT a quick hug from her client, Walt, and he rushed to hug his parents. She closed her briefcase and went out through the almost empty court room to the hall. She was pleased with the outcome of the trial. It had lasted only two days. She had been prepared to bring witnesses who would swear that Walt had been a virgin up to that night in the park. She smiled grimly as she almost danced out the front door and to the parking lot. She had worn her second best "trial" uniform, a sleek all wool Italian made blue suit that had cost her over four hundred dollars. The skirt was modestly cut to the knee and the tailoring was perfect. Only one piece of jewelry adorned it. A small letter T on the left side encrusted with small diamonds.

Her blue eyes sparkled as she remembered the look on the Judge's face when June broke down. Marvelous. She backed her black Lexus from the parking lot, wheeled onto Clairemont Mesa Boulevard to the south ramp on Freeway Fifteen, and raced downtown. She should get to the new Thompson Towers and the offices of Branston, Knox and Tretter well before closing time. She would report her small coup to her boss, Alex Tretter and get back on the heavyweight case they had coming up in a week. It was a socialite murder trial that would be messy, expensive, long running, and make headlines. She would sit in as second chair to Alex.

After two years at this primarily criminal defense firm, she had earned her spurs, and had solid assurances that she would be around a long time. Because she was good. She had won recognition and one promotion and had slept with only one of her bosses, but not Alex.

About five thirty she closed up her desk and her computer and eased the new Lexus into downtown San Diego traffic. She felt like a small celebration, but didn't have the nerve to ask Alex to enjoy it with her. She went to Outlander Steaks, her favorite restaurant. She had a thick, half pound steak with a delicious bourbon sauce, three side dishes, along with a glass of wine. She saw no one she knew at the expensive restaurant. She paid with plastic and then headed out Freeway Fifteen north toward Mission Valley. She loved driving her new Lexus and the traffic was interesting, not mind boggling or totally stalled. She turned off on Friar's Road to her street and into the gated complex where she had a new condominium. She slid into her numbered underground parking slot and beeped the car locked. There were only twelve lawyers in the firm, but they had a good reputation for winning the tough cases. Two of the younger lawyers had come on to her, but she had frozen them solid before they could get warmed up. One called her the ice princess, and he was right. She could turn cold, secretive, and withdrawn in a second if it helped her cause.

Her condo was only six months old and nestled in one of the best spots in Mission Valley along the San Diego River, where the traffic noise was hushed with plantings, architecture, and where 7-24 guards on the gate knew all eighty-seven residents by their name and license numbers.

She had bought the two bedroom because she could afford it, and because it was better for entertaining. Also this one had a better view than most.

For just a moment she thought about last night. Then she relaxed and looked at her computer. She would put nothing in writing or on paper. She had an excellent memory, and a long one. Now was the time when certain elements were coming together and she would take advantage of them.

She stripped off her suit, brushed it and hung it carefully in the large walk in closet. It fit neatly in the rack where her other suits were situated. She rotated six regular day suits, wearing a different one each day. On court days she went to her trial suits, three that she kept only for those days. She bought two new regular suits each year and discarded the oldest two.

She finished undressing and turned on the shower. It was a morning and nightly ritual. She couldn't afford to be at anything but her best in every way at the office. She didn't bother looking at her naked body. She knew it well enough. At five ten and a hundred and thirty pounds, she was trim, sleek, and with good breasts. Men forever would ogle, stare, and grin at big breasts. She couldn't figure it out, but she didn't have to. She just enjoyed it. She watched carefully what she ate, and had a strict exercise routine that included running and two aerobic tapes she played on her TV.

After the shower she slipped into bed and pulled up the one sheet. It was a San Diego summer, with the night time temperature falling all the way to 64. The automatic wake up alarm would sound at precisely 6:30, giving her time to shower, put on her make up, have a quick breakfast of orange juice, mixed fruit, coffee, and be in her chair in the office at 7:45.

Twyla never watched local TV news shows. They were so truncated and distorted. She did skim the San

Diego Union-Tribune morning paper. She devoured the business section and any crime news. The paper would be full of it in the morning. It would be interesting to see how they handled it.

Twyla yawned, spent ten minutes in her resting position, then turned on her side, slipped one hand under her pillow in her sleeping pose and went to sleep within thirty seconds.

At her office the next morning, Twyla opened the paper and read the banner headline.

"Bizarre Killer Strikes Single Mom." Then a subhead: "Six year old eats cereal at breakfast table looking at her dead mother who was murdered by strangulation and hung from the kitchen ceiling fan."

Twyla could almost picture it. "Now that's my kind of a tough little kid." She read the rest of the story, nodded, then moved to the local police blotter type crime update but found nothing interesting. She finished the business section then went to see her boss. He should be in by now. Twyla let a thin smile touch her face. She always felt a surge of anticipation when working on an important new murder case and she knew that she was right in the middle of one.

3

DETECTIVE STACY DEFRAIN got an okay to go back to the Judith Landcaster crime scene late that afternoon after the crime lab had worked over the whole house and attached garage. She started in the kitchen on the refrigerator door. Often it's the center of a woman's universe, with appointments, favorite recipes, specials at the grocery store, and notes from the kid's teachers. She found many of these on the light brown door including one note that fascinated her.

"THE CLUB, yes! Wednesday at eight."

She took a digital photo of the refrigerator door with this note in the center, took down the note, put it in an evidence envelope, and into her purse beside her Glock pistol. THE CLUB, capitalized. That could be a hundred different groups. One stuck out in her mind, "THE CLUB," a small bar with a miniature stage and a ten person dance floor snuggled just off the beach sand at OB. That was Ocean Beach a section of San Diego with plenty of beach front and beach bums. Was that the spot the note was talking about?"

She worked over the rest of the kitchen. Found the usual cook books, dishes, pots and pans, and a small pantry section with enough food for her and the girls for a week. She moved to the living room, but found nothing except a half dozen kid games and magazines. One copy of Redbook Magazine and three days worth of newspapers. She moved to the bedroom and saw a small desk against one wall with a computer and four or five loose leaf notebooks standing on top of the desk facing the wall. They had labels. "Kids medical records," "Household Budget," "Top Survey Outfits That Pay". The last one was a record of child support payments and alimony.

She checked the last notebook first. It had a sheet of ledger paper with only three entries. Two were from three years ago, one from two years ago. Total payments $425. No payments for the past two years.

She checked the drawers. Found Judith Landcaster's checkbook. She put that aside to study later. Nothing else in the desk was helpful. The drawers were mostly empty. She found one file folder marked "Surveys." Evidently she was doing computer surveys for firms that paid her. She showed only two surveys so far and was paid ten dollars for each.

Stacy looked at the computer. She turned it on and six icons came up. She punched up Microsoft Word. It came on the screen with a fill in on the password that it had been filed and was on record. The file tag on the line produced a list of nine most recent files used. Two were marked Surveys, one was letters, and the next was "The Club". She frowned and pulled up the file.

It was a download from The Club's website and

showed the hours, location, services, and the one or two person acts that would be on the tiny stage for the current month.

Stacy saw that the printer was already turned on when the computer came on, so she printed out The Club page.

She went to the hard disk button and the alphabetical listing of files came up. She scrolled down quickly and figured there must be more than a hundred files. She checked at random but saw nothing of interest that would tell her who Judith might have known or who might have killed her.

She looked around the desk. Near the back she found a box with a dozen or so CD-Rom discs. They had labels on them. She read the first one. "Charlie and Linda get Cozy." Sounded sexy. She looked at the next one. "27 Most Popular Sexual Positions." There are twenty seven? Stacy asked herself. She worked through the box and found all but two of the CDs were of suggestive sexual encounters. She pushed the one of twenty seven positions into the CD-Rom slot and it came up in living color and total nudity. The man was young and black. The woman was Latin, slender, and with big breasts. They smiled at the camera then moved into the #1 position with over lettering that said: "The classic missionary position." She stared for a moment. She had never seen any porn movies or CDs. She felt a flash of desire then pushed it down.

Stacy turned off the screen, popped the CD-Rom out, and put it back in its sleeve. Judith had no boyfriends the neighbor had said. Judith didn't need any. What a batch of porn. But what about THE

CLULB? She had the address. She put the box of porn CD-ROMs and the print out page on THE CLUB on the kitchen table and kept searching. The dead woman's clothes still hung in the closet. In the pocket of one cheap suit jacket Stacy found two book matches. One was from THE CLUB. She put them in her purse, picked up the box of porn and headed back to the office in Central.

Nobody was in when she walked into the Team One Room. Just the tack board with the list of everything they knew about the dead woman, Judith. Not quite all they knew now. She called Cain on his cell. He picked up on the second ring.

"Yeah, Cain."

"Boss, you are not going to believe what I found."

"So don't make me try."

She told him about the porn and the tie to THE CLUB. "Seems that our miss purity must have a wild side. Wonder where the kids were when she was out drinking it up at THE CLUB?"

"Probably at Mom's place. She lives just half a mile down the street."

"I haven't been able to set up an interview with her yet," Tracy said. "Tonight I'm going to check out THE CLUB. It's out in OB if you can believe."

"Pay for your own drinks, lady. And don't get sloshed. You don't get overtime for this."

"I know, I know. They won't get warmed up out there until about ten tonight. Maybe until then I'll just watch some porn on our VCR."

"Lock that up in your desk drawer. I'll review it tomorrow."

"Watch the Twenty Seven Positions, Sarge. It could be a learning experience.'

"Not for me. I've seen the Japanese one hundred and fourteen sexual positions illustrated brochure. See you tomorrow."

On every autopsy there is a detective assigned to it who is working the case. It is not favorite duty. This time Kevin had sat in while the doctors did their work. He had brought back a copy of the report and put it on Cain's desk. Stacy saw it there in the familiar envelope and took a look. It didn't say much. The cause of death was cerebral hypoxia due to compression of the carotid arteries by ligature strangulation. Her brain was starved for oxygen due to the carotid arteries that fed it being shut down. So did she die from hypoxia or did she suffocate when her air supply was slowly cut off? Stacy would ask someone.

She read the rest of the report and found that there were no wounds or bruises on the body and that there was semen present in the victim's body probably the result of intercourse within two or three hours before she was killed. There were no signs of vaginal bruising or bleeding so there was probably no rape involved.

Interesting. She went over the autopsy report again, but that was the most surprising part of it. Miss purity wasn't so pure after all even if her neighbors thought so.

THE CLUB. Wednesday at eight. Maybe she went there every Wednesday. Maybe she had a call to meet someone there Wednesday at eight. She had been killed late Wednesday night or early Thursday a.m. Which didn't matter a lot. Judith could even have been a regular on Wednesday nights. Leave the girls at Mother's and go to the "meeting" she had that night. It would work and no one would know exactly what she was doing. She could tell good old Mom that it was a club support group for single mothers. That would do nicely.

Stacy went over the list of what they did know about Judith Landcaster. THE CLLUB would fit in well. Somebody brought her home, had sex with her and then strung her up to die slowly. But why? Why would a man kill a woman if he was having sex with her? Why? Dozens of reasons. All they needed was one.

She checked her watch. Almost seven thirty. She would fire up her two year old Nissan Sentra and go down and grab a fish sandwich at the Crestwood Café on Beacon Street. It was a cop hangout and not overpriced. Then she'd wander out to OB. By the address it couldn't be more than a block off the surf line. She had worn her light brown suit today with the white blouse. She grabbed an orange scarf from her desk drawer and looped it around her neck with one twist. It would give her a little less business look.

AFTER THE SANDWICH AND COFFEE, she headed out I-8 and followed it toward the beach. It's also called Mission Valley Freeway at that point. That changes into Ocean Beach Freeway for a couple of miles where I-8 officially ends and the roadway becomes Sunset Cliffs Boulevard leading directly into the San Diego community of Ocean Beach, or OB as the natives call it. Plenty of sun, sand, surf, thousands of beach bums, bikinis, and yards of bronze summer time flesh.

She found the address just a block off Sunset Cliffs

in a former restaurant that went broke and was reopened as a bar/club/nightspot under the same liquor license. It was doing a booming business. A cracked surfboard and a one man kayak had been fastened to the outside over the door. Beside the outer wall was a planter filled with sand and all sorts of sea shells, fake crabs and lobsters, and a pair of old fishing poles with line and reels. Stacy pushed in the door and heard a soft fog horn blow announcing her entrance. A dozen people looked up. Some waved.

Even at eight o'clock there were plenty of customers. The two man band on the small stage was twanging out Western songs and a few line dancers were trying to wedge onto the small dance floor. Tables around the floor had been pushed back to make more room for the line.

Stacy moved to the bar and ordered a white wine and sipped it watching the action. It looked like a prime pickup spot for singles or marrieds. Two men in their thirties came up to her within the first five minutes and she felt for just a flash like a hooker, but put them down saying she was waiting for someone.

Stacy had taken a picture of Judith from her bedroom and showed it to the barkeep, who wasn't overjoyed with her one dollar tip.

"Have you seen this woman in here tonight?"

The barkeep, about 25, tanned; with wild surfer hair half bleached by the sun had broad shoulders of a paddler, looked closely, and then nodded.

"Not tonight. Brenda, that's her name. She usually shows up once a week. She's real smooth. I mean she has a line of her own to match any of these Romeos around here. She isn't a hooker, I can spot them. But

Brenda usually scores within an hour or so, then it's bye bye time."

"Was she in last night?"

"Damn right. She had two white wines before she hit on the right man. She makes up her mind in a rush."

"Can you tell me anything about the man who picked her up? Is he a regular?"

"Not really. Comes in spurts like every night for a week, then I don't see him for a month. Big guy, must be six four and, what, about two twenty. Really solid. Never get him on a short board."

"Know a name?"

"I heard her call him Bill. But about half the guys who work our bar are either Bill or Joe, so it doesn't mean a damn."

"Is this Bill here tonight?"

"Haven't seen him. If he comes it's usually about nine-thirty or so. Oh, yeah, it helps me to get to know the habits of the regulars."

"Think he'll show tonight?"

"Who knows? This is the night three or four of the guys get together for a friendly little game of black jack. You know, for a change of pace. He usually is in on the games."

"I'd like to meet Bill."

"Why, you a cop or something?"

She showed him her badge. "That's right."

"Why you bugging Bill?" He snorted. "Oh, shit. I ain't stupid. Did something happen to Brenda?"

"It did. And not a word that I'm a cop. You understand?

"Yeah, sure. How's Brenda?"

"Not too good. Her real name is Judith and right now she's stone cold dead in the county morgue."

"Oh shit. Just what we need." The barkeep shook his head. "You sure? She was just here last night laughing and putting down some of the guys. Oh double shit. She left with Bill. You think...."

"It's possible. I'll hang around a while hoping that this Bill comes in to play some blackjack with the boys. Remember, not a peep to anyone that I'm a cop."

4

SHE ORDERED another white wine and took both glasses to a back booth where she wouldn't be so obvious. She put both wines on the table and curled up in back hoping she was sending out a 'not available' signal. Then she thought about Bill. If he was that big, and strong, and tried to run, the only way she could stop him would be with a few handy nine mm rounds. Backup? She considered it. She settled for calling Cain and telling him what she had found and where she was.

"Don't you goddamn move until I get there, you hear me, girl? You stay put. If this Bill shows, don't lift a finger or a Glock. I'm about twenty minutes out. Hang tight. I'll be there. Not a single damn finger, you read me? This could be a real coup if we can land him, if he did it. I'm moving."

"Yeah boss. Not a finger."

She put the second untouched glass of white wine beside her as if someone else would be sitting there. Less than a minute later, one tall redhead with an infectious grin stopped by.

"Hi pretty lady."

She shook her head and pointed at the glass of wine.

"Uh, oh. Yeah. Okay. Maybe next time." He waved and moved on to a blonde sitting at the bar. He slid onto the stool beside her and they began talking.

Stacy tried to concentrate on the men who came in the door. She listened for the fog horn and when it sounded she looked up. She saw half a dozen men, but none of them the size the barkeep had talked about. She sipped slowly at the wine, making it last. When she checked her watch she saw with a sigh that it had been only ten minutes since Cain had talked to her.

Not a finger, she said to herself. If he came in and left, she could at least tail him outside. Maybe she could get his plate. Yeah, that could be an alternate plan.

Another unattached man walked over to her booth, saw the two glasses of wine, and didn't even stop. He turned back toward the front and she lost sight of him.

By that time she figured there were about thirty to thirty five people in the place. More men than women. The line dancers had given up, not enough room to do it right. Now and then two people would get up and do the line dance steps.

More braying of the fog horn. A couple came in, then two single men. No luck.

Another look at her watch. It had been thirty minutes. She had finished the glass of wine. Now she switched it for the full one. The empty one could still serve its purpose.

After she had waited for Cain for over forty minutes, she took out her small notebook with the spiral binding on top and wrote down what she had found at the dead woman's house. She had just about finished the second glass of wine when she looked up in time to see Cain slide into the booth across from her with a beer in hand.

"He here yet?"

She shook her head. "There's no black jack game going either. We may have a dry hole here." Stacy checked her watch. "It's only nine fifteen. The bar keep said Bill usually came in about nine thirty."

"So, I'll enjoy my beer. You've had enough wine that I didn't see you drink. If he comes we play it as cool as we can. "You talked to Judith's mother?"

"Yes. About five this afternoon. Nice little old lady about fifty. A widow. Works for the city as some kind of a clerk. Said the best thing she does is stay with the girls when Judith has to work late or goes out to her meeting. Just one, on Wednesday nights. She was still all broken up about the death. Said that Judith stopped by last night about ten as was her usual time after the meeting with the single mothers. Took the girls home and said she'd get them right to bed, even though school hasn't started. She said as far as she knew Judith had not been seeing any men. She told her mother she just didn't seem to need a man in her life any more."

The fog horn sounded like a mournful sea lion. Stacy looked up and nodded.

"I think our boy just came in with the tide. He's heading for the bar."

"Are you sure?"

"No. I'll go talk to the bar tender again. All I'll need is a nod."

"Then how do we do it? We need to talk to him first as quietly as possible. Depends where he goes.

He's getting a pitcher of beer, so he's planning on being here for a while. Now he's heading for that far table."

"Three men playing cards, looks like gin rummy or poker. He's going over there."

Stacy left the booth and walked up to the bar. The keep came and looked at her.

"Was that Bill? The one who left last night with Brenda?"

"Right. Take it easy. No trouble inside."

"Be up to Bill," she said. She left the bar and headed for the table of four card players. Cain had already moved up near the table and waited. When Stacy came up behind Bill's chair, Cain moved up to him.

"Bill, we need to talk to you outside," Cain said flipping open his leather badge holder.

"What the hell? My name is Harry. What's this all about?"

"Just stand up slowly, Harry," Stacy said from right behind him. "Slowly and turn around so we can see your hands, then come outside with us. We just want to talk to you in private. Don't make this into anything more than a conversation."

"Huh." He frowned, shrugged. "Hell, I ain't done nothing wrong. No way I'm in trouble. Hell yes, I'll talk with you two outside." He turned and looked at Stacy. "You sure you're a cop? Too pretty to be a cop."

He stood slowly, kept his hands in sight, and followed Stacy to the door. Cain was right behind him with his hand near his holstered Glock. The three men at the table sat there watching, surprise lighting their faces.

Stacy stopped outside on the sidewalk a dozen feet down from the club's door.

"Harry, what time was it when you left THE CLUB here last night with Brenda?"

"Brenda? I don't know any Brenda."

"Don't lie about it, Harry, if that's your real name," Cain said, his voice cutting like a whip. "Let me see some identification."

"Sure, why not?" He reached in his back pocket, but instead of taking out his billfold, he pushed Stacy hard to one side so she stumbled and fell to her knees. He darted away down the side walk, scattering a trio of women heading for the bar. Cain charged after him.

Harry had a twenty foot start, but he wasn't in that good of shape and when he slowed after thirty yards, Cain came up on him quickly, tackled him around the waist, slammed him to the ground, and lay on top of him.

A moment later Stacy rushed up, took out her Glock, and held it an inch away from Harry's eyes.

"You move a muscle, buster and I'll blow your fucking head off," Stacy barked.

"Yeah, yeah. Okay. Let me sit up and I'll tell you what you want to know."

Cain had pulled the cuffs off his belt and snapped them on Harry's wrists that he had jerked behind his back. Then he sat him up on the sidewalk.

"Billfold?" Cain asked.

"Left back pocket. Okay. My name is George Funnell. I'm a car salesman at Mossy Ford. I come here sometimes to meet girls. Any law against that?"

Stacy dug out his billfold and read the name off it with a pen light from her purse.

"He's George Funnell all right. He has a driver's license."

"So, what time did you leave here last night with a girl you called Brenda?" Cain asked again.

"Maybe nine fifteen. I'd talked to her before. Last night I hit it off with her and I scored in the back seat of my four year old Cadillac in the back of the parking lot."

"Then when she drove home, you followed her?" Stacy asked.

"Yeah. She said she had to pick up her kids at her mother's place about ten and then she'd get them to bed and I should knock softly on her door about eleven. We'd pick up where we left off."

Stacy held the picture of Judith so Josh could see it.

"Is this the woman you called Brenda?"

"Yeah, but she said that wasn't her real name. Just her bar hopping name."

"Do you read the papers, George?" Cain asked.

"Yeah, headlines, sports."

"This woman's name is Judith Landcaster."

George frowned in the light from the street lamp. "Judith, now that name sounds familiar."

"She was in the papers and all over the TV news this morning. She was tortured and murdered last night, George. And you were the last person to see her alive."

"Dear God, she's dead? Somebody killed her? Oh, damn, it wasn't me. Christ she was a nice lady. Had those two girls and.....I didn't do it. So help me God I didn't hurt her. She was alive when I left."

"Can you prove that, George?" Cain asked.

"Well....no, I guess I can't. But she was alive and

smiling and said she'd see me next Wednesday at THE CLUB."

Cain stood up and helped George stand. "You're under arrest George Funnell for the murder of Judith Landcaster. Stacy, read him his rights."

She did.

They took him back to where Cain had parked and locked him in the back of the unmarked sedan. It had no handles inside on the back doors.

Stacy leaned against the Ford. "Boss, somehow it just doesn't seem right. I mean we'll have the DNA on that semen that will match his, but it's all just circumstantial."

"So why did he run?"

"Maybe he owes a few thousand in child support or even a warrant for something. Two cops dropping in on a guy can scare almost anyone."

"I'll call the lieutenant and tell him what we have and see what he suggests. A night in jail won't hurt good old George." He looked at her with a frown. "You all right to drive? Hate to get you pulled over on a DUI."

"Boss, I'm fine. That little chase washed all the alcohol right out of my blood stream. Steady as a rock."

"Then get on home. You've done enough damage for one night. Hell, you just might have solved this one all by yourself."

"Maybe, maybe not. Call me when you and Hopkins decide what to do with our boy. I'll be waiting."

. . .

HE DIDN'T CALL. At her one bedroom apartment in Middletown across from Balboa Park, she put her car in her slot in front of the eight unit and walked up to the second floor. It wasn't luxurious, but it fit her needs. It was less than a mile and a half from Central and she could ride her bike to work if she wanted to. But usually there was a need for her own set of auto wheels.

She paced up and down in the small kitchen while heating a cup of coffee in the microwave. Something didn't feel right about their suspect. He was big enough to do the kill. He admitted he'd been with the dead woman in her house that night. But still something didn't.....Yeah. George Funnell was a big, strong guy. What did he know about pantyhose? Why would he use that method of killing her? Wouldn't he be more likely to strangle her, or use a knife or a club? The pantyhose just didn't wash.

She grabbed her land line phone and dialed Cain's cell phone. He picked up on the third ring.

"Yeah?"

"Boss, he didn't do it. George didn't do it. He's all wrong for a pantyhose killing. If he'd done it he would have denied even knowing her. He didn't know she was dead until we told him. No way could he have done it."

"Yeah, maybe. We're downtown waiting for the lieutenant. He's gonna have to make the decision. When old George ran I was certain we had the right man. Turns out he has three outstanding traffic tickets. Two the photo kind going through a red light. Those are three hundred and eighty dollar each. I can see why he ran. I'll let you know what the boss says tomorrow. Now get some sleep. You're gonna need it tomorrow."

"Why, we have some new leads?"

"We better get some in a rush if George doesn't work out, or we'll all be hanging by our thumbs. Good Night, Stacy."

"Right. Good luck with the boss."

They hung up and Stacy stared at the clock. Not yet ten thirty. Not sleepy. Newspaper? Game on the computer? Watch some TV? She gave up and dug out a pad of paper, a ball point pen, and sat down at the kitchen table. There had to be some clues they could work from. What? What else did the crime lab guys find? Maybe something they didn't tell them. What about the pantyhose? That was their best bet right now, and it was a long shot. Who would kill someone with pantyhose? Use them for a kind of mask, yes, but not as a killing device. Before she could stop it the idea surged into her mind and she kicked it around a dozen times. Then she nodded. The killer could be a woman. She could have pantyhose available, would know how strong they were. The death weapon was a pair of pantyhose. First thing in the morning she was going to go to the crime lab and talk them out of the pantyhose. Yes. Now she could get to bed and sleep. Suddenly she was drained. It had been a long and exciting day, one that used up tons of nervous energy. Stacy yawned and headed for her bedroom. She had to get a lead from those stretchy, strong hose.

5

TWYLA FARNHAM SWEPT dark hair away from her right ear and put the land line phone up to it.

"Yes?"

"Twyla?"

"Who is this?"

"This is Art. We went out a couple of weeks ago. I wondered if you're free to go to the Stone's Concert with me."

"The Stones. Never one of my favorites. No, Art. I don't think so."

"We were so good together the last time. I just wondered..."

"Art, I said no. I've got a whole pile of work I have to get back to or I'll be shitfaced in the morning. I'm just not interested."

"In me or the Stones?"

"In both of you. I'm sorry. I have to go." She hung up and shook her head. A one night stand and some men thought they owned you. She tried to remember Art, but nothing registered. She couldn't have been that drunk. She shrugged and went back to the large desk in her office. She had turned the second bedroom of her condo into a work space for things she brought home.

She took out her briefcase and the heavy folder marked "Natasha". It was her dream case. A prominent San Diego socialite from an illustrious family worth many millions is raped, killed, and dumped in Balboa Park. Quick and furious police work had come up with a suspect six hours after the body was discovered by an early morning jogger. Two weeks later they had enough evidence and arrested the only suspect, Trevor P. Jamison. He was 38, old money, traveled in the same social set as Natasha did, and admitted having an affair with Natasha his wife knew nothing about. The DA said they had enough hard evidence to choke a pot bellied pig, but Jamison steadfastly denied his guilt. He and Lonnie turned down a man two plea with a fifteen to thirty prison term. The state had said it would go for the death penalty.

She opened the file and stared at her client's picture. A good looking man with dark hair, van dyke beard, hard dark eyes, and his face showing the touch of a grin. He was six-two and in shape at 190 pounds. He had been a pro volley ball player for five years back ten years ago. He had large, strong hands. He was accused of strangling the woman to death, and was powerful enough to do it.

She frowned. The prosecution had so much. Somehow she and Alex, first chair, had to smash it down, to ridicule it, to de-emphasize the importance of the hard evidence. Already they had six men who would testify that Natasha was a sexual manic. She loved to be loved hard and often. She liked to be tied up, chained, went in for all sorts of costumes, sexual devices, and play acting games.

Painting her as a wild sex kitten would be easy, but to take the bite out of hard evidence the prosecution had revealed in the preliminary hearing had taken weeks of hard work. The trial had been postponed for three months so they could gather evidence and build their defense. Those three months were up and the trial was now only a week away.

Fingerprints: the prosecution claimed that the murder scene was the dead woman's condo in one of the San Diego high rises. Yes, of course, his prints were there. He had been there many times in the past six months of their affair. The prints had no date on them. They were not necessarily made the night of the killing. His car, a light blue Lincoln with his plates on it, had been seen near the scene where the body was found sometime after midnight. A night person walking his Doberman pincher along the Sixth Street path beside the park had seen it. He was a numbers nut and had memorized the plate for its interesting balance of numbers and letters: 4-BBB-444. They had brain stormed for hours trying to explain his car being in the area where the body was discovered. The best they could do had been her suggestion that Jamison was in the park dropping off clothing and blankets to some of the homeless who sleep under trees and bushes in that area. He was supposed to leave them in the afternoon but forgot. Weak, but the best they could do. They could show receipts from Goodwill and Veterans of Foreign Wars to show that he regularly donated goods to their pick up vehicles.

She dug into the other evidence, hoping that the

prosecution would make some mistakes they could capitalize on. Sloppy police work would be their war cry. Lack of continuous custody of certain evidence, leaving the door open that the specific item could have been contaminated by unauthorized persons during the lapses.

Alibi. it was weak but the best they could do. Trevor Jamison had worked late that night on a deadline situation, and his secretary/assistant, Valerie, had been with him in the office. After preparing the package for his architectural presentation the next day, he had rewarded Valerie by taking her out to a late dinner. Then he drove her home and she invited him in to see her apartment. One thing led to another and he stayed all night. It had been a quick, unintentional sexual encounter that never happened again. He had explained this to his wife and she forgave him.

The secretary/assistant was a weak link. They had worked late and had gone to dinner, but she had to be persuaded strongly to testify that he had stayed all night and could not possibly had done the murder. If she broke, they were dead in the water, and Jamison was on death row.

Twyla left the desk and looked at the mail she had dropped on the kitchen counter when she came in. It was mostly advertisements. Two letters. One her bill from SDG&E for the gas and electricity. The other had a stamp in the upper left hand corner: "Hoover High Ten Year Reunion". She frowned. It was the first she had heard of it. Ten years since she crawled out of that den of vipers. Her senior year at Hoover had been the low point of her life. She had been miserable and four or five people had been sure to keep her hurting all of her senior year.

She read the letter:

"Greetings, Grads of Ten Years ago. We made it this far. Good for us. Now we can all get together and compare waistlines and hairlines. Thursday night, on August 24, we will have our reunion at the Hyatt Regency Islandia Hotel on Quivira Road. It will be a grand banquet with a great dance by a good band right afterwards. Not formal but dress up fitting the occasion."

She wadded up the letter and threw it in her waste-basket. Then she frowned, lifted it out and smoothed it flat. She'd save it just in case. The letter brought back thousands of memories, most of them from bad to terrible.

She had been born in San Diego and grew up in the Hoover High area. Her father was a mailman and always kept his appointed rounds. Her mother had spent most of her time at the Baptist church and at the food bank they had for the poor. Twyla was an only child and had to shift for herself sometimes.

Her days at Hoover High had started out as a joy, but quickly turned into a disaster as one after another of her plans fell apart and were torpedoed by people who hated her. She had never figured out why. She wasn't brilliant. She didn't bring the GPA up or down. She didn't dress as well as most of the girls and some of them laughed at her the very first day. Then the yell leader's squad dumped her and a boy she really liked got snatched away. She didn't date much and froze up when she tried to talk to boys. Her own damn fault. She had learned but way after high school. One teacher had continually embarrassed her just to see her cringe.

She shook her head and tried to scatter the memories. She had no intention of going to any damn reunion. Ten years: that meant a lot of fat women and balding men. She looked back at her case. The prosecution would present its opening statement first. They had a lot and she and Alex had to riddle it with doubt and ridicule. He did this while playing up Jamison's service to the community, his good works, and his professional standing in the architectural fraternity. A damn big task.

She looked at the crumpled letter. Reunion. It pulled her mind off the case and back into the high school years. Yes, it had been hard. She had tried to make friends, but it wasn't easy. She remembered once in her junior year a boy asked her to go to the movies Saturday night. She said she would. Then later that day she saw the boy talking with some others. They saw her and faded away laughing and pounding her date on the shoulders. They were laughing and teasing him. The boy never showed up Saturday night for the date. When she was sure he wasn't coming she ran into their fenced back yard and cried. When she was done she saw the neighbor's young cat, about three months old. It had crawled under the fence. She picked it up and stroked its fur, then in a sudden rush of fury, twisted the cat's head until its neck broke and it hung limp and dead in her hands. She laughed at the cat and threw it over the fence back into the neighbor's yard it had come from. No one ever asked her about the dead cat.

High school, what a drag. She remembered how her

sophomore year she had tried out for the yell leader's squad. She was filling out a little and with a padded bra was almost as curvy as the other girls. She could do the routines, but there were three girls trying for two positions. The head cheer leader was watching her. Twyla thought she had a good chance. Then another sophomore who was already on the squad talked to the leader and at last she nodded. The other girl came and told Twyla she didn't make it.

"The squad has decided to take the other two girls, Twyla. You're just not quite good enough yet. Maybe next year."

Twyla would never forget the girl's name: Judith Landcaster. She had stayed on the squad and became the leader, but she never asked Twyla to try out again. She leaned back in her chair. She had followed Judith's career after high school. Judith married and had two kids and quickly divorced. She tried to go to college but dropped out and went to work as a secretary. That left her barely enough money to make payments on the house she and her ex husband had bought and still have food for the table. Tough luck, Judith.

Twyla had researched her mission thoroughly, just like she was preparing a case. She knew where Judith worked, how much she made a month, what her mortgage payments were, the kind of car she drove, where she left her kids when she went out, and what she did on Wednesday nights.

Wednesday became the lynch pin of the whole scheme. She would use it, play off it, and have a ready made suspect for the police. The poor slob wouldn't know what hit him. It took her six Wednesday nights before the right elements came into play. Then last night Judith got picked up, fucked in the back seat of a Cadillac in the parking lot and then followed home.

It was perfect. She saw the man go into her house about eleven thirty, and the stage was set. When he left a little after one a.m., Twyla moved in and went to work. She knew that Judith never locked the sliding door from the patio into the living room. It was simple to get into the house and surprise Judith in her bed.

"Don't scream Judith, or I'll shoot you dead. Wake up and look at me. Do you know who I am?"

Twyla turned on the bedroom light.

"Twyla, from Hoover High? Is that really you?"

"It is, Do you remember how you got me black balled off the yell squad our sophomore year?"

"I did? Oh, you tried out you just didn't make it."

"Because you voted against me with the leader. I saw you talking to her and watching me. You kept me off the squad and ruined my whole year."

"I don't remember that. Anyway it was no big deal. What are you doing now, Twyla?"

"No time for chit chat. Get up and get dressed. Slacks and a blouse, right now."

"Why? I don't understand."

Twyla slapped her face hard where she sat on the edge of the bed. She fell sideways.

"Get up and get dressed, right now. No arguments."

After Judith got dressed, Twyla tied her hands behind her back with one leg of a pantyhose she took from her big shoulder purse.

"Why are you doing this, Twyla? What happened ten years ago? It meant nothing. I don't understand."

"You never did understand," Twyla said and put two strips of tape over Judith's mouth. "You never did understand how you hurt me that day. It followed me all through high school."

Twyla led Judith to the kitchen and positioned her under the ceiling fan. Next she tied her ankles together with another pair of panty hose.

She had tested a fan in her condo. She knew how strong they were. She looped the bottom of the panty hose around Judith's neck and tightened it into a noose, then stood on a chair and tied the other end of the hose around the motor on the top of the ceiling fan pulling the stretching fabric until it was tight lifting Judith's head upward half an inch.

"Goodbye, Judith. It was certainly no fun being in high school with you. Now, right now, you're going to pay for all of those sins, all of those sleepless nights you caused me. Goodbye Judith."

Then Twyla pushed Judith over until the nylon noose around her throat came tight, cutting off her breath. Her body had stretched the nylon until she hung there at a forty-five degree angle, the noose tightening more and more.

Twyla wondered how long it would take. It was about two minutes later when Judith's eyes went wide and she stopped breathing. She tired to scream but nothing got past the tape. It took only two or three minutes more before Judith sagged farther against the nylon fabric. She had become unconscious. Twyla picked up everything she had brought, took the tape off Judith's mouth, turned off the night light she had left burning and slipped out the sliding back door closing it soundlessly. She didn't have to wait for Judith to die. It wouldn't take long. The terrorized look in her eyes had been enough to satisfy Twyla. One down. Judith Landcaster was one Hoover High alum who would not be going to the ten year reunion at the Islandia.

6

STACY EXPECTED to hear her cell phone ring as she had a quick shower then her usual breakfast of a whole grapefruit, toast, coffee, and raisins. Then she expected a call while she drove the mile and a half to the new Central garage. No call.

Up in Detective Team Two Room she found Sergeant Cain Baker digesting a report.

"So, what happened to our big suspect?"

Cain looked up and shook his head. "He walked. The lieutenant decided he was too surprised and too dumb to be the real killer. He was broken up by the time I got him down here. The lieutenant had a copy of the ME's report that showed the time of death between two and five a.m. We're keeping him as a person of interest, but we decided not to formally arrest him after all."

"Square one," Stacy said.

"Yeah."

"The pantyhose. Since Judith evidently didn't use them, they must have been brought by the killer. Most men don't walk around with pantyhose in their hip pockets. A woman on the other hand could have two or three pair in a purse."

"You're telling me it could have been a woman who killed Judith?"

"Could have been. No heavy lifting required. Physically a woman could have done it. I'm heading for the evidence room and check out those pantyhose. We might find some kind of a lead there. I don't know what."

She called the crime lab. They said they had sent the pantyhose to the evidence room. They found nothing on or about them that they could use.

"Any other evidence at the scene?" Stacy asked.

"Lots of prints. Small ones from the two girls. Several prints in the bedroom. Mostly hers, but some we can't match with any known felon or in our other print data bases."

"We probably know who those prints match, but he isn't a candidate for the kill. Just some Romeo who scored the same night. Nothing else? Fibers, love notes, nothing?"

"Nothing."

"I'll check the panty hose out of the evidence room."

She did. She took them out of the evidence baggies and looked them over critically. There were two pair. One evidently used to tie her hands and then the other leg to tie her feet once in the kitchen. One pair was stretched out of shape, evidently the pair used in the hanging.

Stacy noted one interesting fact. Neither of the pair had any runs in them. Even with the massive weight on the kill pair there were no runs. Strange. She looked at the panty section for any maker's logo, size, or identifying marks.

She found the small white tag sewn to the top of the hose. It was an inch long and half an inch wide. On top was a maker's name, also the size, medium, the fabric: nylon and spandex, and some numbers and symbols that were evidently the maker's lot number or date of manufacturer. She looked at the maker's name: Span-Perfect ®. She had never heard of a maker of panty hose before, let alone Span-Perfect. She rubbed the fabric between her fingers. It was much different from her own pantyhose. So sheer it was almost invisible, yet strong and stretchable. Who might sell hose such as these? Only one outlet came to mind: Nordstrom. She looked up the number in the book and got a menu of numbers. At last the mechanical voice gave her a number she could use "For lingerie, night wear and hosiery, press nine." She did.

"Good morning, this is lingerie. How may I help you?"

"Do you handle Span-Perfect hosiery?"

"Yes, of course. I believe we're the only store in the county that does. Although there may be one small shop in La Jolla that handles them. Would you like to order some?"

"How much are they?"

"My dear, we never talk price over the phone. I'm sure you'll be pleased.

"I'll come down and take a look."

"We're not open until ten. I'll see you then. My name is Linda."

"Thank you Linda."

She showed the label to Cain who grunted. "A little out of my line."

"I'm going to be at Nordstrom when they open. With my evidence sample in hand. I wonder how many pair they sell a year? They will be expensive. Maybe thirty, forty dollars a pair. If so probably not one in ten thousand San Diego women wear them."

"Cuts down the odds. We've got not a hell of a lot else to work with."

She said hello to the other two men in their five man team that was assigned to another case. Lee Ostrandeder and Fernando Perez were working a homicide down in Shelltown near the National City border. They talked shop for a couple of minutes then Stacy went back to her desk and checked the other pantyhose. It was the same brand. She had worn her plain blue detective suit today with a skirt that cut just below her knee, a white blouse with a bright yellow scarf. She should fit right in at Nordstrom, San Diego's most expensive department store.

Kevin Kirkpatrick, her partner, came in almost an hour late claiming the power was off in his neighborhood so his electric alarm didn't go off. He'd heard about her run in with the man at the bar and she had to give him the whole story, chapter and line by line.

"So we aren't even holding him?" Kirkpatrick asked. "He could be a convincing liar."

"Could be. Look at it this way. If you were going to kill somebody, how would you do it? Say it was a sudden impulse in a fit of fury. How would you kill a woman?"

"Probably knock her out with my fists and then club

her with some blunt object, like a baseball bat or a chair."

"Figures. Most men would. Can you see a guy six two and almost two hundred pounds rigging up a hanging with pantyhose?"

"Uh, yeah. See what you mean. Strangle her maybe with his hands. Damn, just lost our best suspect."

Cain called them up to his desk. "We're going to go full bore on this. Interviews. We talk to everyone where she worked, we talk to the folks down at the bar again, and we get it on the record. Kevin, start making a list of the people we need to interview. Start down at that place where she worked. Then we'll do the neighbors and anyone else we can find who knew her. There has to be a lead here somewhere."

Stacy printed out a new item for the tack board: "Strangled with Span-Perfect pantyhose." She tacked it under the other items then called the crime lab to get two pictures, one of the hanging scene, and another of an 8 x 10 head shot of Judith Landcaster. They would be in the afternoon department mail.

STACY ARRIVED at Nordstrom department store in the up scale Fashion Valley Center at five minutes past ten. She had never shopped in the store. Had been there only a few times just cruising around looking at clothes that were too expensive for her to buy. She found the lingerie department and asked for Linda. She was a tall woman with a swimmer's shoulders, at about forty five looked in good condition, and slender with a well made up face that probably had more than one procedure done on it.

"Linda? I spoke to you on the phone a few minutes ago."

"Yes, the efficient one. You were talking about Span-Perfect. They are remarkable. Never run, last for months. Absolutely the best pantyhose ever made. Right over here."

They walked to a counter that was glass on top and all pantyhose underneath. Linda brought out a package neatly wrapped in plastic. She undid the fastener and took out the hose.

"There is nothing on the market that can beat these Span-Perfect for fit, durability, style, and sheerness. Feel that fabric."

"Could I see the maker's label, please?"

"Oh, of course. Here it is. The maker, this is a medium, and it's made of spandex and nylon."

Stacy took the plastic envelope form her purse with one pair of the hose and showed the label to the clerk.

"Would you say that this also is a pair of Span-Perfect hose?"

The clerk frowned, looked at the label and nodded.

"Of course, dear. They are the same."

"Good. She looked up at the taller woman. "I'm Detective Stacy DeFrain of the San Diego Police Department." She showed her badge. "We need your help. We need some idea of how many pair of these pantyhose you have sold in the last three months."

"Oh, well, that is unusual. I would have to consult my computer records. All sales are computerized now."

"A rough idea? Do you order them from the factory?"

"Yes, I'm the department head, so I order. Let me think. The last order was for four dozen in two sizes."

So you sell maybe fifty pair every three months?"

"I'd say that's about right. Why the interest by the police in pantyhose......Oh, God. Now I remember that picture on the front page of the paper. That poor woman was strangled and hung by a pair of pantyhose." Her eyes flared and mouth dropped open. "By a pair of our pantyhose?"

"Yes, that's right. This pair right here. That's why we need your help. We'd like a copy of your list of customers for these pantyhose during the past three months."

"Oh no. That's impossible. We can't allow that."

"Linda, this is vital police business. We can get a court order instructing you to give us that list."

"That would be awkward."

"If you don't obey the court order, you and your store manager would go to jail."

"Jail? Prison?"

"County jail until the list was given to us."

"Oh, dear. Let me think about this. We have names and addresses on about three-quarters of the customers, those who use credit cards. Cash sales we have no records."

"Thirty five to forty would be better than what we have now. Talk to your manager. I'll wait. We need that list this morning."

"Oh dear. Mrs. Black is going to be tremendously upset about this."

"Just think how upset she will be when uniformed officers come and arrest her and put here through a skin search in the jail and she lands in a holding cell wearing nothing but a blue jail jump suit."

Linda shuddered. "I'll go see her right now."

The department manager was back in a minute and a half with a short wiry woman wearing a thousand dollar tailored suit with a large diamond pin on the left breast, and a pair of granny glasses perched on the end of a small, stylish nose. She looked about sixty, with soft blue eyes and a small mouth that was slightly pursed to go with her frown.

"You have some identification, young lady," the boss asked.

Stacy nodded. "I'm Detective Stacy DeFrain." She showed her badge. The woman took it and studied it carefully. Than handed it back.

"I'm Theta Black, manager of this establishment. What is this about demanding our customer list?"

"Mrs. Black, this is a murder investigation. Your Span-Perfect pantyhose customer list may be vital to our investigation. We will not reveal the list to your competitors, or anyone else. We will be looking at it with the hope that it might contain the person who murdered a woman yesterday."

"Yes, I saw it in the newspapers. You said something about a court order."

"We can get one requiring you to turn over the list. But I had hoped we could get your cooperation."

"Yes, I hope so too." Her frown had moderated. She turned to her employee. "Linda, about how many names are we talking about?"

"Thirty-five to forty."

"You have a customer file on Span-Perfect?"

"Only on the charge customers."

"Print it out and give it to Detective DeFrain."

"Yes, Ma'am." Linda hurried away.

"Detective DeFrain, I've always admired law enforcement people." Her face had relaxed into an engaging smile. My eldest son was a Lieutenant in the LAPD for years. He's retired now. Can I get you a cup of coffee?"

"That would be wonderful, Mrs. Black. We appreciate your cooperation. If I may ask, what type of woman buys these pantyhose?"

"Only those who can afford them. Many from La Jolla and Del Cerro. They are expensive but some women wear them for six to eight months. They never run." She motioned to the left. "Come into my office, it's just around the corner. I like to stay in the thick of the retail trade."

FIFTEEN MINUTES LATER, Stacy was on her way back to her car with a spread sheet safely folded into her purse. It showed the number of items purchased, the price, the buyer's credit card number, home address, telephone number and E-mail address. What a gold mine. It was just a list for now. They would keep it on file and hope that somewhere, somehow they would find a suspect who would cross check on the pantyhose list. Then they would have a starting spot.

Before she drove, Stacy dialed Cain's cell. He picked up on the second chirp.

"Yeah?"

"Boss, I got the list of women who bought those expensive pantyhose. Thirty seven names, addresses, and phone numbers. It could prove productive if we can cross it with a suspect."

"Yeah, good. Head on back here. We might have caught a small break. Tell you about it soon as you sneak into the barn."

7

SERGEANT CAIN BAKER stared at the two boys who sat across the table form him in Interrogation One. Both were nineteen or twenty maybe a little younger. Both looked concerned, serious, and not used to being in a police station.

"This is Friday afternoon," Cain said. "You just told me that you saw this on Wednesday night or early Thursday morning, you're not sure which?"

"Yes sir, Sergeant Cain. It was part of a frat initiation, you know how those go." Phil Alder was talking. He was blond, over six feet, relaxed more now. "You know a lot of booze, a few broads, a lot of bullshit, and a treasure hunt where we had to bring back certain obscure and embarrassing items."

"I've seen a lot of frat guys in this room trying to explain things, but never like this. So you were hung over Thursday."

The other frat pledge looked up. He was shorter, a little heavy, and dark. His name was Ed Grogan. "We didn't get back to the house until almost six a.m. It had been a horrendous day and night, so we slept in. We finally got with it last night and tried to remember what happened. That's when we recalled the car. Then we saw the news about the dead woman around that same address and tied the two together."

"So, Ed, tell me again what you saw."

"We were up there on Judson Street hunting squirrel shit. I used to live up near there in Linda Vista and I knew where there were a lot of squirrel holes, so there should be droppings all over the place."

"A truly noble cause. So what did you see?"

"We had just driven up to the place and turned off our lights when this Lexus turned into the street and came to a stop about thirty feet ahead of us and parked on the other side of the street. It was a Lexus, far as I could tell a brand new black one. I know the Lexus always wanted one. That was weird because this ain't the neighborhood where the folks can afford an expensive set of wheels like that. It was about two a.m. I figure. We were both in the car and we hunkered down since we didn't want somebody reporting us wandering around the area. Some of those blocks got wide eyed Neighborhood Watch teams. So we waited. After about five minutes somebody got out of the Lexus and looked around, then ran up to the side of a house and vanished."

"You get a good look at this person?"

"Oh, hell no. Too dark. We could see that the person was dressed all in black and had on a baseball cap."

Cain turned to the blond kid. "Is this what you saw, too?"

"Yeah, Ed has it right. We figured maybe a guy

getting home late and not wanting to wake up his wife. Or maybe a burglar, who could say?"

"So you just sat in the car and didn't look for the squirrel holes?"

"Actually, Ed watched the Lexus and I went out and grabbed what I thought was squirrel shit next to a pair of holes in the ground. It turned out to be dog poop."

"Then you just sat in the car?" Cain asked.

"Well, yeah. I was afraid to start the car. Didn't know when that person might come back and have a gun and shoot both of us just for fun. Hey, it was past three a.m. by that time."

"So you waited?"

"Yeah, probably wasn't as long as it seemed. Then this person came out of the side yard of the house, got in the Lexus, turned on the lights and drove right past us. But we both bobbed up and had a look at the rear license plate."

"You could see the plate even in the dark?" Cain asked.

"Hey the plate holder has a light on it," Ed said. "Comes on with the headlights and taillights. I saw it; I just can't remember all of it. For sure the first part of it was Four LOT."

Cain looked at Phil. "You saw the number too?"

"Yep. My dad is a cop back east. He taught me to read plates before I could read anything else. It was Four LOT but beyond that the beer and shots and the tequila rubbed the rest out."

"Man or a woman driving the car?"

"Not the slightest, man." Ed said.

"No way to tell," Phil said. "Dark out there. The

person was wearing pants, a black jacket, and that baseball cap. Could have been a man or a woman."

"Then today you were sober enough to put it together?"

"I love mystery novels," Ed said. "Read them all the time. When I saw the newspaper with the story about the hanging and the address up there on Judson Street the bells rang loud and clear. We drove up there and the police were gone but there was still the yellow crime scene tape around the house. That's when we knew we had to come in."

Cain had their names, addresses, and phone numbers. It was a San Diego State University frat house. He stood. The boys stood.

"Well, guys, I think we're though here. I want to thank you for coming forward. Sometimes these are the only clues we get in a killing like this." He gave them his card. "If you remember anything at all that you didn't tell me, give me a call day or night. That's my cell number. You guys did good coming in with this information. We'll put it to good use."

Cain led them out to the front lobby and shook hands with them before they headed for the big doors.

Stacy came in one of the other doors and angled over to her boss.

"Those guys the big news?"

"They brought it. We might have a partial plate of a new black Lexus that the boys saw at the crime scene the night of the kill. Let's go upstairs."

IN DETECTIVE TEAM ROOM ONE, they found Ostrander and Perez working on their case. They waved at them. Cain called Kirkpatrick over and grinned.

"Boys and girl, we might have a lead on the Judith case." He outlined what the frat boys had told him.

"So how many new Lexus cars are there in San Diego right now?" Kirkpatrick asked. The others shook their heads. "Four dealerships, say they sell two hundred new a year that would be eight hundred. How many black ones? Who knows? How many with that partial plate? Maybe ten, maybe two, maybe twenty. I'll call the DMV and find out. What's that direct line we have to them?"

Ten minutes later he put down the phone. "The Department of Motor Vehicles was most cooperative. They are sending me an E-mail with the full plate numbers along with the names and addresses of the registered owners. He said we should have it within a half hour."

"If one of those partial plate names matches up with anyone on my pantyhose list, we could be in business," Stacy said.

"Could be," Cain said. "Partial plates are always a tough call. Depending on how many we get, we may have to chase down every one of them."

"Let's hope not," Kirkpatrick said.

TWYLA FARNHAM, Esq., spent most of the day tracking down three witnesses for the defense in the big society murder case she was working on. Two had refused to testify until she threatened them with subpoenas and possible arrest warrants. She was drained by four o'clock. That's when she remembered she had a dinner planned with a lawyer from the biggest law firm in town. It was a business appointment, and she figured it was a "look over" by the partner in the firm to see if they should make her an offer to come work for them. She'd heard that the firm was hunting a good criminal defense lawyer to fill out their band of almost forty lawyers working in most fields.

The dinner went well and she figured she had a chance for an offer. She knew the salary would be well above the hundred thousand she was making with Branston, Knox & Tretter. Something to look forward to.

By seven thirty she was home and a unsettling itch burned in her mind. What was it? She remembered the night with dear Judith. That had worked out rather well. The police were baffled. She tried to relax, but the urge to do something came again and again. At last she took out the folder that she had kept since high school and looked at it. Inside were dozens of pages, pictures, the year book, and some hand written promises that she had made to herself ten years ago.

To her surprise she saw the ten year reunion letter right on top. Then she remembered she had filed it there the day it arrived. She read it through then looked at the next hand written note on blue lined paper.

"Something has to be done. I am so angry and furious and mad at myself for trusting him. He was the football hero, Bert Showley the half back who won the games with his flashy runs down the field. One day he came up to me in the hall and flirted with me. I was so surprised I blushed and wanted to run. He touched my shoulder. I stayed and he asked me out. A week later we went to a movie. At least he said we were going to a movie. He had his father's big Cadillac. He told me I was his girl, his steady and that we would be together all through our senior year. He asked me to the football banquette which is the biggest thing at our school next to the senior prom. I was thrilled and didn't even realize what he was doing. We had moved to the big back seat so we'd have more room to talk and almost before I knew it he had my blouse open and my bra pulled up around my throat. He seduced me. Actually he raped me because I kept telling him to stop. He didn't stop. He tried to do it again, but I fought him off,, got dressed, and *I* demanded that he take me home. He did and said he'd see me Monday at school.

"He never spoke to me again. That was when I saw the guys laughing and slapping Bert on the back. The word got around quickly. Bert had won a twenty dollar bet by having sex with me. I was so embarrassed and furious that I stayed home a whole week from school. I told my mother I was sick. I was sick at heart and worried about getting pregnant. Well, this is two months later and I'm not pregnant, but I'm still furious and some day when the time is right, I want to take care of Mr. Bert Showley and make him pay for what he did to me. I'm waiting. I hope it comes soon."

Twyla took out another file folder marked: "Bert Showley" and opened it. There were clipping from the newspaper about his game winning runs. More from the school newspaper. Then the announcement in the Union-Tribune that he had won a football scholarship to San Diego State University. There was a big story when he reported to practice, than not much more until the third game of the year when he was booted off the team for drug use.

He had settled down in nearby La Mesa and took training on computers. He took out ads in the local papers that he was a mobile computer repairman. He would come to your home or office and fix your computer and get you back into operation quickly. The last time she checked, a year ago, he was still in business. She took out the ad and phoned the La Mesa number. It rang. No one picked up. The recorder came on:

"Hi, sorry to miss your call. This is Bert Showley's Mobile Computer Repair. I come to your place, which is probably why I'm not home answering your call. Just leave your name, number, the time of day, and I'll get back to you just as quickly as I can. Usually no more than four hours unless you call in the evening. Please leave your number. You have a nice day."

Twyla sat back and shook her head. Still a big talker. She would take care of that. Two months ago she had driven past his La Mesa address. It was less than ten miles from her Mission Valley condo. He still worked out of his house. No business rent to pay that way. Which told her that he was probably barely scraping by. She had no idea if he had a family. Now in the early evening, she took another drive by. Even in the dark she could see a small wheel bicycle and some kid toys in the front yard. It was on a residential street that had been spruced up a bit, but Bert's place needed a paint job and some new grass. One tree in the front yard looked starved for water. As she drove home, her anger level rose. The bastard. He probably didn't even remember her. He must have spent the twenty bucks he won on the bet for fucking her buying beer and sharing it with the guys who got the biggest kick out of his winning the bet.

She drove back to her condo. She had several books on early methods of execution. She looked in one and leafed through it. She liked the early English method of piling on stones. In this practice, the accused or guilty one was placed on his back on a hard surface, and then a wide board was placed on his body from his throat to his knees. Now large stones were put on the board. One after another stone slabs were stacked on the top of the pile. If it were an interrogation, the additional stones were stopped when the accused confessed. If it were an execution, the stones were increased until the guilty party's chest was crushed and his heart exploded.

She liked that one, but it would require a lot of effort. She moved on. The book was filled with all sorts of deadly devices, from a simple gallows, to the guillotine, to four horses tearing a man apart with chains attached to his arms and legs. Colorful but hard to duplicate. She couldn't make up her mind and went to bed with dozens of deadly methods circulating in her head. One thing she had decided for sure. She was going to kill Bert Showley and do it soon.

8

ALL THE NEXT day at work Twyla was busy on the socialite murder case. They had some strong evidence and were looking for more. She vetted two possible witnesses. One of them turned out to be an outright liar who had faked his name and his residence as well as his contact with their client. The other one was pure gold and would stand up well in court as a character witness.

On her lunch time, she ordered in Chinese sweet and sour pork and chow mein. That with a diet Coke got her into the afternoon. Before she went to vet another possible witness, she thought about her other situation: Bert Showley.

The method of his demise should be something that would be in keeping with the crime of rape. She could castrate him. That would be messy and she wasn't sure she had the balls to do it. She smiled at the male term for courage. That's what she got working around so many criminal type men. Some of the other criminal lawyers were just as foul mouthed. She had found that it helped her image if she threw in a shit or fuck once in a while when talking with the men. But what about good old Bert?

Strip him naked and drag him behind her car down the street with the tow rope around his prick? No it would tear off too quickly. Nice thought though. What else?

Stuff his mouth full of unrolled condoms until he gagged, vomited, and died of his own vomit? Getting closer.

Take him to a motel and fuck his brains out, then spread eagle him on the bed, castrate him, and let him bleed out and die. Closer yet.

Use a butcher knife and chop off his prick? She shivered. That would be messy and she wasn't wild about the sight of blood, even his. But if that was the final solution, she could live with it.

Brainstorming. It was called that. Write down every solution you can think of that has any relevance at all to the project or problem, and then sort them out later. She kept at it.

Tie him down and shoot his balls off with a hand gun. Get one of the nine millimeter Glock 18's that some cops had. They would fire semi automatic and could use a thirty three round magazine. Dreaming. She wasn't good with a pistol, although she had one, a neat little thirty two caliber she carried sometimes for protection. She had been through the basic shooting training at a range.

She had written some key words for each of her wild brainstorming. She would remember the details of each one. She folded the paper and put it in her purse, then got back to work on running to ground three more potential witnesses. They were going for good character witnesses. But they wanted solid ones that the prosecution couldn't cut to ribbons on cross.

That night in her Mission Valley condo while she watched a DVD horror movie she went over her list for Bert's entertainment again. One by one she rejected them. She liked the condom idea and underlined it. When she finished it was the only idea that had an underline. She tried to picture it, then expanded on the idea a little and combined it with another one. She grinned and took the list to her fireplace and with the trigger fire starter burned the page into ash which she stirred and mashed and made totally unreadable. Twyla nodded with grim satisfaction. Now, all she had to do was pull it off.

How? She would phone him and set up a computer repair at a house for rent in one of the poorer sections of town. First she had to spot a suitable house. Then she would need a different car, not her Lexus. She knew cons who had taught her how to steal a car. They said the best way was to roam the parking lot at a huge shopping center. Walk up and down the cars until you found one where someone had left the keys hanging in the ignition. Jump in and drive away. Then keep the rig on ice in some parking garage until needed. She could put it in a visitor's slot in her condo garage. Yes! It was coming together. Getting into the rental house? How would she do that? She'd look over the place. Park a block away and walk back to it. Find one with glass in a back door or a small window she could break the night of the do on Bert. Break the window and take Bert down as soon as he came to the front door. She'd hide the for rent sign at the side of the house as soon as it got dark. She'd offer to pay Bert more for a night visit. He wouldn't have a clue.

She would hold the gun on him; make him go down on his stomach. Yes, tie him up, it would work.

Now when? She got in her car and drove into the raunchy side of San Diego into one black and Mexican area where the houses were old and run down. It was past ten o'clock that evening that she found the ideal house. It was in the Paradise Hills district, down by National City just off Alleghany Street. The houses on each side of it had been abandoned. Only two places in the block looked lived in. The sign out front said "For Rent," but it looked like it was a "by owner" situation. No big post hole sign buried in the front yard. The place was old, needed paint, and the yard was mostly weeds and rocks. Perfect.

While she was on a roll, she went to Mission Valley Center near one of the theatre complexes. Lots of people still at the flicks. She parked making sure she remembered the row and position where she left her car and then began looking at cars. She quickly determined that it was too hard to see inside the cars at night. She should have thought of that before. She drove back home and checked her supply of condoms. Only six. She would need how many? Maybe twenty or thirty. She would buy a dozen at each of three different stores. No suspicion that way. Yes. Tomorrow she'd find a car. She would call in sick. That migraine she couldn't shake, the excuse she had used before and it still worked. Nobody at work thought it strange that the migraines never happened on a court day.

. . .

THE STORES in Mission Valley Center opened at ten, and Twyla was there trolling for a keys-in-ignition car by ten thirty. She had parked her new Lexus half a block away from the nearest car, knowing the area would fill up. She hated car door opening dings in the sides of her baby.

It took her only two rows of twenty cars to find one with keys dangling in the ignition. It was some kind of an older Ford and looked ideal. She slid into the driver's seat, turned the key, which started the engine, backed out carefully, and then drove away. What a rush! She was a car thief. Now to get it into her Mission Valley Condo garage before a cop stopped her. It was only about five miles.

She made it ten minutes later, went up to her condo, and called a taxi. He came quickly and the driver grumbled about the short run. She gave him an extra five dollar tip and he brightened up. She had him let her off at one of the stores, and when he was out of sight, walked back to her Lexus, got in, and took a deep breath.

She was set. She would make it for tonight. She went to three different stores and bought condoms. Now she had thirty-six. Even a big mouth like Bert's should fill up with those all stretched out. Next, twine, rope or string. Did she have any? No. She went back to Rite-Aid and found in the package wrapping section some heavy string. It was tough and no way she could break it. Several wraps of it should work fine. She bought two rolls of the string. In the kitchen section she found a butcher knife, a heavy one with a ten inch blade. It was sharp. Yes, that would do nicely. She thought through the scenario. She had everything that she needed. Now all she lacked was Bert.

That afternoon about four she called his business number from the yellow pages. He was in.

"Bert's Mobile Computer Repair."

"Hi, good, you're in. I have this lap top that is giving me fits. I loaned it to a tenant of mine in a rental and now t won't work at all. Can you help me?"

"What brand lap top is it?"

"Wow, I have no idea. They are all a lot alike, aren't they? Oh, I'm Mrs. Johnson."

"Mostly they are alike. About what did it cost new?"

"That I know, about four hundred."

"One of the simpler ones. Okay, where is the machine?"

She gave him the address of the kill house.

"Not the best part of town."

"I know I never should have bought the house. It was cheap and I thought I could make money. Oh, I can't get there until about eight o'clock. Can you come then?"

"Late. I usually don't do night calls."

"This is important. I'll give you an extra twenty five dollars on top of your bill. I really need to get it fixed tonight."

There was a pause. She frowned at the phone.

"All right. I can make it. Turn on the porch light and stand outside so I'll know where I am. Lighting is lousy down there."

"Good, I'll see you about eight."

. . .

SHE WORE HER BLACK OUTFIT: shoes, socks, pants, jacket and baseball cap. She tucked her dark hair inside the baseball cap so it wouldn't show. At a distance she would look like either a man or a woman.

She arrived at the address down in Paradise Hills fifteen minutes until eight. By then it was almost dark. She parked a block away, carried her tools in a plastic grocery bag, and walked quickly to the house. Then she went around back. The rear door with the glass panel yielded quickly. She smashed the foot square pane out with the handle of the butcher knife, reached in, unlocked the door, and was inside. She stopped and didn't move for two minutes. No reaction from outside or inside.

She went through the house using her pen light. It was sparsely furnished. She found the front door. It was double locked from the inside. She opened the locks and swung the door outward. Then she tried the lights. They hadn't been shut off yet. She waited until eight o'clock, turned on lights in the front room and the porch, and stood at the door. The place had minimal furniture, a typical low priced rental.

A small van rolled slowly down the street, evidently the driver was hunting an address. She took off her cap and let her hair down. Bert was looking for a woman. She stepped out on the lighted porch and waved. The rig pulled to a stop at the curb. A moment later a man came around the van, opened the back, took out a large carrying case, and came up the sidewalk.

"Mrs. Johnson?" the man asked. She couldn't see him well, but she remembered his voice. He was Bert. His voice was a little on the low side and she used to think sexy. This was Bert for sure.

"Yes. You must be Bert. Come on in." She held the .32 caliber pistol behind her hip and let him come into the room. Then she could see him plainly. She was surprised at the change in him. She took a step back. He was Bert, all right, but with about twenty extra pounds and a hairline that had wandered half way back on his head. Bert had the same sloppy grin.

"Hey, where's the laptop?"

"Right here," she said bringing the pistol out. "Bert get down on your knees on the floor then stretch out on your stomach. We have some talking to do."

"Hey, not a chance." He lunged toward her and she fired one shot. It hit him in the leg and he cried out then dropped to the floor. The shot shook her. But she didn't let it show. Just like on the range. She centered the pistol on him again.

"What the hell is this?" he brayed. "I don't carry any money with me."

"Flat on your belly, Bert, then I won't have to shoot you again."

"What the hell?"

He turned on his side then to his stomach.

"Hands behind your back, lover boy. Now."

"Not a chance."

She kicked him in the side about where his kidney should be. One of her clients had been convicted of doing that and got two years in State. Bert bellowed in pain.

"Okay, okay, don't kick me again."

He put his hands behind his back, she took out the precut lengths of string, and tied his wrists together. He jerked them apart once. She kicked him in the side and he stopped trying to get free of the bindings. When she was sure they were tight and knotted good, she made him stand up.

"Going to take a little walk, Bert, see if you remember me. Doubt if you do. It's been ten years. But then you must have fucked half the girls in our class at good old Hoover High our senior year."

He jerked his head around and stared at her.

"Should I know you?"

"Damn right you should. Now get walking through that door. We'll go into a back room where the light won't show and attract attention. You don't remember me, do you? You bastard, you fuckhead. I should just shoot you about five more times. Now move." As they left she turned off the front room and porch lights. In the back bedroom, which could not be seen from the street, she turned on the lights. There was a bed and a dresser in the otherwise bare room.

He stared at her. "Sally?"

She hit him in the middle of the back with the side of the pistol.

"Down on your belly on the bed you rapist asshole."

9

THE E-MAIL from the DMV had not come in that afternoon as they had promised. It was there the next morning in an attachment. Kirkpatrick downloaded the attachment and printed out the file.

"One hell of a lot more names here than I expected," Kirkpatrick said as he showed the sheets of paper to Cain. "I counted. There are twenty four owners in the county with new Lexus cars with the first of their plate showing 4 LOT."

Stacy looked over the list quickly. "I don't see the name of any one on my pantyhose list," she said. "Let me check it again, I just did a brief glance. She took the list to her desk and compared the two reading one name from her list and going down the twenty-four on the plate sheets. Five minutes later she came back.

"No way. Those plate names don't mesh with any name in my pantyhose bunch."

"Might have been a cash buyer," Cain said. "Or maybe knowing she was gong to do something criminal, she gave a fake name and address. That's what I'd do."

"Wow, boss. I didn't know that you wore pantyhose," Kirkpatrick jibed. Cain threw a waded up ball of paper at him.

"So where are we?"

"Damn near close to nowhere," Stacy said. "I hoped I could find a match."

Cain did a walk around of the room. "Let's say this was not just some casual murder of someone who got in the killer's way. Whoever did it must have selected Judith, followed her, and knew her habits. Knew that she used that club to pick up men. Then waited until Judith brought one home for a fling. That was a set up he or she needed providing a built-in suspect. Zappo, she waited until good old George Funnel made a late call on Judith and then our killer struck.

"So why did someone want to kill this woman? We need to do our interviews over again. People at the office where she worked. Her little girl's teachers. Any neighbors who knew her in any way at all. There has to be a reason a non-descript regular person like Judith was murdered."

"Back to basics," Stacy said. "I'll take her next door neighbor, the one who found her."

The others picked people who had been talked to before, including Judith's mother and her co-workers. It was going to be a long day.

STACY SET the tea cup down on the saucer on the living room coffee table. She smiled at Mrs. McLoughlin who urged another homemade peanut butter cookie on her.

"Well, I guess I didn't know Judith really well. I

mean she lived here for two, maybe three years. She moved in just after my Harry died. Her with the two little girls. Not so little now. But as near as I can tell, I never saw a gentleman caller coming to her house."

She stopped and frowned. "Well, now let me think. I do remember her saying something about a man at work who kept bothering her. She said at last she went out with him just to get him off her back. But it didn't work. He started dropping by at unusual times without calling."

Stacy perked up and took out her small notebook with the spiral at the top. "Do you remember the man's name?"

"Actually I do. It was Norman. I recall that name because it's the same as my first son, Norman, who is back east now working in computers."

"You don't know a last name?"

"My goodness, no. that was all six months or so ago. I'm not what you'd call good on names, especially after six months. Can I get you more tea?" Her eager smile betrayed a touch of loneliness.

"I'm fine, Mrs. McLoughlin. You said he worked at the same place that Judith did?"

"Yes, A & M Placement. They get jobs for nurses all around the country and even in foreign countries. I wish I'd been a nurse. They do so much good for people." Her now wan smile faded as she thought about her missed chances in life.

"Did Judith go out much? You know to plays or movies, or take the kids to the park or the zoo?"

"Not a lot. Now and then she'd speak about a movie they saw. Always it was a children's movie."

"We're trying to figure out who might have killed her, so I have to ask all these questions."

Mrs. McLoughlin smiled and nodded. Her glasses jiggled on her nose. "I understand, dear. Now, one more cookie. If you don't help me I'll just have to eat them up myself."

Stacy had another cookie and some more tea. After another fifteen minutes of gentle probing, she was sure that she knew everything Mrs. McLoughlin knew about Judith Landcaster. She eased her way out and went to the unmarked police car. Inside she used her cell phone. Cain had gone to A & M Placement. He answered on the third chirp.

"Yeah, Cain."

"Boss, see what you can find out about a man called Norman. That's all I have. Some of Judith's friends there might know about him. He put the rush on Judith about six months ago. He could have done a payback to her for cutting him off."

"Norman, no last?"

"Afraid not. Lucky to get that which is all I did get from the next door neighbor."

Cain said goodbye to Stacy and went back to talk to Milicent. She was a small girl, maybe 25, with soft blonde hair and a sweet round face. She wore a pretty white blouse, tan pants, and worked in the booking and travel section.

"Sure, I knew Judith. I was as close to her as anyone. She had been badly hurt in her marriage and protected herself at all times. Some of the guys tried to hit on her for a quick weekend, but she wouldn't even talk about it with a married man. We don't have a lot of singles around here."

"What about Norman?"

Milicent laughed. "You mean Norman Vuylsteke?" She shook her head. "Yes, there was Norman. He's a bit of an odd duck, even for this business. He's in credentials and contracts and wanted to be a lawyer. But a Romeo he is not. He liked Judith and kept bugging her until she said she'd go to a movie with him and that would be it. Norman is about forty, never been married, is a poor dresser, can't keep his hair combed, or his tie on straight. He's a bit of a loser. Twice I saw him with his zipper down after he came from the men's room. She got him out of her hair quickly, but I'm not sure how she did it."

"Is Norman the violent type?"

"Did he hang poor Judith? Not a chance. The cars in the parking lot scare him. He never drives on the freeway. He lives with his mother in Clairemont. You can forget about Norman as a suspect."

TWYLA HAD JUST FINISHED her work with Bert, put all of her equipment back in the plastic grocery bag, and went to the front door in the dark to relock it. To her amazement a black and white San Diego police car pulled to a stop directly in front of the house and a cop got out, put his baton in its belt holder and started up the sidewalk. No time to lock the door.

She ran to the back door, slipped out and closed it quietly. She had already turned off the bedroom lights. She went to the side of the house and could hear the cop knocking on the front door. Then he called out something and she heard him try the front door.

There was no fence around the house, few fences

anywhere in the area. Twyla hurried across the open space to the vacant house next door, then to the one beyond that. Her stolen car should be another fifty feet up the street and was heading away from Bert's final sex scene. She walked casually to the street and down toward her car. She saw the police car well behind her with its roof lights flashing. Someone across the street snapped on a porch light and came out to see what was going on.

She eased into the stolen Ford, started the engine, and drove slowly away from the area back to Allegheny Street. She turned left and soon came to I-805 freeway which she took heading north toward Mission Valley. She would be home in fifteen minutes. She took the car back to the parking lot in Fashion Valley and caught a taxi to her condo about five miles away. A five dollar tip to the cabby made him happy. She walked up to her condo and went inside. Twyla checked all the rooms, then dropped on her bed, reliving the final few minutes of that bastard Bert Showley's life.

OFFICER DONALD CHASE rattled the front door of the house in Paradise Hills. This was only his second month on this beat but already he knew that some of these old vacant houses had been used by kids to shoot up or have drinking or sex parties. A resident had phoned in a complaint about lights being on in this vacant house. Something was going on. Or had gone on. With his lousy luck lately it would be all over and the kids gone.

He rattled the door again then tried the knob. It turned and he pushed the door open.

He smelled something strange, but didn't pick up on it. Not booze or pot he was sure of that. Nobody was cooking meth here. He used his three cell flashlight and checked the living room from one step inside. Sparsely furnished, like a cheap rental. Maybe that's what it was.

The odor puzzled him. He checked out the kitchen, and bath, both lightly furnished and without any odor. He went down a short hall to the first bedroom. No bed. He pushed open the door to the second bedroom and his light flashed on the cheap bed. He staggered back a step. On the bed tied spread eagled on his back lay a naked man. His crotch was a mass of blood. Blood pooled on the sheet under his body. That's when he recognized the odor. The copperish smell of fresh human blood.

He took a deep breath, steadied himself with one hand against the door, eased back out of the room, and grabbed his radio.

10

STACY LAUGHED at the antics on stage at the Civic Theatre where she was enjoying a road company show of "Hello Dolly." The first act was about half over when the vibrator on her cell phone buzzed through her purse and into her hip. She dug out the little darling and saw the coded number: 999. That meant something wild had just happened and she must call in pronto. She slipped out of the row climbing over four matrons and two men who tried to grab her rear end as she pushed past them. Once in the lobby she flipped open the cell and dialed Sergeant Cain Baker's cell.

"Yeah, Stacy?"

"What do we have?"

"Another one," Cain said. "I'm on my way. It's down in Paradise Hills." He gave her the address. "Soon as you can get there. Kevin and Lee are on the way."

She hurried out of the entrance and to the elevators on the parking structure that stood across a block long walkway next to a convention center. None of the four elevators seemed to be working. She pulled open the door to the stairs and ran up two flights glad she hadn't parked on the top floor.

FIFTEEN MINUTES later she stopped her Sentra behind a black and white that still had its bubble machine on the roof pounding out colored lights. Eight cop cars were already there and the yellow crime scene tape was out. She showed her badge, gave the uniform guarding the scene her name to record, and hurried up the walk to the open front door. Lights were on all over the house.

She found Cain and Kevin in the back bedroom. The medical examiner hadn't arrived yet. The crime lab guys had started their work dusting for prints, finding the broken out pane in the back door and the two front door locks that had been found open by the first officer on the scene.

Stacy saw the body on the bed and took a step back, her hand coming up to her mouth in an involuntary protest. The man had been tied spread eagled on his back on the bed. The cheap sheet under him was pooled with blood around his crotch. She frowned as she looked closer. There was no sign of the man's scrotum or his penis. His right leg showed what she figured was a bullet hole. It was a puckered round black mark with a tiny fringe of blood around it. Other than that she could see no other marks or injuries to the man.

"Not a pretty sight," Cain said. He watched her reaction and waved one hand.

The photographer who traveled with the crime lab crew took three more flash shots with his digital camera.

He backed up and got several pictures of the room, then looked at Anderson, his boss.

"Anything else?" he asked.

"You've got him in situ, and everything else. Go back and make prints. Cain is going to want a set yesterday." Anderson grinned at Cain.

"Damn right, detail man. You find anything we can't see?"

"Not yet. Did you look at his mouth?"

Cain stepped forward and bent closer. He came away with a frown. "Is that a condom half way out between his teeth?"

"Quite right inspector general," Anderson said. "From here it looks like he may have a mouth full of them. We'll have to wait for the ME to be sure."

As if on call, an assistant Medical Examiner Cain didn't know came into the room with his black bag. He wore a paint spattered pair of blue jeans and a white shirt outside that also had splotches of blue paint.

"Yeah, I was painting the bedroom, all right? Just one?"

Anderson said just one body and the man leaned over the bed and touched the man's carotid.

"Okay, he's dead. He have any clothes?"

A uniform brought in a pair of pants, work shirt, and underwear. The ME dug into the pocket and took out a billfold. He checked the driver's license.

"Tentative I.D. on the victim is Bertrand D. Showley. He's twenty eight and lives in La Mesa. Will somebody cut this guy loose so I can examine him?"

One of Anderson's men clipped the heavy cord and saved the salvage ends in a plastic evidence envelope.

The ME rolled the body over, examined it quickly

and then rolled it back. He pulled the condom from the man's mouth and handed it to Anderson who bagged it. Then he fished more condoms out of the subject's mouth.

"Be damned," the ME said. A minute later he shook his head. "Fifteen unrolled and stretched condoms in his mouth. None seemed to have been used. The last few show signs of vomit. Right now I don't know if he regurgitated and sucked the vomit down into his lungs and suffocated, or if he died when somebody chopped off his genitals and he bled to death. Could be a close call."

Cain looked at Stacy? "So?"

"Lots of sexual rage," she said. She frowned and pushed strands of hair back behind her right ear. "Lots of anger and fury and frustration. Could be a man whose lover was stepping out on him."

"His crotch looks like it took a hacking job," Kevin said. "Cuts on both thighs and the genitals are missing. Anybody found them yet?"

"Not yet," Anderson said. "If they're here, we'll find them."

"What kind of a knife?" Cain asked.

The crime lab man shook his head. "Not sure. No stab wounds to use. I'd say a big knife. Four inch switchblade, a hunting knife, even a kitchen butcher knife."

Stacy looked at the pile of condoms on the bed beside the body. "I like the condoms idea to suggest it could have been a woman. Somebody who wronged her, or stepped out on her and used a condom. She stuffed his mouth with them to gag him, never thinking it might kill him. Then she hacks off his cock and balls and knows that he'll bleed to death. Yep, could have been a woman."

"Weak, pretty weak," Cain said. "Kevin, check the kitchen and see if the furnished plan here included kitchen knives."

Larry Anderson came over showing a pained expression.

"Damn near nothing. Might be some fibers. The cord is generic. Buy it in dozens of stores. Did find a used tissue in the living room. Has lipstick on it. He pushed an evidence baggie toward Cain. Stacy grabbed it first.

"My area," she said. She looked at it, turned it over and studied it a moment, then she grinned. "Another vote for a girl. This one blotted her lipstick and pitched the tissue. Bad habit."

One of the crime lab guys came up and handed Anderson another evidence bag. He crime lab chief belched.

"Hell, we might have something for you yet. Looks like a .32 caliber casing recently fired. Victim has a bullet in his leg. It didn't come out the back. Might have good ballistic marks on it. We'll find out soon as the doc does the auto and gives us the slug."

"Weak, you say, my leader? A thirty two is a woman's gun, agreed?"

"Could be."

"I've never taken one off a man, or seen a man use a thirty-two. A twenty-two, yeah, but not it's bigger cousin. I think we have a woman serial killer. The panty hose on the Judy Lancaster kill, and now the lipstick and the thirty-two, the chopped off genitals and the condoms stuffed...."

Cain shrugged. "Yeah, sure, possible. Give me a name and address."

"Poor loser."

"Good winner. Lee, you and Stacy get two uniforms and go with them up and down the street to see if anyone heard a gunshot or saw anything unusual. Double check on the guy across the street who made the call about the lights."

"Yeah, I'm on it." Stacy laughed. "It's a woman who has guts and a gun." Stacy left quickly before she pushed her luck.

"Kevin. Call dispatch with the plate on the rig outside and run Bert for wants and warrants. He's probably clean."

Anderson came back. "We've got a black roll along case in the front room. We dusted it and looked inside. Full of electronic and computer stuff. You want us to look over the small van at the curb? Paint job says it's "Bert's Mobile Computer Repair." Probably belongs to the victim."

"Check it out."

Twenty minutes later the four detectives gathered at Cain's Chevy Cavalier and compared notes.

"Only six houses occupied on the whole damn block," Lee said. "What a crummy neighborhood to die in."

Stacy chimed in. "As far as I could tell, no one saw any thing except the man across the street. He said he saw the porch and front room lights come on for about ten minutes. Then he saw the van pull up and a man went up to the front door. Said a woman came out on the front step and met the man. Then they went inside."

"Woman, huh?" Cain asked.

"Right. He described her as a woman with long dark hair. Said she wore all black. That was all he could see."

"Bring him down to the house and get him on tape," Cain said. "So far he's the best thing we've found. Yeah, yeah, it could be a woman."

"Boss, don't be a sore loser. We just nailed it.. Our killer is a woman."

"I checked with dispatch," Kevin said. "No wants or warrants on Bert. Only one traffic ticket. Has a city business license in La Mesa. Works out of his home in La Mesa."

"Okay. Somebody has to talk to the widow." Cain looked around and the three detectives quickly found something else to look at. "Okay, I'll do it. What the hell time is it?"

"A little after nine fifteen," Stacy said.

"Thought you had a..." Kevin started.

"Yeah, I do. Martha gave it to me. Half the time I can't figure out the damn hands. But I have to wear it." He shrugged. "So, write up your reports first thing in the morning. I'm off to see the widow. Maybe she knows something about who he called on tonight."

"It was a set up," Stacy said. "A for rent house. One of our guys found a for rent sign stashed at the side of the house. Call out at night. One quick shot in the leg. She puts him down, ties him up and marches him on the bed. He had to walk to his own execution."

"Yep, maybe. But why?" Lee asked.

"That, gentlemen, is what we're going to find out," Stacy said.

11

STACY AND KEVIN talked to the eye witness and took him downtown for a formal interview that could be tape recorded. Cain copied the dead man's address and headed for La Mesa, a suburb that butted up against San Diego's east border.

He found the home, a modest two bedroom on a fairly nice street where the lawns were green and trimmed and the houses painted. A modest pride of ownership area. He went up to the door with his usual dread of bringing death news to new widows. It was never easy. After he rang the bell, the door opened slowly and he could see the chain in place.

"Mrs. Showley?"

He held up his badge. "Ma'am, I'm Sergeant Baker from the San Diego Police. Could I talk with you for a minute?"

"My husband isn't here. He says don't let nobody in unless he's here."

"This is about your husband. Could I come in please?"

"You sure you're a cop?"

"Yes, ma'am. Have been for the past nine years."

"Is Bert all right?"

"No, I'm afraid he isn't. We need to talk."

"He's hurt. An accident. I knew it, I knew it. I tell him bout jumping red lights." The door closed and a moment later opened. She was a small woman, Hispanic with long dark hair, a round face and deep set brown eyes. She looked to be about six months pregnant.

"My Bert, how bad is he hurt? Should I go to hospital? Where is he?"

"Mrs. Showley, can we sit down? Then I'll answer all of your questions."

She waved him to a brown sofa that had seen much use. She sat in a rocking chair facing the sofa three or four feet away.

"So, my Bert?"

"Mrs. Showley, you husband was not in an accident. Tonight when he went on a repair call, someone killed him. Your husband is dead."

He watched her. Every one acted differently when they received such news. Mrs. Showley sat totally still, her hands folded in her lap. Her face worked into a frown then she looked up at him confusion in her features.

"My Bert. I don't think I heard right. You say he is no hurt in accident. But he is.....you say he is muerto?"

"I'm sorry, Mrs. Showley. That's right. He is no longer living. Someone murdered him tonight in an empty house in San Diego."

Her sudden scream rattled the windows. It blasted out of her small body, washed over him and a moment later she flew at him with her fingers curled into claws as she tried to rip him apart.

"Nooooooooooooooooooooooooooooo" she screamed. The sound spewed from her mouth again and again. Cain saw her coming at him just in time, dodged to the side, and caught one of her hands. She kept lashing at him with the other one.

"You kill him. You bastard, you kill him." She said the words over and over. After a dozen times shouting the words, she shrilled a wild, high scream of terror, pain, and agony.

He set her gently down on the sofa and let go of her hands. The fury had burned out. She collapsed into a thin shape and seemed to wither. Only her eyes remained the same, sad now, the anger gone, the wild and savage outburst quelled. She shivered and put both hands on her rounded belly.

"You not kill my Bert?"

"No. I'm a policeman. It's my job to find out who did. Do you know who called him to come and fix a computer tonight?"

"No. No name. He did business. I don't know computer. All mystery to me. He do business."

"Could he have written down a name on a pad or some paper? Does he have an office here?"

She nodded, stood, and motioned for him to follow her down a short hall and to the left. At the first door he found a small office. It probably had been a bedroom. An old wooden desk sat by a window with four card-board file boxes perched precariously on top of one another at one side. A computer sat on a special table on the other side. Near the telephone lay a scratch pad and a ball point pen. Several messages were there. Including one that read: "Extra $25 for night run. Down in Paradise Hills. Ugg. Better go."

"Did he mention any name where he was going tonight?"

"No. No name. Address. He said bad part of town."

"He was right about that." Cain looked over the desk again. Nothing. There would be nothing. If the killer gave Bert a name it would have been a false one. Taking his office apart would be a waste of time. They went back to the small living room.

"Did your husband have any enemies? Anyone who would want to hurt him?"

"My Bert? No, no. No bad people hate him. He like everybody. No enemies. Didn't owe nobody no money. My Bert was big pussy cat." Tears flashed into her eyes. "He waiting for the baby. Boy, we're having a boy.'"

"Mrs. Showley, do you have any other children?"

"No, just little Bert." She patted her swollen belly. "Named him Bert."

Cain felt himself slipping down a slope. He cleared his throat. "Is there someone I can call for you? A relative, a friend. You should have someone stay with you tonight."

"No. I go to sister's house. Just down street. I stay with her for a while. When can I see my Bert?"

"Someone will call you. You'll need to go to the county morgue to identify him. That's important."

"I have cell phone. I give you number."

Cain took down the number and the name of her sister.

"Had Bert been talking about anything? Making any plans? Maybe thinking about a vacation or a trip?"

Maria Showley pinched her face and slowly shook

her head. "No vacation. No money. Oh, he was excited about something. What? He said it would be a chance to see old friends after such long time."

"What was that, some meeting?"

"He didn't say. I think he got letter. He not show me. I don't know. That weeks ago. Letter gone in trash."

"See if you can remember anything else about it. If you do, call me." He gave her one of his cards, said goodbye, and then got out of there as quickly as he could. God, but he hated these muerto calls. Back in his Chevy he punched up Stacy's number. She answered on the third ring.

"Hey, you do any good with the witness? He remember anything else like a strange car in the neighborhood?"

"A Hi, Stacy, how you doing would be good. Nope. He had nothing more than what he told me at the house. He said he checked the street the way he does every night just before dark and he didn't see any strange cars. He knows the cars, who owns them and the plates. But he said there were no strange ones on the block."

"I got zilch at the widow's place. A note on his desk showed the address and that he was getting twenty five bucks extra for the late night call. This bitch thought of everything."

"Except showing herself on that lighted front porch. She wasn't thinking about that. Maybe she figured nobody would be paying any attention."

"Her first big mistake. That tissue. Maybe we'll get some DNA off the lipstick."

"Doubt it, mostly just color. Afraid the tissue is too soft to pick up any fingerprints. It could have been a great chance to I.D. her, but I don't think so. Anderson will tell us tomorrow."

"Yeah."

"You heading home?"

"About time. You going out on the town?"

"Sure, I've got a late date. We've going to cruise all the hot spots down in the Gaslight District. I probably won't get to sleep until three or four."

"Yeah, sure. Hey, good work tonight. Your woman theory seems to be holding up. Now we have a bitch hunt."

"We can't pick our poison. See you tomorrow."

"Yeah, you do that." He put away the cell then got the Chevy back in motion. He never used the cell when he was driving. He didn't think anyone should and it was against the law. Driving was hard enough when a person's whole attention was on the road and the traffic. Fuddy-duddy. Yeah, he was an old fuddy-duddy. At thirty-two he felt ancient. He didn't know a tenth of the hot new bands and singers. The movie stars were teenagers and he couldn't understand half the music he heard. He'd go home and have a beer and yell at Martha. She'd grin, kiss him, give him some of her terrific home made potato salad, and he'd grumble and she'd call him an old man. Billy and Grace would be in bed by the time he got home. Maybe by then he could put aside for a few hours what he had just seen in that murder house. He would never forget it just shift it into the background for the rest of the night.

A half hour later he pulled into his driveway in the Claremont section of town. He hadn't parked in the attached garage for months. Too many school projects going on and too much junk. The porch light was on.

Inside Martha had been waiting for him. She brought him a beer but no potato salad.

"A bad one?"

"Might say so. Think we have a female serial killer."

Martha frowned. She was a solid woman, about five eight and wider at the hips and waist than last year. She pushed some hair off his forehead then kissed his cheek. She had an oval face with green eyes that often showed wonder. Her nose was classic and she had a long elegant neck. She grinned and dropped beside him on the couch.

"TV or do you want to mess around?"

"Been waiting all day for you to say that. Where were we when that damn telephone went off?"

"Not sure, we could start over."

He grunted and grabbed her. "Fine idea."

STACY ARRIVED in her apartment on Juniper Street. It was home for her. She'd been there for almost a year and had planned on getting a room mate to help cover the rent. She had put a note up on the bulletin board in the cafeteria at work, but nobody had responded. She might try it again. The rent ate up more than half of her monthly pay. Be good to have another female cop to bunk with. Maybe soon.

She yawned and stretched. Shower time, then a good night's sleep so she could hit the case first thing in the morning. She'd get to work by seven thirty and get her report written up.

The shower was good. It was in a combination tub and shower and she almost pushed in the plug and had a long soaking bath, but decided not to. She always closed the bathroom door when she used the toilet or took a shower. She wasn't sure why. Nobody else in the place. She wondered if others did the same thing.

The big blue fuzzy towel soaked up the moisture from her. She stared at her naked body for a minute in the full length mirror on the bathroom door. She had heard some women say they never looked at their naked form. They must be fat. She wasn't. Maybe a few extra pounds around her middle. Those were the hardest to lose. Waist still trim, hips under control and her boobs......not as big as she had wished for as a teen but she'd never had any complaints. She shook her head making her short brown hair spin. She pulled on a large sized Sea World tee shirt and dropped on her bed. A bitch hunt. Oh, yes, that's what they had on their plate. If this bitch was also a witch they would be in deep trouble.

She had been thinking about going to City College and get some law enforcement credits. The cost wasn't much, maybe forty dollars a credit hour. Books would be more. She could afford it. She'd talk to Cain about it tomorrow. He had suggested that she start working on a B.A. degree.

"So what if it takes you six or seven years to get it, you'll be learning good stuff you can use all the way through. Work on it."

Maybe when they got this bitch hunt over. She grinned. She liked the play on words, it was appropriate. Cain came up with a good one once in a while.

She groaned. It had been two weeks since she had talked to her mother. Her parents lived in El Cajon, just east of town. She should take them out to dinner.

They loved that. Denny's or Coco's would do just fine. She'd give her mother a call tomorrow. Too late tonight.

She adjusted the stuffed animal on her night stand. He was Frisky, one of the new panda cubs at the San Diego Zoo. Frisky was her good luck charm. She patted him on the nose and turned out the lights.

Now if the damn phone didn't ring she could get a good night's sleep. She drifted off still thinking about the butchered dead man on that bloody bed in Paradise Hills.

12

THE NEXT MORNING at the office, Stacy and the rest of them were waiting for the autopsy report from the medical examiner. Lee had been the detective assigned to baby sit the autopsy.

Cain threw the crime lab report on Lee's desk.

"A whole lot of fucking nothing," he said. "The lipstick on the tissue was worthless. All it did was tell us that a woman had been in the room at some point in time, and not necessarily last night. No fibers that were of any use. No sign of the genitals. No knife and no gun. Outside of that, we've got an open and open case."

"Not a thing?" Lee asked.

"We've got the eye witness who said he saw what he thought was a woman standing at the front door in the porch light. Could have been a thin man with a long hair wig. So far that's about it. The condoms weren't any help. Common type that you can buy in every other store in the country. By now we've checked the county recorder's office so we know who owns the house. He lives in New Jersey and an agency here in town rents it out for him. They hadn't been to the property since they put up the last for rent sign a month ago."

He looked around at his four detectives. "Any of you geniuses have any good news for me?"

One chair scraped.

A small cough sounded.

A throat cleared.

"Figured. Okay, we're looking at our two murders this way. Kevin and Fernando, you two stay on the Judith Lancaster kill. Stacy and Lee, you're on the Showley case. First order of business for Kevin and Fernando has to be the plates on the twenty-four new black Lexus buckets of bolts. Don't just look at the women owners. The men owners could have a wife or girl friend who drives the car, so investigate everyone. Watch for nervousness and alibis for the kill time. Should keep you busy for a day or two."

Cain turned and looked at Stacy and Lee. "Showley is an unknown quantity. Check him out right back to kindergarten if you have to. We want to know everyone he knew, look at his records on customers, and see if his wife remembers any complaints. Go to neighbors, relatives, his parents, stay with it until you turn up something."

The mail room girl dropped an inner office large brown envelope on Cain's desk. He grunted and picked it up. His name was on the "to" line. The previous recipient was the medical examiner. He opened the flap and pulled out the ME's autopsy report. He scanned it quickly reading what he wanted to learn.

"Yeah. Death by asphyxia after he aspirated his own vomit into his lungs and couldn't breathe. He was dead before he would have died from loss of blood in his genital area. The bullet, a .32 caliber, was recovered with good rifling showing four grooves. No other signs of trauma to the body. No other wounds or bruises. The castration and penectomy appear to be the result of intense sexual rage against the sexual activity of the deceased. Death declared a homicide."

"That was a big help," Stacy said.

"Sexual rage is the key here," Cain said. "You two get on your horses and see what you can track down. You know the routine. Start with his wife who is staying with her sister down the block." He gave them the address. "Then see his parents, old girlfriends. He'd been married three years, somebody said. Get to it. His wife is Mexican but speaks enough English so you won't need Fernando."

"On our way, boss," Stacy said.

They checked out an unmarked and Stacy drove them to the La Mesa address of the wife's sister. A short, fat Mexican woman came to the door and looked blankly at them when they said what they wanted. Maria appeared right behind her sister Guadalupe and asked them to come in. Her eyes were still red ringed. She asked them to sit on an old couch in front of a modest sized TV set.

"What you find out?" she asked.

"Little so far," Stacy said. "May I call you Maria?" the small pregnant woman nodded. "We know someone was tremendously angry with Bert. We don't know why. We're doing everything we can to figure out who did it. May we ask you some questions?"

"Si, yes."

"Did Bert have any enemies, business or personal?"

They worked through the usual questions about

business and friends. Then Stacy moved in another direction.

"How long have you been married?"

"Three years."

"Did you know any of Bert's girlfriends before you married him?"

"No. He live here. I live in San Ysidro." She stopped and frowned. "One. One woman came to door after wedding. Not nice. Yelled at Bert, threw things at him. Bert laughed at her and told her go. She screamed at him and call him names."

"Do you remember her name?"

He wrote down name. Told me not to talk if she call. Name still on refrigerator door."

"At your house?" Maria nodded.

They drove up the block to Maria's house and went inside. At the refrigerator she took down a faded yellow piece of paper with a name and phone number. Stacy grinned.

"This is good, Maria. Muy bueno. I'll write down the name and number. You put it back on the door." Stacy put down the name in her small notebook. Wanda Werring. Three years later the phone number probably wouldn't be any good but she put it down. 463-5847.

"Did Bert have any men friends he went to football games with, or went bike riding or running? Anything like that?"

"My Bert play softball. Old man ball he call. Saturday morning."

"Where did they play?"

"I show you. Don't know name."

They drove to the La Mesa Recreation center that

still proudly displayed the La Mesa Little League World Champion banners from years ago.

"Play here all year round," Maria said.

"Do you remember the name of the league?" Lee asked.

Maria shook her head. "No, but Bert has paper at home with his batting average. He happy about that."

They drove back to Bert and Maria's home. She unlocked the door and they went inside. In the small office she showed him the sheet of paper with the name of the league: The Over The Hill 27 League.

"Have to be twenty-seven years to play," Maria said.

Stacy looked at the sheet. It listed six teams with the players and their at bats, strike outs, walks, runs batted in, home runs, and batting average.

"Can I take this?" Stacy asked. "I'll bring it back." Maria nodded. While they were there Lee had a question.

"Did Bert owe anyone any money? Besides a mortgage on the house, I'd guess."

Maria frowned not understanding.

"Did he borrow money from the bank?"

"No borrow. Bad credit, he tell me."

Lee frowned this time. "Did Bert ever go out with the guys from the team, drinking?"

"Drink?" she frowned again. "Bert like beer."

Stacy was scowling at Lee as if he were asking dumb questions. At last she poked him and when he turned she talked to Maria.

"Thanks for your help. We've got to go now. Can we take you back to your sister's house?"

"No. Stay here a while. Think about Bert."

Later in the car, Lee drove. He looked at her with a lifted brow. "What was that poke in the ribs about?"

"I want to get back to the office and see what we can do with the list of softball players. Could lead somewhere."

"Like maybe one of the boys is a woman?"

"Hey, good idea. I hadn't thought of that." She snorted. "No dummy, like maybe some of them know more about Bert's business affairs than his wife did. This could be partly a money motive kill."

"Not a chance. A woman did it who was incensed with Bert's cock hound lifestyle."

"Didn't look like he was sexually active lately, not with a baby on the way."

Lee looked over at Stacy. "Hey, what does a killer bitch do with a scrotum and penis once she chops them off?"

Stacy shook her head. "I have no idea."

Lee laughed softly. "Hey, I wonder if there was a food grinder in that sink."

Stacy whacked Lee on the shoulder with her hand. "Now that is sick." She frowned and looked back at him. "Sick but a great idea. You should call Anderson over in the crime lab and ask him if they checked it. My guess is they didn't."

BACK IN THE OFFICE, Cain took their report on Bert's wife.

"Not much," he said.

"We didn't expect much. The softball team might be more productive. Could be some jealousy there, some vibes, we'll check for anything."

"The license plate guys are out pounding the pavement. They cut two off the list. A second DMV report we just got in showed that two of the cars were resold two weeks ago."

Lee told Cain about the food disposal under the sink idea. Cain guffawed.

"Yeah, phone Anderson. Bet he never thought to check that. I want to listen in."

Lee looked up the number and dialed the four digits. It took two more minutes to get Anderson to the phone.

"Lieutenant Anderson, this is Lee over in homicide. We were wondering about what happened to the victim's genitals. Did you check the disposal under the kitchen sink?"

"You pulling my crime scene leg, detective?"

"No sir. It just occurred to us that it could have been a way to dispose of the evidence."

There was a long pause.

"Damnit," Anderson said. "Hell yes, there could be a chance our killer did that. It would have left some residue, but what would it prove?"

"Not much, I guess," Lee said.

Anderson chuckled. "We'll check. I've been looking for some shit detail for a guy. This should work in nicely. Thanks for the tip. We'll keep you informed."

Lee, Stacy and Cain hung up and they all laughed.

"Had him stopped for a minute," Cain said. "Now where do we go from here?"

"I was thinking about commonality," Stacy said. "Do we have any between the two kills?" They went to the tack board and looked at the list of evidence, speculation, and facts listed below each homicide.

Lee pointed. "Both of them were 28 years old."

"Both of the motives could have been sexual rage," Stacy said. "Granted we might have a bitch hunt here. She could have been going both ways."

"Not likely," Cain said. "Sexual rage in the last one is for sure. Rage maybe in the first one, but not sexual. None of the usual signs. Rather a strange way to kill someone, and with stranger yet device, the pantyhose."

"Is that all we have?" Lee asked.

"That and the bitch theory that Judith could have been killed by a woman as well," Cain said. "Not enough. We don't know for sure right now whether these two deaths were at the hand of the same person. Let's try to tie that down, people. Go work on Showley. Follow up on that softball team. Catch some of them at home tonight, then go to the game on Saturday and talk to them. You might dig up something. And, Stacy, call that old girlfriend. Looks like she might be mad enough at him to cut him up before she killed him. The condoms play a role there, too."

Lee went back to his desk. "I'm going to run him for wants and warrants. Not much hope but we need to do it. Then I'll check out his credit rating and any business group he belonged to, like the La Mesa Chamber of Commerce."

Cain got up from his desk favoring his right knee. "I'll go talk to the lieutenant and try to explain why his best detective team is dead in the water on two homicides that could be the work of a female serial killer. But just as well might be two different perps."

Stacy checked the phone book. There was one listing for Wanda Warring and it showed the address. She dialed. It rang four times then someone picked up.

"Yeah?"

"Wanda"

"Yeah, so what?"

"Did you know Bert Showley about three years ago?"

"Not a chance. I only been in town a year or so."

"Okay, thanks."

She hung up and called information. She asked for a county wide search for the name and the operator gave her another one with a La Mesa address. She called.

"Wanda?"

"That's right. Who is calling?"

"I wondered if you knew Bert Showley about three years ago?"

A long pause.

"May I ask why are you calling?"

"If you knew him, we need to talk to you. Are you still at 8484 Linda Way there in La Mesa?"

"Yes. Curious. Who are you?"

"I'm Detective Stacy DeFrain with the San Diego Police Department."

Another long pause.

"I don't understand. Is he in trouble?"

"You could say that."

"Just lock up the sonofabitch and throw away the fucking key. I hope he starves to death." The phone connection broke off.

Stacy checked the address.

"Our friend Wanda is home in La Mesa, knew Bert and hopes that he'll starve to death. I'm going out and have a girl to girl talk."

. . .

THIRTY MINUTES later Stacy eased an unmarked to a stop outside the address of Wanda Warring in La Mesa. It was a well kept four-plex. Wanda lived on the first floor right. When Stacy rang the bell no one answered immediately. When the door opened it was a two inch crack and Stacy could see the safety chain on.

"Wanda? I'm Detective Stacy DeFrain. We talked on the phone about an hour ago."

"Oh. Yes. Let me get the chain off."

Inside a moment later Stacy found Wanda to be a tall blonde with short hair, a slender body and wearing a slack suit you don't buy off the rack. Her face held the classic high cheek bones and pristine clear skin that looked soft enough to smudge. Her eyes were hazel with flecks of green and her nose the perfect finish on a beautiful face.

"I've been gone for a day on a job in LA. I just saw the paper when I got home. I read it after you called. Bert is really dead?"

"Positively."

"Murdered, the paper says."

"I'm afraid so. It's my job to find out who did it. Did you kill him?"

Her face took a slack almost hurt expression. "No, of course not. I've been in LA on a two day shoot. I can give you people to call to confirm it. My agent for one."

"You're an actress or a model?"

"Both, trying to break into film. It's horrendously hard."

"What can you tell me about Bert?"

"I haven't seen him or talked to him for over three years. I yelled at his wife just after they married. I was sure that Bert and I had something special. Kids ruined us."

"How so?"

"He wanted five or six kids, I said one or two but not for ten years. He said goodbye." She took a deep breath. "What I said on the phone about him starving to death. I didn't mean that. I was just suddenly remembering our last few days together."

"Do you know anyone who might want to hurt Bert?"

Wanda shook her head. "No. He made friends quickly, easily. Everybody loved Bert. I was only with him for six months or so, but he was one great guy."

"Somebody really hated him."

"The story was true about the condoms and his genitals missing?"

"True, and it isn't helping us any."

"Look for a woman."

"What?"

"A woman killed him I'll give you a hundred to one. Consider the rage with the knife on his privates. And then the condoms. It has to be a woman he had a sexual relationship with that went bad. Hey, it wasn't me. I was out of town and working. Let me give you those phone numbers you can call. Check me out. I'm not a part of this."

"I will. Oh, do you have a gun for protection?"

"Yes, is that important?"

"Bert was also shot. What caliber is your weapon?"

"It's a little thirty two caliber automatic."

13

SHE HAD JUST TURNED fourteen and gradually realized that boys were looking at her differently. That night just before she went to bed, she stared down at her chest. Yes, they were larger, not as big as her mother's, but bigger. Much, much better than last year. Slowly the hormones were charging through her body and she didn't know how to handle them.

She talked to her mother, but mom had stammered, shook her head, and changed the subject. No help there. Her father was out of bounds.

Then a week later on a soft summer night she had been playing tag with the boy next door she had known since they had both been in the first grade. She had noticed changes in him lately, too. His voice was lower and he kept staring at her breasts. They laughed and rolled on the grass then they bumped into each other and caught hold to stop. His hand brushed her breasts. He leaned in and kissed her. She lay still for a moment, then reached up and kissed him back. She didn't remember how many times they had kissed, but at one point she was so worked up that she took his hand and put it on her breast. He made a strange sound and his hips pumped six times and he yelped in delight. He took her hand and put it over his crotch where she felt a long hard object. Was it his....? It had to be.

She rolled away from him, scrambled to her feet, and rushed into her house. She didn't speak to him for a week. It was so embarrassing. Or was it? She was totally confused and so mixed up emotionally that she had a super big fight with her mother about how short a skirt could be. She had raced up the stairs and slammed her room door. She wished she had a lock on it. She pushed a chair against the door and threw herself on the bed. Why was it so hard? Damnit, why was growing up so hard?

That afternoon her mother went to the store and she begged off. She wandered into the back yard and found their three month old registered Cocker Spaniel pestering a bone made out of dried cow hide. She threw it for the pup a few times, and then grabbed it. Puppies had no problem growing up. No problems at all. She pulled at his leg until he barked in protest. She felt strange. Hurting the dog satisfied something deep inside her. She smiled as she jerked the small leg again and the dog howled in pain.

She laughed. It felt so good.

A half hour later the small dog lay dead at her feet. Its eyes had been gouged out, all four of its legs broken, its tail cut off and its belly sliced open with a paring knife. She laughed softly at the carcass and made no attempt to hide it. She went back into the house and had a Coke and cookies.

Her mother freaked out when she came home and

took the puppy a new kind of food. There had been a lot of yelling and screaming, and tears from her mother. Her father had been soft spoken and that scared her more than anything. They had talked. She told them how she felt, that everything was against her, and everyone was trying to take advantage of her. She told them about the boy and her grouping each other on the lawn.

Her father peaked his fingers where he sat in his den and stared through the opening. He told her that such sexual experimenting was entirely normal, and she shouldn't worry about it. Her father was smart, and she believed him. He had been a licensed psychologist before he switched to real estate so he could make more money.

When they talked about the puppy, she cried. Then it had seemed like exactly the right thing to do. To take out her anger and hatred on the small dog. He father held her hands and talked quietly.

"Twyla what you did to the puppy was wrong. Thinking that way is not normal. You must be extremely careful thinking that way, or doing anything like that again." Then he had hugged her and let her cry. She said she would never ever hurt another animal as long as she lived.

She never did. The next thing she hurt was Sarah Jane, a girl about her own age who said embarrassing things about her to other girls and boys at high school when she was fifteen. She had hated Sara Jane on the spot and let the anger and fury churn and build all afternoon. Then after school, on the walk home, she had waited for Sara Jane and chased her into a wooded section. She caught her and without a word began beating her and tearing off her clothes. When Sara Jane was naked, she let her up from the ground, picked up the discarded clothes and held them as she ran back through the woods toward her house. Sara Jane lay on the ground sobbing. She didn't come to school for almost a week. When she did come back she had bruises on her face and arms and one arm held a pristine white plaster cast from wrist to elbow.

Sara Jane evidently never told anyone who attacked her, because no one came to her house with the police. It had been a highly satisfactory experience, one she would never forget. The best of all, she didn't have to talk with her father about Sarah Jane.

14

IT HAD BEEN one hell of a tough day, Twyla decided as she let herself into her condo. They were jury picking and she didn't have anything to do with that, so she was out vetting some more witnesses. They needed all the favorable faces and voices they could find. Sometimes that was hard trying to get a friendly person who was willing to testify for this creep...their client, Trevor Jamison.

She had eaten on the way home and now had a quick shower and dropped into bed. There was more vetting to do tomorrow. She didn't know when she'd get back to the trial. She tried three sleeping positions and none worked. For just a moment she thought about Bert Showley. What a loser. He blubbered for his life before she got his fucking mouth jammed with condoms. What a jerk.

"But you loved it when he fucked you in high school."

Twyla snorted. Her damn voices again. "I didn't love it, he raped me."

"Sure, sure, and you screamed and hit him and told him no, no, no a dozen times. Ha. You loved it. Your first time and you were out of your muff with excitement."

"Shut up, bitch, when I need any...."

"You're more foul mouthed now than before. Killing people has changed you."

"I don't kill people. I pay them back for what they did to me ten years ago."

"Hot shit. Now there is some perfect rationalization. What do you think the San Diego cops will call your little pay back episodes?"

"I don't care. Now leave me alone."

"Why? You're a mean assed fucking serial killer who is planning to do in some more totally innocent people. You're scum you and your big fucking law degree and passing the bar doesn't make you..."

"I said, shut up." She whirled, her face grim, her hands in front of her as if to push someone away.

"So why did you wait ten years? Why didn't you nail the bastards the year after graduation?"

"I needed resources, to get established. So I'd have the cash and the ability to do the job right."

"Sara Jane."

"Don't you dare mention that name." Twyla sat up in bed swatting as if swinging at a marauding mosquito. "I won't allow you to use her name."

"Sara Jane, Sara Jane, Sara Jane."

"Just go away and leave me alone."

"Why, so you can plan more killings, more murders most foul?"

"Yes, yes, plan more. Two more, maybe three if I could get my hands around your scrawny, scratchy voiced neck."

"Now you're getting personal."

Twyla threw back the sheet and rolled out of bed. She went to the bathroom and picked out the Tylenol PM and downed two pills with a glass of water.

"No, no. Not those damn blue pills. I hate those pills. Now we can't continue our little chat."

Twyla grinned and slipped back into bed. She hit the pillow and just as she heard the voice screaming at her again, she nodded off to sleep.

THE NEXT DAY Twyla was in the social set of La Jolla for the first three contacts. Two of the women said they had interesting memories of Trevor Jamison, but that was in their far, far past. They absolutely would not testify for him in any way. The third one said she remembered Jamison. He was a little old for her but she would be glad to testify on his behalf, if she were not going to Switzerland in two weeks. She'd be there for six months.

Twyla had lunch on the firm at a swanky little hotel in La Jolla and drove back to the downtown section of San Diego. She hated La Jolla. It even had its own post office, when it was just a section of San Diego. A lot of rich creeps lived out there. Tremendously rich ones she hadn't met yet. It might take some time. She wouldn't mind meeting a rich young bachelor.

Twyla checked her watch. Time to go see Shadow. Dear Shadow Enright. She was the one witness for the defense who had to hold up or their alibi for Trevor was shot down. Shadow lived on Point Loma in one of the better homes perched on the side of the hill with a beautiful view of the San Diego Bay, the Pacific Ocean, and most of San Diego. She was a stripper and dancer by night, and a volunteer to help poor readers in the second grade where her daughter attended school in the afternoon. She saw no conflict in the activities.

Shadow answered the door on the first ring. She was almost six feet tall, with brilliant red hair, glowing skin and simply a gorgeous figure. On top of that she was beautiful even at one thirty in the afternoon.

"Shadow, I'm Twyla, we talked on the phone."

"Yeah, I remember. This Trevor Jamison guy. The big society bird we read about in the paper. He said he was with me that night? Not that I keep any kind of records, but I'm not at all sure..." She stopped. "What? Why the look?"

"You told me over the phone that you were sure that Trevor was with you on February 12, a Tuesday, from after work at two a.m. until noon the next day." She took an envelope from her purse and waved it. "You may remember that we had a viable verbal contract."

Shadow motioned Twyla to a couch that looked new and had a blue and brown pattern.

"Oh, yeah, I forgot. A contract. Yeah. Okay. It was Trevor, I'm sure and I remember, because he drove me home in this small Humvee. I'd never been in one before."

"Good girl. Now you know the prosecutor is going to cross examine you and ask questions."

"Yeah. He'll ask if we had sex and I say sure. He'll ask me if Trevor paid me for sex, and I'll say not exactly. He gave me a present. He'll say what kind of a present, and I'll say a present in a box. And he'll say what was in the box. And I say five brand new one hundred dollar bills."

"Good girl. You know we're relying on you to remember it exactly that way. He was there with you in the club from nine that night, took you home about two a.m. He stayed at your place until the next morning and was there until noon."

"Yeah, gotcha. He was."

Twyla held out the envelope. "There are five thousand dollars in there. Don't deposit it in your checking account. If you have a savings account, don't put it in there. Hide it somewhere here in your apartment where nobody could find it. If you are asked by the prosecutor if you were paid by Trevor or by the defense to testify, you lie. You say of course not. Clear?"

"Clear. Yeah, clear as crystal." She frowned. "Never seen any crystal that was clear. It's always got those cuts and marks on it."

"True, Shadow. Remember, don't deposit this anywhere or give it to anyone to keep. It's our little secret. And lie when they ask you if anyone paid you to testify."

"Gotcha."

BACK HOME TWYLA did some work on her own agenda. She got on her computer and did research. She had almost all she needed. Number three on the list was Ron Ingram, 36 years old, and a teacher at Hoover High School. Yes, he was still there after ten years. He had moved into teaching American and World History. She had his address and phone number. She didn't know his Email address. There was no Web Site with his name on it.

How to get to him? How to get him under her

control so she could carry out the several little activities she had planned for him? He had embarrassed her almost every day when she was in his classes at Hoover. Now it was pay back time. But how?

She would have to use the gun again, at least to get him under control. She wouldn't shoot him. A bullet would tie her in with the Showley kill. That would not be good. Out of the house. When did he go out of the house? Survey time. He wouldn't be home this time in the afternoon. His wife. Twyla took out his phone number and called.

"Hello, Mrs. Ingram. Is your husband home?"

"No, he's still at work."

"We're from the Western Research Group and taking a quick survey. Could you help us?"

"Well, if it won't take long."

"Good. Is your husband a member of any of the men's service groups like the Lions or the Optimists?"

"Why, yes, he does go to the Lions meetings at noon on Wednesdays. Every Wednesday, he never misses."

"Any others like a bowling league, or adult softball?"

"No, he gave up on ball years ago. Arthritis. Anything else?"

"Which Lions meeting does he go to? There are many of them in town."

"Oh, the North Park one, at a Denny's there."

"Thank you, Mrs. Ingram, you've helped the survey results."

Twyla hung up and showed a big grin. Wednesdays, Denny's at the North Park restaurant. She'd be there tomorrow. She had some preparations to make. Her digital camera and printer were right where she had left them. They were ready to work. She'd take the camera with her tomorrow. She picked up a pair of the plastic riot cuffs like the police use. They are plastic strips with notches in them. You thread the end through the loop and notches click in as you pull it tight. Impossible to get out of until someone cuts the plastic. Did she need a mask? No. There was no way he would remember her. He'd had more than a thousand students in his classes since she'd been there.

She remembered his classes with absolute clarity. She had never been so embarrassed in her life. He delighted in picking on her and asking her to answer the toughest questions. Then when she didn't know the answer he'd make some smart remark just to get a laugh from the class. Not just once, but almost always one or two times a day for the whole school year. She had never got used to it.

More than a year ago she had done a lot of research on Ron Ingram. He had claimed to have graduated from a small college in Northern California. She contacted their alumni association and they reported no such person had ever attended the college, let alone graduated. She wrote a letter to the college registrar and asked the same question. She got back a letter on the school stationary that no Ron Ingram had ever attended Pacific Ocean University.

Next she wrote to the California agency that issued teaching credentials. They quickly wrote back that no Ron Ingram from San Diego had ever applied for a teaching credential or been issued one in the past twenty years. She had the ammunition. She just hadn't figured out how to use it. The man was a fraud and a bully.

Now she had the plan. It was Tuesday night. She called for a taxi and had the driver take her to Fashion Valley Shopping Center, just a few miles away. She roamed the parking lot. She needed a van, new or old, she didn't care. It took her an hour to find a van with keys in the ignition. It was harder at night but she spotted one, a Dodge Caravan maybe ten years old. She got in and drove it back to her condo complex and parked it in the visitor's space at the rear of the building. No cop was going to come in there looking for a stolen car.

Twyla took out her old high school year book and studied Ingram's picture. She wanted to be sure that she would recognize him. He'd be ten years older, maybe a little gray and with at least ten more pounds. He always wore glasses, and he had three or four tweed jackets. She figured he still wore them with a white shirt and tie.

Twyla looked over her digital camera. It was fairly new but she remembered how to work it. She took two pictures of her office in the second bedroom. Yes, she could use it just fine. Then she had a long hot tub bath and tried to relax. Her nerves were twanging and jumping. She had never felt so keyed up before a pay back.

"Well, aren't you the sneaky little serial killer working on your next victim."

Twyla closed her eyes and shook her head. "Not you again. I simply won't listen to you. I won't. You are nasty and evil and I won't let you say a word."

"Try to stop me, bitch. You can't and you won't. You know that you're out of bounds. You're a lawyer for god's sakes, you know the law. You're way outside it just the way you have been for years. The problem is, nobody ever suspected you so you got away free and clear."

Twyla splashed water at the end of the tub. "Shut up, shut up, shut up. I won't listen. You can't make me listen. I won't."

"Marybeth Hughes."

Twyla screamed. The sound echoed inside the bathroom, slanted out the half open window and faded out in the alley behind the condo. She sat up in the tub, her face flushed and twisted into a vicious mask.

"I wish I could strangle you, you bitch. Why do you bother me this way? Why? Leave me alone. And never, never say that girl's name again."

"Marybeth Hughes. Marybeth Hughes. Marybeth Hughes."

Twyla screamed again, this time she choked it off, stepped out of the tub, and grabbed a large towel. She hurried out of the bathroom to her bedroom, dropped on the pink and white bedspread, and let the tears roll down her cheeks.

It took ten minutes for the tears to stop. Then she sat up and shook her head. Reality. She had to get back to reality. No more voices. No more memories. Just the pay back motive. That was all she needed. Yes PAY BACK, in capital letters and in bold face type. That's all she needed. That's all she would ever need – at least for right now.

15

THE MORNING after Stacy talked to Wanda Waring, she told Cain about the meeting and that Wanda owned a .32.

He harrumphed and stared at her. "You say she's a model and actress. Is she pretty?"

"Gorgeous, thin and lanky and....just beautiful."

"So why did the jerk ditch her?"

"Kids, she said. He wanted five. She said wait ten years. He gave her back her key."

"Keep her in your file. But she doesn't sound like the type. Especially with that alibi. Did you check the people in LA?"

"My first job this morning." She talked to them and indeed Wanda had been working both days she said she did, and a hundred and forty miles away from San Diego. A perfect alibi.

Kevin and Fernando were bitching about not being able to find some of the Lexus owners.

"Two of them just left on long driving trips,"

Fernando said. "Be gone two or three weeks. Most of them work."

"We've cut the list down to twelve, and some of them we just can't locate. For two of them their DMV address isn't the right one anymore."

Cain's phone rang and he grabbed it.

"Homicide, Cain." He listened a minute then grinned and hit his speaker phone with the volume up.

"...so I didn't know if you were joking or what. I sent one of our guys out there to check the food disposal under the sink. Yeah, there was one and whoever used it last didn't bother to run much water. We found enough blood and tissue to make a definite DNA match with Showley and his privates."

"You're welcome, Anderson. But that doesn't help us one damn bit to find the killer."

"Yeah, I know. But figured you might want to know. You just keep the old dobbers up."

There was a silence.

Cain grunted. "Yeah, we used to say that back in high school. I never knew what it meant back then, and I still don't."

"Don't worry about it," Anderson said. "I don't know what it means either. Take care."

They hung up.

"One small step for man, no step at all for mankind," Stacy said.

"They owe us one now," Cain said. "I'll remind Anderson of that next time I see him. Now, what the hell we got working?"

"Not much on Showley," Lee said. "We've about ruled out any business motive. He was a loner who did his thing with computers and didn't interact with any high powered types."

"Which leaves his personal life," Cain said. "Get back to work digging him out. I want to know everything he did and said from the time he was in grade school. You talked to his parents yet?"

"Next on my list," Stacy said. She looked at her notes. "He had a kind of pro arrangement with one of the big computer stores out in Grossmont Center," Stacy continued. "He'd refer clients there or he'd buy parts he needed or whole computers, lap tops, screens and get a discount. I'm set to see the manager later this morning."

"Doesn't sound like killing money," Cain said. "Lee, you go see his parents. Mother may be home. See what she can tell you. She might remember the jobs he had just out of high school and before he went into business for himself. Some people have long memories when it comes to getting shafted by another person."

"Especially women," Stacy said.

"Did he go to college?" Can asked.

Both detectives shrugged.

"We don't know," Lee said.

"Find out. He played softball. Maybe he was a jock in college or high school. Some of those guys did unkind things to girls."

"I'll ask his mother," Lee said.

Stacy went over and looked at the pin board that showed both cases, the clues, and data on both. She concentrated on the Showley case, but there was almost nothing there. Nothing she could follow up on. Not a damn name or client or source she could touch.

She went to the women's locker room and the john.

She was washing her hands when a redheaded sergeant came in. Stacy knew her but they had never been close friends. Her name was Alice Schatzman and she was about thirty. She was in uniform and it fit her perfectly.

"Hey, Stacy. I've been thinking about you."

"Hey, I didn't do it, I've got an alibi." They both laughed.

"No not work thinking. You look so sleek, in good shape. You must run."

"When I get the chance."

Alice walked over closer to her, her eyes sparkling. "You been getting laid lately?"

Stacy laughed. "Not often no."

"I was just wondering. Hell, Stacy, I'll just say it. I go both ways. I love the softness of a woman between my thighs, the light touch, the tenderness. You know?"

"I'm afraid...."

"Stacy, what I'm wondering could we get together one of these nights to just, you know, fool around a little? If you don't want to more than cuddle a little, what the hell?"

"Alice, I don't go both ways."

"You ever tried it? Hell, how do you know? With women it's different than men. We can go both ways and have a ball at both of them. Want to do a little experiment?"

"What do you mean, Alice?"

"Just a little kiss. A trial balloon. If you don't like it we go no father. You know, a kind of test. See if it gives you a little thrill, makes your old muff jiggle a bit."

Before Stacy could move, Alice pushed up against her, her mouth covered Stacy's, and she felt a tongue on her lips.

"Hey, no fair," Alice said. "Open up, for just a little test." Her mouth went back on Stacy's who hadn't moved. She opened her mouth and felt Alice's tongue push in and work around. At the same time she felt Alice's hand caressing one of her breasts. The kiss lasted longer than Stacy wanted it to. When they broke apart, Alice eased back, but kept rubbing Stacy's breast through her blouse. Stacy felt nothing, not a whisper or a whimper of any sexual excitement.

"Wow," Alice said. "Stacy honey, you are hot."

Stacy stepped back disengaging the hand. She blinked and shook her head a moment. "Well, I don't know, Alice. A kiss is just a kiss. That was, yeah, hot. But I think it was all your hot. I don't think that it would work out. I mean we could cuddle, but there would be no way I could do anything else."

"Not even a little magic fingers?"

Stacy laughed and held up her hands and moved her fingers. "So that's what you call it." She shook her head. "No, Alice, I think we've gone about as far as we can go. Hey, no problem. It was just a test. You take care now." Stacy didn't exactly run from the room, but she did hurry a little. Once outside the locker room she leaned against the wall a minute. That was the second time a woman had come on hard to her with the same results. Where the hell were all the good looking men?

Back in the office she looked at the board again and added an item. "Softball." She went to her desk and phoned the widow Showley at her sister's home. She was in.

"So, Mrs. Showley, I wondered if you had the name of the manager of the softball team?"

"Yes. Name is Mark.'

"Do you have his phone number?"

"Number on league paper you took."

"Right, I should have thought of that. Thanks."

She got the paper from Lee and found the team and the manager with his phone number. She called.

"Mark's Used Sports Goods. How can I help you?"

Stacy grinned. "Mark, you're the team manager of the Bobcats, right?"

"One of my fun jobs. Yeah."

"You heard about Bert?"

"That I did. Shocked right down to my number nine iron. I mean he was one okay guy."

"Could I come talk to you about Bert? This is Detective Stacy DeFrain of the San Diego Police."

"Really? Sure come out any time. I'm in a little shopping mall in La Mesa just off Dallas." He gave her the address.

"I can find it. I'll be there in about half an hour."

MARK'S USED Sporting Goods was squeezed between a Better Burger and an arts and crafts place. The whole store was no more than twenty feet wide and forty feet deep. Mark was up front showing a man a set of bar bells.

"Free weight the only way to go, man. You can adjust it exactly to what you need. These damn new machines are a bunch of crap."

He looked up and saw Stacy. "Hey, you the cop? Don't know if I can tell you much."

"Finish with your customer," Stacy said.

"Him? He's no customer. Just comes in to kill time.

He's waiting for prostate cancer to kill him and he dreams a lot."

Mark was a little heavy, wearing a Padres tee shirt and brown shorts. When he grinned his face broke into pieces and came back together slowly showing sharp green eyes, thinning hair and jug handle ears.

"You want to talk about Bert. No glove but he could hit like crazy. We kept him in right field since the fewest balls go out there. What do you want to know?"

"Who would want to kill him?"

The cancer guy's ears perked up and he had found a new way to kill time.

"That's what's been making me wonder. Hell, we just played ball, but I thought I knew him."

"He mixed up with any kind of dope operation, coke, meth, heroin?"

"Oh, hell no. Bert was a straight arrow. He didn't believe in none of that shit. Pardon the French. He didn't have no friends into that stuff either. It was mostly work for him and then we played ball every Sunday morning. He was some hitter. Highest average on our team. He loved to bang out singles, drilling the ball between the infielders. He had a good eye and a great bat."

"Was he in trouble with any women?"

"Bert? Not a chance. You got to be kidding me. He had his wife and he just worshipped her. She's pregnant and that's all Bert would talk about. Her and the baby. They knew it was a boy and they named him already Bert junior."

"How long have you known him?"

"We been playing ball for five years. We play all year around. No off season. Started even before he got his computer thing going. I've never known him to step out on his wife or before her a girlfriend. Steady and loyal. That was Bert. And he sure knew his computers. Got me all set up here so I know exactly what I have in stock, even if I can't find an item sometimes."

"Anything else about Bert?"

"Naw. He was a good Joe. What a hitter. Gonna have to find myself another hitter. The team used to go out for beer after a game. Kind of cool out and calm down. Once Bert had four or five beers and got to feeling maudlin and even cried a little. He said he really fucked up in high school. Something about this chic his senior year he really liked and then one night he got carried away and did her in the back seat of his car. After that she wouldn't speak to him. I think he really loved that high school girl. He only talked about it once."

"High school. That must have been eight or ten years ago. I don't think we can do much with that." Stacy took a deep breath and shook her head. In fact they couldn't do a damn thing with that. So he boffed a high school girl, big deal. Happened all the time. She closed her small notebook and put it and her pen in her purse.

"Tell you what, Mark. If you think of something that might tie Bert into anything with a killing edge, you give me a call." She handed him her card, waved and went out the front door to her car. Not a damn thing there. Not a damn thing anywhere.

Before she drove she called Cain on his cell and told him what she didn't find out.

"Yeah figures. On your way back stop in at Grossmont Center and talk to that computer guy, most likely the manager or sales manager about the deal Bert had with them. Might turn up something."

"I'm about a mile from there. Good timing. I'll swing by there now."

THE SALES MANAGER talked to Stacy in his cubby hole office. His name was Reggie and he was thin, nervous, with a whiteside haircut like he'd just got out of Marine boot camp.

"Yeah, we heard about Bert. Not one of our big customers but he did throw business our way. And he bought parts and boards here and whatever he needed. Good guy."

"Any idea who might want to kill him?"

"Oh, hell no. Everybody liked Bert. Went out of his way to talk to the guys. Not stuck up at all."

"Any way he was involved with dope?"

The sales manager laughed. "Now you are kidding. I don't think Bert could recognize pot smoke if he smelled it all day or what crack cocaine even looked like. He was as straight as anybody could be. I think he even went to church."

"Right, but that doesn't help us find his killer. I've been hearing a lot of this." She took out a card. "If you think of anything about Bert or his friends that might help us, give me a call. That's a cell phone and good seven twenty-four."

Stacy went outside, stepped into the unmarked, and drove back to the office. It had not been a good morning.

16

EARLY WEDNESDAY MORNING Twyla went scouting. She needed a construction site where they were doing block work. A wall preferably. She found one in the east end of Mission Valley. The wall was half up and all the blocks needed sat on pallets. Ideal. They wouldn't be done with it today.

When it was nine o'clock she called in to the office that she was vetting two more witnesses. The secretary said they were still choosing a jury so she was free.

Next she put on a blonde wig and a black light sweater and stage glasses with large black frames and no correction and went to four book stores. At each one she bought three different books on history, American and British. Then she stopped at a costume shop, still in her disguise and paid cash for a cap and gown in traditional black. That done she checked her watch. Time to get back to the condo and move the books and gown into the van and get the party underway.

She felt a thrill drill through her as she backed the van out of the visitors parking at her condo and drove toward Denny's restaurant in North Park. It was mid-priced and hosted several service club meetings each week. She eased the stolen van into the front of the parking lot at 11:30 and waited. A few customers came, then a string of lone men who could be club members. None looked like she remembered Ron Ingram.

As she waited she thought about it. She had to do this. She had waited too long. She had suffered too much at his hands, at the hands of the other four. Yes, she wanted to kill him, to make him pay. But should she? She was an officer of the court. She was a lawyer. She had passed the fucking state bar. And she had suffered. She felt the hatred and the anger rise up in her again. It was a powerful feeling that she could not deny. Didn't want to stop. It grew and grew as she waited. It boiled inside her head and made her eyes flare. Her breath came in short quick gasps until she thought she might hyperventilate. She had to do it, to get the relief. The pressure was so intense she closed her eyes for just a moment and she was back in his class. The embarrassment, the humiliation was overpowering.

A horn honked somewhere and she opened her eyes. Her watch showed almost noon. As she waited a two year old Ford wheeled into the lot quickly and parked. A man jumped out and hurried toward the restaurant. His car was in the back of the lot and she studied him. Yes, he was Ron Ingram. He had to walk past her to get into the front door. She got out of the stolen van and banged her hand on the door three times. She didn't have her disguise on now. She looked up and almost cried just as Ingram came up to her.

"Sir, oh, could you help me? I can't get this old thing started."

The man slowed, stopped. "Well, I'm late but I guess a good deed is called for. Let me try the ignition. He sat inside the van and at once she pushed him over into the passenger's side seat and held the .32 automatic pointing at him.

"Ron Ingram, right? School teacher."

"Yes, I'm Ron Ingram but I don't know you. Look. Miss. I don't know who you are or what this is about. If you want money I have almost twenty dollars in my pocket that's all I...."

She cut him off. "I don't want your damned money. Put your hands together in front of you."

"Why?" His hands trembled. Sweat popped out on his forehead and he kept looking out the windows.

"No fucking questions, weirdo. You yell for help, I'll gut shoot you and let you die slowly. You understand me?"

He nodded. She slipped the plastic around his wrists, put the end in the slot and pulled it tight.

"Now, we go for a little drive." She had picked out a dead end street there in North Park where there was no foot traffic and most of the people seemed to be at work. She parked, put a towel over the side window and then moved Ron into the back of the van.

It took her ten minutes to cut his clothes off with a pair of scissors she had brought from home. She had a bandana tired around his head and across his open mouth to stop him from yelling. He tried to fight when she began cutting off his clothes, but after she slapped him four times he gave up. When she had him naked, she removed the gag, took out the digital camera, and shot six pictures of him sitting on the rear seat. Then she tied his ankles together with plastic riot cuffs, laid him down on the seat and covered him with a blanket.

"You don't know what's going on, do you Ron? That's good, it makes you sweat and piss blood. Why would I want to take pictures of you nude? What the hell is happening to you? Hey, you'll get all the answers pretty soon. Just think about the past years that you've been teaching school at Hoover High. Think about them and wonder who I am." She laughed then got the van in motion.

She drove back to Mission Valley, parked the van in the visitors slot at her condo, and went in with the camera. She put on latex gloves, loaded the pictures from her camera into the computer, and checked all six shots. Then she chose the best one and printed out twenty of them in four by six inch size. They were fantastic. She giggled all the way through the process.

At her desk she took out the copies of the letters she had from the college and the California State Department of Education. When she got the letters in the mail she had put on latex gloves to be sure she didn't get her fingerprints on them. She had done the same thing when she made copies of them. No prints anywhere. Now she used the gloves again and folded the two original letters and put them in an envelope addressed to the Hoover High principal.

Now she was ready. She had the letters, the pictures, the cap and gown, and the history books. All she needed were a pair of planks or boards and the concrete blocks. She would teach Ron a history lesson he'd never forget. For now, all she could do was wait. She couldn't get to the school until well after dark. She had scouted it and there were banks of lockers accessible. She watched TV. She had a frozen TV dinner for lunch. When she thought of Ron Ingram she snorted, then giggled. He wasn't all the man she thought he might be. He was strictly short stuff. Not that it mattered. She went down and checked on him twice before dark. He was seething but couldn't get a word out past the gag. She rolled him over and stared hard at him.

"Mr. Ingram, you don't remember me, do you? I was one of your students ten years ago and you made me the butt of every joke you ever made in our class. You embarrassed the shit out of me. Now it's pay back time. Oh, I know that you never attended the college you claimed to have graduated from. Pacific Ocean College never heard of you. And I know that your teaching credential is fraudulent. The state board of education has never heard of you. Pulled it off, didn't you? But no more. You're through teaching for good. Just settle down there and relax. I'll be back soon and we'll go for a ride."

He tried to shout but the sound came out as a gurgling mumble and she laughed at him and went back to her condo.

JUST AT TEN o'clock that evening she drove up within a block of the new Hoover High and took her package of pictures, the envelope, a roll of Scotch tape, and walked into the campus. There was no security on the area. She had checked. She found the lockers and pushed a picture into every fifth one, and taped two on the pillars next to the door. She took the principal's envelope down closer to the office where she taped it to the door of the assistant principal. Then she walked out the other way and back to her van. She checked Ron under the blanket. He was still alive and his face red from anger. She laughed at him again.

"Won't be long now, teacher. Not one hell of a lot longer and I'll get you out of the van for a history lesson."

She drove back to Mission Valley to the east end and found the same construction site she had passed that morning. They had put up a lot more blocks, but they were still only half done. She checked again for a security guard, but there was none. The housing complex behind the wall had been finished, rented, and now just this sound reflecting barrier remained to be completed. She stopped near the spot the block men had been working and turned off the van's lights. She looked around. Nobody in sight. No parked cars. Nothing. She found what she wanted in the darkness, two boards a foot wide, two inches thick, and six feet long. She carried them to the van and cut the plastic tie off Ron Ingram's ankles.

"You're getting out of the van now, Ron. You try to run and I'll put six slugs into your worthless hide. You understand?"

He nodded, his face slack now, all the fight gone from him. He looked resigned to being tortured or hurt some way. She walked him ten feet to a level spot of ground.

"Sit down, Ron. Sit down or I'll knock you down."

He sat on the rough ground and she pushed him

over on his back. Then she brought the two boards and put them across his chest side by side. The ends of the boards went up to his chin and the other ends rested on the ground.

"Ron, remember the old English and some of their laws? How sometimes they had ways to get confessions from suspects? This is one of them. A history lesson for you." He frowned. She went to the van and brought back the cap and gown and draped them around him, then replaced the boards.

"This is the cap and gown you never earned, Ron. I figured it was ironic to let you die in them instead of live in them. God, no?"

She went to the stack of concrete blocks. They were eight inches wide, eight inches high and sixteen inches long. She guessed they weighed about thirty pounds each. She put on work gloves and carried one block to the boards and placed it carefully on the two inch thick board directly over Ron's chest. She put another one beside it and looked at Ron in the eerie darkness.

"This is what the English called the stone confession. They didn't have concrete blocks back then so they used stones, heavy ones."

She put two more of the blocks on the boards making them three long. Over his chest she stacked two blocks high.

"The authorities figured that if the suspect confessed they would stop piling on rocks and hang him. If he didn't confess they just kept on putting on the stones until the poor bastard's chest crushed and he couldn't breathe."

She added two more blocks, now six of them and

she figured they must weigh at least a hundred and eighty pounds. Ron wheezed when he breathed and he coughed several times.

"Isn't history wonderful, teacher? You learn so many things to use in real life."

Now there were nine blocks on his chest, three high. She watched him closely. He passed out once then struggled back to consciousness. She cut the gag off his mouth but he had no energy to talk. Two more blocks. She had to struggle to pile them four high. Eleven blocks, three hundred and thirty pounds. Was that enough? She checked him again. She could hear him breathing. She brought two more blocks and heaved them on top of the others. Now thirteen of the thirty pounders, almost four hundred pounds. She bent and looked at him in the darkness. Blood seeped out of his nose and his mouth. His eyes had closed. She couldn't hear him breathe. She checked his neck with her fingers. His carotid artery showed no pulse. Ron Ingram had been paid back.

She took a deep breath and sat on the ground exhausted. She got up quickly, took the history books out of the van and arranged them on the blocks. Then she stared at the silent form a moment.

"Yes, Mr. Ingram. No Mr. Ingram. Good bye Mr. Ingram." She laughed one last time, got in the van and drove away. She left the van near Broadway downtown and walked a half mile to a hotel where she caught a taxi. No way they could tie her taxi ride to the van even if it was identified as used in the pay back for Mr. Ingram.

. . .

AT HOME in her Mission Valley condo, she had a long hot shower, then crawled into bed. Three down. Two to go. Tomorrow. Tomorrow she would be a lawyer again, sitting in the second chair at the biggest murder trial San Diego had ever seen.

17

TWENTY FOUR CARS drove past Ron Ingram's body the next morning as early to work men and women hurried past noticing only a stack of blocks for the new wall. The crew came to finish the wall a little after six-forty five for a seven o'clock start. The foreman saw the stack first and knew he hadn't left the blocks there the night before. He drove up, stopped, and saw the feet and legs sticking out from under the blocks. He grabbed his cell phone and ran around the stack.

"Holy Jesus," he said and hit 911 on his cell. He gave his location and the problem and closed the phone.

Three minutes later a beat cop in the area whined up with his siren screaming and red lights flashing. He parked in back of the foreman's new pickup and hurried up to the stack of blocks.

"What in hell is this?" the cop asked. He had been on the force for two years and had never seen anything like it before.

"Looks like somebody got himself crushed to death with all those blocks," the foreman said. He was Irish and had the red hair and freckles to prove it. "Hell of a way to die."

The fire department's red truck came from the other direction with its siren on, and four paramedics swarmed the scene.

"Don't touch a damn thing," the cop yelled at them. "Them blocks didn't jump up there by themselves. We've got a homicide here, so stay the fuck back."

One paramedic touched the man's throat and shook his head. The ambulance came next with three more paramedics and they all stood around not quite sure what to do.

By the time Cain drove up in his Chevy Cavalier there were ten cop cars there, including the crime scene guys. He had taken the call at seven oh five and called his team. The murder location was just off Camino Del Rio North between Qualcom Stadium and Mission Valley Shopping Center.

Cain saw the photographer at work and then Lt. Anderson removed the history books from the top of the stack of blocks. He asked the construction guys to take the blocks off the body. By the time they had all but the last three blocks off, Stacy and Lee pulled up and stared in surprise.

"Now that's something new," Lee said. "The old English stone crushing confessional. I bet nobody has been killed that way for eight hundred years."

"Why is he wearing a graduation mortar board and gown?" Stacy asked. "And what's with those books?"

"History books," Cain said. "They were on top of the thirteen blocks that crushed the poor slob."

They pulled the last three blocks off the planks, and then Anderson and his team took off the boards.

"Naked under the robe," Anderson said. "Not a stitch of ID on him."

An assistant medical examiner rolled up in his city car with his black bag. Anderson filled him in on the crushing weight and the method. Under the robe the ME found the body's chest had been crushed, caved in five or six inches. He looked up.

"No I.D. Preliminary is death by suffocation when his lungs were crushed and probably punctured by broken and smashed ribs and he couldn't breathe. That's about all I can say now."

Anderson moved everyone back twenty yards and began a detailed search of the immediate area. They found tire tracks, but nothing else. He came over to Cain shaking his head.

"Clean as a nun's habit. Not a damn thing that doesn't belong there. Some cigarette butts, some junk food trash, and plenty of construction boot prints."

"Any smaller women's shoe prints?" Stacy asked.

Anderson frowned. "Heard about your theory. We'll check again for small prints. Not much chance on this hard surface area but we'll take another look."

"Doesn't follow the pattern," Cain said. "The first two were young, late twenties. This guy is late thirties at least."

"You think your lady serial suspect could pile those blocks up that way?" Lee asked. "Four high they said."

"Yes, with the right motivation," Stacy said. "Hell, I could do it."

Cain asked Anderson to get finger prints right away so they could take them back and try for a match. When he had the prints, he waved his team away.

"See you back at the barn," Cain said.

. . .

BACK IN THE OFFICE, Homicide Team One gathered. Stacy put up a new list on the board without a name as the third kill.

"A graduation cap and gown and those history books," Stacy said. "Our killer was trying to make a point. Was this man a student or a college professor? How does the cap and gown have anything to do with it?"

"History books," Lee said. "The stone confessional is a historic form of torture and execution. That fits."

Cain took the prints to the crime lab as soon as he got back. They promised a report in ten minutes. It took only five.

"We have match, a hundred percent sure," one of the crime lab experts said on the phone. Cain had it on the speaker. "Match is through the San Diego Unified School District. They do a background check and print all of the teachers they hire. Guy's name is Ron Ingram. The data we have on him is over thirteen years old. Better check with the School District."

"Thanks, you've made our day." Cain hung up and Stacy was on the phone to the Unified School District to check with personnel.

When she asked about the name, she was switched to the Principal at Hoover High School.

"Mrs. Wilforce? This is Stacy DeFrain of the San Diego Police Department. We're looking for information about one of your teachers, Ron Ingram."

There was a silence on the end of the line.

"I've been afraid something might have happened to him. Is he in trouble?"

"I'm afraid that it's worse than that. Someone has killed him. Evidently last night. Can you help us with his address and phone number?"

"I think you better send some detectives over here to the campus. We have some pictures and letters that showed up this morning that you should look at."

"We'll be right there."

Stacy told the others about the call. The three grabbed an unmarked and drove out to 4474 El Cajon Boulevard to the high school.

A campus security guard met the police and took them directly to the principal's office. She was waiting for them. After the introductions, she took an envelope off her desk and passed it to Cain.

"One of our janitors reporting to work at six a.m. found these two pictures taped to the building near the entrance. We understand there are more. Evidently someone pushed them into student lockers through the vents."

Cain looked at the picture of a naked man sitting in a vehicle of some kind. His hands and feet were bound.

"Is this Ron Ingram?" Stacy asked.

"It is. You told me he's been murdered?"

"Evidently sometime last night out in Mission Valley."

"His wife called this morning and said he hadn't been home last night. Who would do this?"

"That's what we're trying to find out," Cain said. "Have there been any recent lawsuits by parents against Mr. Ingram?"

"No, none in all the time he's taught here, over thirteen years. There's something else." She took out another envelope in a plastic bag and handed it to Cain.

"This envelope was taped to the assistant principal's office door. He opened it and looked at it, then put in this bag and brought it to me. His fingerprints will be on the envelope and the letters."

"What do they say?" Lee asked.

"One says Ron Ingram never attended the college he told us he graduated from up in Oregon. The other is the disturbing one. It's from the State Board of Education and says that no teaching credential has ever been issued to Ron Ingram."

"And you think the letters and the pictures are related?" Stacy asked.

"Absolutely. Someone wanted to embarrass him and his memory, and wanted to destroy his teaching record. I'll phone the state office for confirmation, but the letter is on their usual stationery and I assume it's legitimate."

A woman came into the room and handed the principal a large envelope. She looked inside. "Six more of the pictures. The students are turning them in. I have no idea how many might be on campus." She shook her head. "The pictures are of little importance. You say he's dead. How was he killed?"

Cain told her what must have happened and the touch of the history books and the cap and gown.

"Yes, it's all connected," the principal said. "Someone found out that he was not trained as a teacher and had no right to teach, and took the pictures, got the letters from the college and the state, and then to add insult to the murder, draped the graduating gown around him and put the mortar board on his head. An ironic jolt of shame for him."

"What about any of the other teachers? Did any of

them have any trouble with Mr. Ingram? Any build up a hatred for him so intense they would question his credentials, find out, and then kill him?"

"Not a chance. I know my teachers. Ron taught history, so the reason for the history books on the blocks. But he knew his field well. He was one of the best teachers that we ever had here at Hoover."

"Could you give us the name of two or three of the teachers here he was closest to?"

"Yes, of course. Also you'll want to talk to his wife. She will be devastated. She's not the strongest woman anyway. Do you want to talk to the teachers right now?"

"That would be good," Cain said. "Then Stacy can go see the widow. No one has notified her yet about what happened."

A half hour later, Cain and Lee had talked to two teachers, one woman and one man. Both said that they were totally shocked by Ingram's death. They had absolutely no idea who might have done it. One said Ron didn't have an enemy in the world. He was a kind man, gentle with his students, excellent in his field of history, and dedicated to teaching.

Cain took the envelope with the letters in it and one of the color pictures of the naked man back to the office and ran them over to the crime lab. They waited for the testing. Only one set of prints came off the letters. A check showed that they belonged to a teacher at Hoover High, the assistant principal at the school who had looked at them that morning.

"We won't get any good prints from the pictures, either," Lee said. "Whoever did it was smart enough to use gloves. So this is no help."

Stacy called the office.

"Mrs. Ingram broke down completely when I told her about her husband. She made me call the crime lab and get them to confirm that the prints were those of her husband. Then she pointed to the door and told me to leave. I didn't get a word out of her about possible enemies. She was crying, screaming, and throwing things when I left. We need to give her a few days to settle down, but I'd be surprised if we got anything worthwhile from her."

"Come on back," Cain said. "We'll regroup and see what to do next."

Cain sat down in his chair and pointed to the wall board. "We put up kill number three with a name, and what we know about him."

Lee went to work on the tack board. He put the name up and under it bullets.

. Crushed to death in Mission Valley.

. History teacher at Hoover High School.

. No college.

. No teacher credential.

. Everyone loved him. (all except one)

. Naked pictures taken and posted at school.

. The naked picture tacked on their board.

Cain looked at the list and grunted. "Not a hell of a lot. Is this killer this good or just lucky?"

"Right now, I'd say she's this good, if it's a woman."

Cain looked at the picture again. "Looks like the back seat of a car or a van, probably a van. Take this over to auto theft and see if they can figure out what kind of a rig he's in. They might have a clue."

Lee left with the picture and Stacy came back.

"Nothing from the widow. The next time you get to do the informing the next of kin about a death in the family. That woman wanted to scratch my eyes out. If she had a gun she would have shot me dead. I was glad to get out of there without a lot of serious wounds."

"That bad?"

"Worst I've ever seen. She came apart and was totally furious."

"Okay, the next one I do." He watched her gradually cool down. She was pretty when she was mad. He grinned. "You still think our serial is a woman?"

Stacy slumped in her desk chair. "This one could go either way, unless they found some small shoe prints at that block wall. Anderson ever tell us?"

Cain shook his head.

Stacy made the call. Anderson came on sounding tired.

"Hey, Stacy, we've got less than nothing for you. No physical evidence on the scene. Just nothing. Zilch."

"What about those small shoe prints in the dirt?"

"Oh, that. Yeah, we did find some. Quite a few looks like they went from a pallet of blocks over to the kill."

"Ah hah!" Stacy said. "Send me an email with that information. I owe you a cup of coffee."

Cain looked up. "He found some?"

"Lots, going from that pallet of bocks to the kill place. Lots of small, woman sized prints in the dirt." Stacy looked at the bulletin board, went over and added to the list: small shoe prints in dust near body.

"Boss, I'd say that ties it, our serial killer is a woman."

18

TEN MINUTES after they found out about the small shoe prints at the third kill scene, Lee called.

"Hey boss, we might have a winner. The guys at auto theft said we lucked out. The body is on the rear seat and there's a seat belt hanging beside him against the window. The latch on that belt has a distinctive style. The guy said he had a van like this one. Says it's a ninety to ninety five Dodge Caravan. We're running the stolen vans right now for the past three days. Figure it must have been stolen. He's waving at me. We have a ninety four Dodge Caravan stolen two days ago out of Fashion Valley parking. He's putting out a special alert to see if the troops can find that van. I'm coming back."

Cain had the call on his speaker phone. Stacy frowned.

"So, if we can find the van the crime lab guys can go over it. If she's been as careful this time as she has been so far, we won't find zilch."

"Never can tell, Lone Ranger. We might get lucky. What else you have on your plate?"

"You said a couple of days ago that you wanted a complete work up on Showley and Judith," Stacy said. "How about I start with the first kill and talk to her mother again, and get a detailed biography on Judith. Birth date, early schools, grade and high schools, college, marriage, all of her work places. Get all the details. Then if we do the same thing on Showley and Ingram, we might be able to come up with something that ties all three of them together. Right now it's the only thing I can think of that might produce some results."

"My idea, huh?" Cain said. "Damn but I'm good. I think I'll put me in for a medal. Yeah, do it. We've got nothing else going. Maybe we can dig out something on Ingram. From what the principal said he looks like a straight arrow."

"Maybe. But every arrow has a little bend in it somewhere. I'm going to call Judith's mother. I'll get a meeting set up for just after lunch at the woman's home."

Lee came back looking pleased with himself. "Those guys nailed it, I was amazed. Now if the beat cops can find the stolen van, then we might have something."

Fernando and Kevin came back to the office looking wrung out.

"Not a damn thing," Kevin said. "We've checked out all twenty-four of the black new Lexus that had that partial plate. Four were owned by women but three of them were out of town on the kill date and proved it. Business trips. The fourth had no alibi and we went out and called on her. She was home. She also spends most of her time in a wheel chair, can't walk and uses hand controls to drive the specially outfitted Lexus. We're no where."

"Weird," Cain said. "Like the rest of these cases. You heard about our third kill. Probably the same woman. I want you two to take the Showley and Ingram cases. Do a complete biography on the two. Date of birth, early schools, high school, and any college. Total run down on every job they ever had and for how long, addresses, girl friends, anything that might give us a commonality fact. Kevin, you take Ingram. His wife is crazy wild right now. Work the school, Hoover High first and let the widow cool down. The principal there will cooperate. Check with the widow tomorrow. Fernando, you've got Showley. Dig up everything you can find on him."

"We've got nothing else?"

"Damn little."

"We're on it. Where's the kill file?"

STACY HIT the SDPD cafeteria line for lunch. She went by herself so she could think through the case. The cases. Sometimes if she got by herself and let the facts of a crime flow out for her, she could come up with some new angle or new idea. She tried as she waited in line, then took the crab salad and a diet Coke and looked for a table. Crowded today. She spotted an opening and got there in time and sat down.

"Well hello Stacy. It's been a while."

She looked up to see Hal Young smiling at her.

"Hal. What's a nice vice cop like you doing in a classy pace like this?"

"Looking for snitches," he said. They both laughed.

"You must be busy with your situation. The word is we have ourselves a serial killer maybe a woman."

"That's what I'm pushing. So far it looks good. We just don't know who she is or why she's killing people in rather strange ways."

"What I heard. Weird."

They talked a little as they ate, and when he finished, he got that lopsided grin that she found attractive. She'd known him at the office for over a year, bumping into him now and then. But nothing ever happened.

"Hey, could I steal you away from Homicide tonight for dinner out?"

She felt a real thrill. She'd hoped more than a few times that he would ask her out. She wasn't pushy enough to make the first move. "Gee, viceman, I don't know. My plate is pretty full already."

"Bullshit," he said with that damn grin.

"Yeah, right. My social calendar is a total disaster. I'd love to have dinner with you. No place expensive. Hey, I know what your salary is."

"But you don't know how much I get under the table. These vice guys have tons of money. Good. I'm tied up until six. Meet you in the lobby downstairs?"

"Sounds like it will work. I've got a one o'clock with one of the bereaved. No fun but somebody's got to do it."

"Great. See you then."

She watched him go. He was about thirty, single, in good shape, with dark hair, clean shaven, and with a face she had always liked that she thought of as soft and gentle, not like a tough vice cop's face should be. He had brown eyes over modest brows that he must keep clipped. His nose was almost perfect except for a slight twist at the end. She'd have to ask about that fight. His chin was solid, but not square and his shoulders were wider than his slender hips. Put it all together and he was one of the best looking cops she'd ever seen. She smiled. Hey, she had a real date. Now she wished that she'd worn her best white blouse. Oh, well, maybe next time. If there was a next time. She set her jaw. Damnit, she'd make sure there was a next time with Hal.

TWYLA FARNHAM SHOWED the guard on the door her pass and walked into Superior Court number three, Judge Harlan Sanchez presiding. He wasn't there yet. She went to the defendant's table and sat beside her boss Alex Tretter. He shuffled some papers on the wide table in front of them and then turned toward her.

"You're looking lovely today, Miss Farnham. It's a waste today. Opening argument which I'll handle. But I'll want you to do some of the questioning on some of the witnesses. We've got a long haul before we get our shot. The prosecution has shown me twenty eight witnesses, and they figure it will take about three weeks to present their case. Then it's our turn. I want you here as it progresses. Find all the holes in their case as you can. We have to punch and puncture and drill holes all over the place. It's going to be a heavy load. How did you come out with that fu fu girl he slept with the night of the crime?"

"Wanda Warring. She's on board. A bit flighty, but for the value received, she's going to swear to anything we want her to. She should be a solid witness."

"Good work."

The jury members came in and took their places. Six men and six women, two blacks, one Hispanic and one Pilipino. The rest Caucasians.

The defendant, their client, Trevor Jamison, was brought in by his jailers. He wore a suit and tie, both in the average cost range, and a white shirt. He had a grin that the jurors would surely resent on sight. They had made sure he didn't come in a four thousand dollar Imperi suit and five hundred dollar shoes. That would turn off the jury in a rush.

Twyla watched the prosecution lawyers enter. An assistant DA she hadn't met but heard he was the number two man in the department. He would be tough. The spectators were allowed in and quickly filled the available seats. The front row was reserved for lawyers and the press. No cameras were allowed.

"All rise," the bailiff said. They stood and the judge strode into the high bench, whipped his robes around, and sat down.

"Continuing the Jamison case from yesterday. Is the prosecution ready?"

Two men stood. "Ready your honor. Braithwaite and Clawson for the state."

The judge looked over at the defendant's table.

Both lawyers stood. "Yes, your honor Tretter and Farnham for the defense," Tretter said and they sat down.

Twyla took out a notebook computer and opened it on the table. She saw the prosecution had one set up on its table. Her job for the next two or three hours was to brief the prosecution's case on the screen, and make notes of any possible gaps or holes in the logic or the trail of evidence. She was good at this. She watched as the prosecutor left the table and went up to the rail surrounding the twelve jurors.

"Ladies and gentlemen of the jury. This morning I will show you in brief and undeniable strokes the fact that the defendant, Trevor Jamison, is guilty of the first degree murder of Linda Natasha. Let me set the picture for you."

Twyla hit the keys on her notebook, getting down the salient points as the assistant district attorney talked. She would be able to transcribe her notes almost word for word of what the DA had said. A lot faster than getting a transcript from the court reporter. Much easier to annotate and take apart on the screen and reassemble it the way the defense wanted it.

She listened intently. It would be a two hour session at least.

AT A QUARTER TO six that same evening, Stacy went to the locker room where she fixed her make up, combed her hair and studied herself in the mirror. Not bad. With some advance notice she could do a lot better. What the hell, it was just a first date. Now the second one would be outstanding.

He waited for her as she came out of the elevator. She was five minutes early.

"I like a man who's on time," she said. He had changed shirts and had on a different sport coat. He looked good enough to eat for dinner. Hal Young grinned and she walked beside him toward one of the four big doors in the lobby.

"Your car or mine?" he asked.

"Yours, I'm tired of driving today. Where are we going?"

"Your choice, Italian, Chinese or the French place Jaque en la Boxe."

"Since I'm French and hate Chinese, let's do Italian."

They drove in his two year old Buick and found a parking spot at the Olive Garden, a mid priced Italian eatery with a good reputation. Inside they were seated at once since they were early for the rush.

Hal looked at the menu and then up at her.

"What's for dinner?"

"I like it all. You order for me and just one glass of wine."

Stacy still thought about her serial killer. A woman. She couldn't get it out of her brain. She didn't remember what he ordered and was half way through the big Italian green salad before she realized she hadn't been talking much.

"Sorry, the damn woman serial is getting to me. I'll dump it for the rest of the night. Now, tell me about yourself, first date regulation question."

He chuckled. "It's going to be real veal parmigiana and a tasty sauce on the spaghetti. You demolished the green salad and bread sticks. You were a dozen miles away."

"Sorry. Now about Hal Young."

"I'm in vice and happy in my work. Been a cop for just over ten years. Did four years in the Marines, and decided I didn't want to stay longer. I had a commission through the ROTC route in college. The politics were overwhelming. So I cut out as a first lieutenant and came here. I was married when I was twenty. We didn't have any kids and called it off almost to the day a year later. No regrets. Single since then. My folks live in the LA area where I have an older brother who is into complicated advanced computer things I don't even try to understand. My sister is a doctor, pediatrics, and works here in town with Kaiser Permanente. The only time I ever heard that word before was the name of permanente cement. Now, what about you? I know you're a detective in Homicide One and you've been there for a little over a year. Oh, you drive a three year old Nissan Sentra and you live in the North Park area across from Balboa Park a ways."

"You ran me?"

"Sure, there isn't much there. You did have a speeding ticket when you were in high school, but nothing since. Unless you got them wiped out."

"I wouldn't do that. I'm a good driver, a legal driver. I even signal when I'm making lane changes. Now, what else? I graduated from high school here in San Diego, from Patrick Henry out in San Carlos. My parents still live out there in the same house where I grew up.

"I'm trying to get out there once a week for a meal but I don't always make it. My dad runs a small copy shop and office supply store and is making a living, but not getting rich. My mother does some charity work and is at a food bank place out in El Cajon one day a week. I've never shot or killed anyone and hope to God I never have to. Cain is trying to get me to go to City College and work on a degree, but so far I haven't tried it. That's about me. You want my weight, height and bra size too?"

He laughed. "Not necessary since I'm a good guesser. Hobbies, clubs, churches?"

"I run when I get a chance, used to do open ocean swimming, but no time to stay in shape for that. I'm not afraid of the ocean but I respect it, especially those damn rip currents. Cain is trying to get me on his bowling team. He says he needs my high handicap."

"What's your average?"

"I bowled league one year. A straight ball, kind of slow, and my book average was 132."

"Hey, not bad. What about music?"

"I grew up with rock and roll. Went to about a million concerts, but now I'm more moved by a really good jazz combo belting it out about three A.M."

"When the club was supposed to close at two."

"Right, just a little illegal makes it sweeter."

"Dessert?"

"Crumb crust apple pie alamode with some lemon sauce."

"You're terrible." He caught their waiter and ordered.

"Sir, we don't have lemon sauce."

"Then have the chef make some. It's really tough to do. Most of the homeless living on the street down by Petco Park can do it." The waiter's brows lifted in surprise then he grinned and hurried away.

"What a smooth touch with the hired help," she said.

"Comes from long talks with perverts, slimes, and weasels trying to con pretty teenagers into being call girls."

"You save some of the younger girls?"

"Some of them. Most don't want to be saved. Hey, no shop talk. Where is that lemon sauce?"

The waiter came back smiling. "The chef sends his compliments and the lemon sauce. Told me he hadn't thought of it for years. Now he'll probably put it on every other desert we serve."

Hal watched her eat.

"You always eat this much? How do you stay so slender and in such good shape?"

"Salad and diet Coke for lunch, remember. Besides, the women in my family have always had generous bosoms. So it's no direct achievement of mine."

He laughed. "Now you have embarrassed me. I didn't mean...."

"Yes you did. Men always do. So, are you ready to go?"

In the car on the way back she leaned her head on his shoulder. "Hey Vice, I really enjoyed our camping out tonight. How about coming to my place next week for some really, really good food?"

"You cook, too?"

"Of course. Say Wednesday night, if we both don't get last minute assignments."

"Wednesday night sounds great."

He drove into the police parking garage and to where she said her car was parked. There was an awkward pause, then she leaned in and kissed him softly on his lips.

"I'll see you around and call me for sure about Wednesday. I'm in the office book."

"I can do that."

He let her out right behind her car and waited until

she pulled out before he left. Stacy smiled all the way north to her apartment on Juniper Street.

19

CAIN TOOK the call at his desk just after eight o'clock the next morning. It was from auto theft.

"Found your van, the right make and year for the one you think was used in the last killing, the teacher."

"Good."

"We told the crime lab and they had it towed and are working it over right now. Anderson asked me to give you a call."

"It's at the impound lot?"

"That's a Roger."

"Thanks, we owe you one."

"I'll take a beer on Thursday."

"You got it." Cain hung up and reached for his suit coat. He was going car diving.

ANDERSON SHOOK his head when Cain showed up at the impound lot and found the crime scene guys vacuuming the interior. It had just one bench seat in back, then an open space up to the driver's and the passenger's seats.

"Plenty of room to strip him and shoot the pictures," Anderson said. "But so far we don't have much."

"What does 'much' mean?"

Anderson took from his lab coat an open top glasses case. He pulled out a pair of glasses and held them up. "Some of the new bend won't break glasses frames. Twist them and they pop right back. Expensive. These seem to be reading glasses, mostly magnification. Just inside the case is a sticker with the optometrist's name and phone number. We assume this is the person who examined the owner of the glasses, prescribed the Rx for them, and had the lens made to fit."

"How old are those new frames?"

"Been out for about a year."

"Can an optometrist tell us who he made these glasses for?"

Anderson shrugged. "Got me. You're the detective. Best I can do for you. Hope it helps."

Cain took the glasses and drove back to the office where he met with the rest of the team and told them about the find in the stolen van.

"So we might have something?" Lee asked.

"First we get the tag on the van and check the owner. If that person wears glasses and left them in the van, we're out of luck. If she doesn't, we move on up the ladder."

Cain put Stacy and Lee on the glasses and told Fernando and Kevin to keep on their bio search on their two victims.

Lee got the plate number from the impound lot and

talked to DMV. They showed the van was owned by Olive Quarter. She was in the book. Stacy called her and asked the woman who answered if she owned a 1994 Dodge Caravan. She did and had reported it stolen.

"The police found it last night, Mrs. Quarter. I'm sure you can pick it up soon. Incidentally, do you wear glasses?"

"Just for long distances. Need them for my license."

"You don't have reading glasses?"

"Heavens no. I read good. Who do I call about my van?"

Stacy told her and then hung up and called the Clear Vision Optometrist's number listed in the glasses case. A man answered and said the office was open and that they did take walk in clients. She and Lee took an unmarked and found the Clear Vision office on El Cajon Boulevard half way to La Mesa. It was crowded between a fast food café and a Big O Tire store.

Inside a bell rang as they entered. It was a tiny office with a counter half way across the front with three soft waiting chairs and a magazine rack.

"Be with you in a minute," a voice sounded from the back. The man who came out almost five minutes later was short and heavy, with drooping jowls and pale blue eyes behind thick lensed glasses. His head was small for his short body and hair had refused to grow on his head for some years. Stacy figured he was over sixty.

"Now, what can I do for you kind people? I'm Wilbur and this is my place."

Stacy showed him the glasses case. "Is this one of yours?"

Wilbur took the case, looked inside and nodded.

"Yep. It is. Those are one of my best frames. Expensive but good for life they tell me."

Stacy flipped open her badge. "I'm detective Stacy DeFrain with the San Diego Police Department. This is my partner Detective Ostrander. We're interested in who you made these glasses for."

"Why?"

"Because the person who owns these glasses may be a serial killer. Does that give you some incentive?"

"Helps. I've only had these frames for six months. Sold a batch of them."

"You keep record who you sell to, what prescription goes with each set, right?" Lee asked.

"Yep."

"Don't you have one of those machines that looks through the lens and evaluates it and tells you the prescription?" Lee asked.

"Nope. Too damn expensive."

"Do you remember who you fitted these glasses for?" Stacy asked.

"No, too many of them but it would be a woman, fairly young. They go for these frames"

"How many of them have you sold in the past six months?" Stacy asked.

"Just put in a new order yesterday. I'm getting in fifty in the most popular sizes. I'd say I've sold maybe seventy-five to a hundred."

"Could we go through your orders looking for this particular prescription?" Lee asked.

The man frowned, rubbed his balding head and shrugged. "Will I get in trouble with the privacy laws?"

"Not a chance. We can get a court order if it takes that," Stacy said.

Wilbur thought about it a minute, rubbed one hand down his side and back up. "Hell, why not. I'm not a good record keeper. The sales slips are in a box. I'll go through and pick out the Flex-O-Flex frame customers, and you guys can check the prescriptions."

"Sounds great. Is now a good time?"

He held up the glasses and then put them on and checked a chart. "Wow, these are strong. You're looking for a plus 4.25 right and left."

Two hours later they had waded through almost seventy five prescriptions and orders. They found two pair of glasses ordered with the right correction and the right frames. They showed them to Wilbur.

"Oh yes, this one is dated just two weeks ago. I remember her. Has some macular degeneration in her right eye and is blinder than a bat in it. But we put the correction on anyway. Helps some with her depth perception, you know, two eyes looking at something in the distance."

"So the other one?" Stacy asked.

"Don't remember her." Too long ago. Date is five months ago. Wait a minute. This is the wrong prescription. It's for 2.5 plus. Not strong enough for the pair you brought in. So we have just one match."

Lee wrote down the name and address:

Yolanda Gomez, 2434 Aztec Drive, La Mesa.

Stacy used her cell and called Cain. "We might have something." She gave him the name and address. "Check out wants and warrants, the DMV, and San Diego Gas and Electric. We're out in La Mesa not too far from the address. We'll swing over on Lake Murray and check out Aztec drive. I used to go past it every day."

They thanked Wilbur and told him they would come and see him the moment they needed glasses. He waved and started putting the paper work away.

THEY PROWLED Aztec drive off Lake Murray Blvd and found no number that came anywhere near 2434.

"Fake address," Lee said.

"Probably a fake name, too. It still could be our girl. If she had planned this whole sequence, she could have set up a fake name she could use when a name was required with no I.D. If she was really serious she could go to the DMV and with minimum I.D. get a driver's license in her fake name."

They headed out Lake Murray to Interstate 8 and back down town.

BY THE TIME they drove to the office, Cain had more news.

"We checked out the name you gave us. She doesn't exist, at least at the phone company, or SDG&E, the DMV, the City Water People, and there are no wants or warrants. We got a call from traffic. They towed a car from a restaurant after the manager complained. Turned out to belong to Ron Ingram. So she might have grabbed him from the parking lot. His friends inside at the Lions International meeting said he didn't attend the last session at Denny's Wednesday noon."

"Not good news," Stacy said. "I still think there's a connection between the three kills. I know two are in their late twenties and the teacher is ten years older.

But there has to be something that ties them together, and generates all of her hatred of the three."

Cain looked up and scowled, then rubbed his face with his hands. "There is one different factor here. No sexual component. Not much in the hanging, lots in the second one, none in this one. Should that be a factor?"

"The Ingram killing was slow and deliberate." Lee said. "It took some time to pile those blocks up. They get heavy in a rush. So she was in no hurry to kill him. Make him sweat and suffer more. Is that a factor?"

"Makes me wonder," Stacy said. "The principal said there were no lawsuits against Ingram by parents. That wouldn't rule out sexual harassment. He could have been accused of that and it never got beyond the school, never to court. They might have taken care of it internally."

"Stacy, do some girl talk with the principal. Find out about any sexual harassment. She might not have wanted to bring it up since the whole thing is moot now. If there were any charges at all, we want to know about them and the name of the girl or girls."

"I'm on it. You have the principal's number?"

Cain gave the number to Stacy and then kicked his feet up on a pulled out drawer in his desk and worked over the three autopsy reports on the three murders. He was searching for any common factors. He studied the medical language carefully, but nothing even looked promising. Entirely different causes of death. Totally different methods used for killing the individuals. That would usually point to three different killers, but not this time. They had a tie of sorts in the woman angle, but it was flimsy and not one the DA would ever take to a jury. They needed evidence, some hard facts that pointed to one individual. It had to be there, somewhere. They just hadn't found it yet.

Cain was between a mild depression and downright anger at this current problem. He'd been on a lot of tough homicide cases, but this one was strange, different, and had him mystified. There had to be some evidence that pointed toward somebody. They just hadn't found it. He could think of no angle that they hadn't investigated. Damnit, why were they all so hard?

Stacy bumped his desk. He looked up and saw concern on her pretty face.

"Hey boss, you ok? You look a little down."

"I'll live. Anything from the principal?"

"Yeah, we might have something. I finally got her to admit there were two sexual harassment charges against Ingram two years ago but nothing since then. Both girls have graduated. They handled it all inside the district and nothing leaked and there was no legal action.

"I'm going over there now to get the names and the files on the cases and then see if I can find the girls."

Cain brightened. "Good work Stacy. We might get a break on this case yet."

20

SHE HAD BEEN fourteen that warm summer. Strange and wonderful and frightening things were taking place with her body. Her breasts took a spurt of growth and she really needed a bra now. She had flashes of fire and ice and sometimes she wanted to crawl into her bed and sleep all day.

That was the summer she realized that the kid across the street was something more than a brat who teased her a lot. Nelson was his name and she'd known him since they started kindergarten just years and years ago. Nelson was almost as tall as she was. Most of the boys in her class had not caught up with the girls yet in height. A month ago he had came across the street where she was planting some flowers with her mother and told her he could teach her to throw and catch a softball.

"Hey, maybe then you could get on the girl's softball team. Nobody on there now is very good."

She had shrugged. Her mother pushed her on the

shoulder. "Go on, do you good. A little activity. You sit and read too much."

So he got his softball, two gloves, and they tried. She wasn't good at it but after the second day she got better. He didn't seem near so nerdy now. After playing catch a while she wanted a Coke and invited him to the back yard where she brought out Cokes and some donuts. They talked about school coming up and then went to the old lawn swing that was barely working and sat and talked and went back and forth. Once Nelson lost his balance and leaned against her. She pushed him back and he apologized. They were out of sight of the kitchen window. No one else was around.

The next time he pushed against her she looked over at him and he reached in and kissed her cheek.

"Your first kiss," he said.

"That doesn't count. All the girls at school say it has to be on the lips."

"Like this?" he said and kissed her lips gently then harder. She liked it and kissed him back. They both laughed and worked the swing some more. Before they could kiss again her mother called and she had to scoot into the house.

The next day they found a more secluded spot and kissed more and he tried to put his hand on her breasts but she pushed it away. They talked and kissed some more and he got a funny look on his face and then groaned and turned away from her. He was back in a minute.

For two weeks they practiced softball and she got better and each day they had Cokes and cookies in the back yard where he mother couldn't see them. Twyla had never been so thrilled in her young life. Then

Marybeth Hughes had her birthday party. Marybeth lived three doors down the block and was in their class and for years had been Twyla's best friend. She didn't invite Twyla to her party but she did invite Nelson. Twyla stormed into her room and didn't come out for dinner. Her mother brought her some ice cream and sympathy. She confessed she was upset about the birthday party.

"It happens, dear," her mother said. "Life's little bumps and problems. It'll all work out. Did Norman go?"

Twyla said he did and wouldn't eat any more ice cream.

Then it was Thursday, and Twyla knew that Marybeth always walked to the branch library taking back books and getting new ones. Twyla slipped out of her room and hurried to the little patch of woods near the library. She waited for Marybeth and when she came called to her.

"Hey, Marybeth. I think I borrowed one of your books. It's overdue. What should we do with it?"

Marybeth shook her head but stayed on the sidewalk.

"I have all of my books," she said.

"Come take a look. I'm sure you checked it out."

Then Marybeth went into the woods and when she was out of sight of the sidewalk, Twyla ran at her and knocked her down. An intense fury surged up in Twyla. Her heart pounded like a jackhammer on concrete and her breath came in ragged surges. She pinned Marybeth down and slapped her twice in the face. Then she saw a fist sized rock nearby and grabbed it.

So far she hadn't said a word. Marybeth didn't look concerned. Twyla always won the wrestling matches they had when they were little girls.

"Twyla, let me up. You're going to ruin my new blouse."

That's when Twyla hit her in the face with the rock. It smashed in her cheek and Marybeth howled in protest. Twyla put her hand over Marybeth's mouth to stop the sound. She also covered her nose. A moment later Marybeth began to struggle to get the hand away so she could breathe. Twyla hit her again with the heavy rock, slamming it into the side of her head. Marybeth's eyes went wild for a moment then slowly closed and she gave a long sigh.

Marybeth didn't move. Twyla felt the rage flow out of her. She sat up away from Marybeth.

"You can get up now, boyfriend stealer," Twyla said.

The other girl didn't move.

Twyla frowned. Now her fury vanished and she watched Marybeth carefully. Was she breathing? Twyla couldn't see any movement of her chest. She touched the girl's throat as she had seen paramedics do on TV. The artery that went up the neck. She couldn't feel any pulse.

Marybeth was dead.

Twyla knew in an instant what she had to do. She pulled Marybeth's shorts off and then her panties. She scraped her thighs with a stick until they were raw, then she hurried away through the woods and out the other side. She got home quickly and back into her room. Then she told her mother she was going to take a shower.

The searchers found Marybeth the next day about noon. Police said it looked as if an attempted rape had gone bad. They were on the lookout for a known pedophile who had recently been released into the area after spending twelve years for child molestation and rape. They never did find him and after two weeks the story dropped out of the newspapers.

Twyla and her mother went to the funeral and to her surprise, Twyla cried as the coffin lowered into the ground.

21

STACY PHONED the principal at Hoover High and told her what she wanted. There was a short silence on the phone.

"Detective, I want to stay as far away from this as I can. I've already turned down three reporters and TV people to talk about Mr. Ingram and his work here."

"Mrs. Wilforce. This is somewhat different. We're the police and we're on a murder investigation. We can talk with you there, or come and get you with three squad cars with sirens and red lights flashing. Then we take you downtown for our little chat. Which is it going to be?"

Another silence on the line this one longer.

"All right. Yes, I'm here until nearly five. Come this afternoon."

"I'll be there in half an hour."

STACY TOOK HER TAPE RECORDER, small camera, notebook, and made the run out to Hoover

High. She'd been there before. The secretary opened the closed door and let Stacy into the inner office. Mrs. Wilforce was as she had been earlier.

After pleasantries, Stacy got down to work. "Mrs. Wilforce, you said there had been no parent or student lawsuits filed against Mr. Ingram. That's noted. You said there were two sexual harassment charges against him in the past ten years. What the police need are the tiles on those charges and the names of the two students so we can talk with them."

"That's a strange point, Miss DeFrain. It involves the privacy of any student who may have made the charges."

"I'm sure the court would not agree with you. This is a murder investigation. Those sexual harassment charges, even if they were settled or taken care of internally in your school or with the school board, they could be a vital link to a student with a long memory. One of those students may have killed Mr. Ingram."

Mrs. Wilforce blanched. She put one hand up, adjusted her glasses, touched her chin, and then let her hands fall into her lap.

"Oh my. I hadn't thought it through that far. As you might expect in a high school with all of these sexually excitable teens we do have our share of girls who get a crush on a teacher and try to move it further. If it fails, sometimes then they make charges. Most of them are discounted and the girls back off and admit that maybe it was just their over active imaginations. Now and then one is for real and we try to settle them out of court and out of any legal entanglements.

"Since our talk earlier, I checked our sexual harassment files. They are listed alphabetically and I show three girls who insisted that Mr. Ingram had fondled them after class when no one else was in the room. He said, she said. Impossible to prove or disprove. Two of the cases were talked down and the girls backed off. The third one was with a girl with unusually large breasts and a good figure. She swore up and down that Mr. Ingram had teased her about her breasts and asked her to bare them for him. She said he'd show her his genitals if she showed him her breasts."

"When did this happen?"

"Two years ago, when the girl was a senior. We talked to other students. Several said the girl had a reputation as an easy lay; she'd go to bed with anyone with male genitals. We had a knock down discussion with her and her parents, told them of the reputation the girl had and advised them to back off and withdraw the charges. We also had the girl forcefully transferred to another high school for the second half of her senior year."

"I'll need her name, her parents' names and address."

"Oh, I'm afraid...."

"I can get a court order in two hours if that's what it will take. Then three or four police cars will come with sirens and lights flashing...."

Mrs. Wilforce waved her hand. "Yes, all right. I won't tell our lawyers about this, so they'll never know." She reached in a drawer and took out a file. She opened it on her desk and read a moment then looked up. "The girl's name is Tamara Kelly. She graduated two years ago."

"Her parent's address?" Stacy asked.

The principal hesitated, closed her eyes and gave a

big sigh. "I guess I have to. Nothing good will come out of this." She looked back at the file. "Her father is Joseph Kelly and he lives, or did two years ago, at 3429 Monroe. That's in the Normal Heights area."

"Can I see the file?"

Mrs. Wilforce hesitated, then her jaw firmed. "No, I don't think so. I'm sure I've provided you with whatever information the court order would tell me to. You have what you need."

Stacy stared at the woman a moment. She wouldn't change her mind. Stacy stood, turned off the tape recorder, and picked up her purse with the Glock pistol inside. "Oh, do you remember what Mr. Kelly's occupation is?"

"That I remember vividly. He's a plumber."

IT TOOK Stacy ten minutes to drive to the address she had been given. The house was more of a bungalow, the kind that were being bought up three or four at a time in a row, torn down and six to eight unit condos or apartments being erected on the lots.

This bungalow was painted white, with light blue trim. The yard was well tended and flowers graced the area next to the house. She went up the sidewalk and rang the bell. She heard the sound it made inside the house. Stacy waited her usual time before ringing again. She had never figured out how long that was, but it was ingrained. Just before she hit the button again, she heard movement, then the door opened on a chain. A slice of a curious woman's face showed through the two inch slot between door and jamb.

"Yes?"

Stacy held up her badge. "San Diego Police. Are you Mrs. Kelly?"

"Yes. Has my husband been hurt?"

"No, nothing like that. I just need to talk to you a minute."

"So, talk. My husband says not to let anyone inside when he isn't here."

"I'm with the police."

"I saw the badge. What do you want?"

"Is your daughter Tamara home?"

"Gracious no. She's been in Los Angeles now for two years, ever since she graduated from high school. Claims she's going to be a big famous actress. So far all we know is that she has done one local commercial, has an agent, and asks us for money on a regular basis."

"She hasn't visited you lately?"

"Ha. That girl hasn't been here for six months now. Last time she came because she wanted her father to fix her car. That was the only reason she came down. Showed us her new head shots and a brochure. A big time nobody is what she is. I keep telling her to get a job as a waitress. Anything else?"

"No, Mrs. Kelly. Thank you. You're doing the right thing about not letting anyone in the house. You have a good day now."

Stacy used her cell phone and told Cain the bad news.

"Right, one real case but it was dropped or settled, and the girl graduated two years ago. She's in Hollywood trying to be a star. I'm heading back to the office."

"We tried. Get on back here; we may have a new lead."

"What?"

"Tell you when you show up."

WHEN STACY WALKED into the team room, the other three detectives had gathered around Cain's desk. She saw something on his desk but didn't recognize it.

"Good, you finally got here. We have news. The crime lab guys weren't happy with what they found in the van, so they did a second search and cleaning on it. Guess what they found?" He pointed down at the plastic cuffs on his desk.

"Not some of ours, Lee said. "They're too thin."

"Quite correct Dr. Watson," Cain said. "They are thinner, not as strong, and the notching cuts are different."

"So where did they find them?" Stacy asked.

"This one had been pushed down into the crack between the rear seat and the backrest. Out of sight and the guys missed it the first time."

Fernando reached in and turned over the plastic. There was a sticky label on the inside. "We know who makes them: Ace Plastic Novelties, of Waterville, Maine."

"We're talking costume shops, joke stores, magic stores, those kinds of places that would sell these," Lee said. "Can't be more than a dozen of them in the whole county area."

"Who wants to check out these shops and see if you can get a make on any recent customers?"

All four held up a hand.

"Yeah, figures." Cain rubbed his face and picked up the plastic cuff. "Trouble is I still am not happy with that work we did on the partial plate on that black

Lexus. You two guys sure you checked out every one of those leads?"

Kevin scrunched up his face and shrugged. "Hell, we did them. Maybe we missed one or two. We had so damn many. I agree that the plate is our best tie so far." He hit Fernando in the shoulder. "Let's take another look at them. Remember those three who were on vacation? We can check them out again. Might be home by now." Fernando grunted and the two went back to their desks.

"Which leaves you two," Cain said pointing at Stacy and Lee. "Find the names and addresses of the stores and then call them and see if they sell this particular brand of riot cuff. Should keep you guys out of trouble for a while. Doubt if they sell a lot of these. They are damn hard to get off once they are cinched up tight." Cain scowled. "Get with it, I've got to go alibi you guys with the lieutenant for not having these cases solved by now."

There were the most costume stores listed in the phone book, so Stacy took them. The joke and magic stores had about half as many listings.

Stacy made her first call.

"Good afternoon. This is the Grove Costume shop."

"Hello. I'm Detective Stacy DeFrain with the San Diego Police Department. I'm wondering if you sell the plastic riot cuffs, the kind that cinch up tight and you have to cut them off."

"We used to sell quite a few of those. Then teenagers began buying them and we had three irate parents who threatened to sue, so we dropped them. Sorry. I know some of the other shops sell them."

Stacy thanked her and hung up. She looked at the next number in the phone book and dialed. There were seven costume shops in the county, all in the San Diego immediate area except for one in Escondido, twenty miles north. Three of them sold the name brand of plastic cuffs the killer had used.

Stacy looked over at Lee. "Hey, buddy, I've got three hits out of seven. How are you doing?"

"No positives on five calls. One more to go. You heading out?"

"Soon as I can get an unmarked. Want to ride along?"

"Does the Pope like brown gravy?"

Stacy frowned. "Brown gravy?"

"Thought I'd change around the old cliché a little. Let's go."

The closest shop, San Diego Costumes, was downtown so they hit it first. The manager was a small man with an oversize head and floppy ears. His eyes were small and deep set and he looked almost like one of his hundreds of masks that dotted the walls. He lurched out of a chair near a counter and moved toward them with an exaggerated limp. His right arm trailed uselessly at his side.

"Help you folks?" He paused. "Cops, right? I can tell."

"Right, I'm Detective DeFrain and this is my partner Detective Ostrander. You do some time?"

"Nothing major. A year here, a year there. What can I help you with detectives?"

"I called about the plastic cuffs?"

"Oh, yeah. I've got them. Don't think I've sold any in six months. Mostly around Halloween. I can check on my computer. Keep everything on there now. Know exactly what my inventory is."

"Please take a look,"

He moved back to the chair and used his left hand on the keyboard.

"That was Ace Plastics?" Stacy nodded. He hit some more keys with his left hand and studied the screen. "Yep, just as I figured. Sold the last pair to a teenager who wanted to scare his girlfriend. That was almost four months ago."

"Nothing since then?" Lee asked. "None to a woman?"

"I get some women who like them. Masochists I'd guess for some rough sex. Nope. Nothing like that in a long time."

They thanked him and went back to the unmarked.

"Next on your list is Party Time in El Cajon on Main," Lee said.

"I've been there," Stacy said. "Mostly party stuff. I got some decorations for a friend's birthday once."

The store was next to a tattoo parlor and just down the street from a Jack In The Box fast food place. A bell tinkled as they went in the front door. A woman came through a beaded curtain. She was nearly six feet tall, with line backer shoulders, a well filled white blouse and an expression that left no room for argument. She had short blonde hair a pretty face and an attitude.

"You the cops, right?" she demanded.

Lee introduced them and asked about the cuffs.

"Yep, I've got them. Not against the law. I checked that out. Should sell these at the sex stores. Right back here."

She led them down an aisle filled with party decorations and table favors to a locked glass case. Inside were the cuffs and costume jewelry. She unlocked the case and took out a pair of the cuffs.

Stacy checked the label inside. "These are the same ones. Have you sold any of them recently?"

"Hey, I don't keep tabs on what I sell. When I run out of something I order it. I ain't no damn computer freak."

Lee grinned. "Hey, know what you mean. Neither am I. Do you remember selling any of these in the past month or two?"

"Two months? Damn. I lost a week in there somewhere. Booze and pills really knocked me out. But I made it. Store was closed then, though. Let me think. Damn pills. Cuffs, cuffs. Not a big seller. Like I said used mostly by sex freaks. Oh, yes, wait a minute let the old synapses close and do their stuff up in the cranium. Okay, yep, got something. About a month ago this lawyer woman came in saying she needed some cuffs for a demonstration to a jury. Said the damn cops wouldn't loan her a pair. So she had to buy them."

"A lawyer. You remember what she looked like," Stacy asked.

"Oh, yeah. Not my type but interesting. Too damn smooth and fast talking. Damn lawyer. Yeah a blue eyed brunet, hair around her shoulders. Dressed in an expensive sleek business suit. Must have paid five hundred bucks for it in La Jolla."

"About how tall?"

"Too short for me. Maybe five six or so, good figure at no more than a hundred and twenty. Stacked, you know, busty."

"Any idea how old she was?

"My guess about twenty seven to twenty nine. Ripe and good but, like I said, not my cup of java."

"She wear glasses?" Lee asked.

"No. But with all her lawyer reading, I'd guess she had laser surgery, you know that cutting thing."

"Did you get her name or address on a sales slip?" Stacy asked.

"Oh, hell no. I don't bother with that. Cash is cash. That's what I like. I don't do credit."

"Anything else you can tell us about her?"

"Good shoes. I always check out the shoes. Nice little round bottom on her, but she had that prissy, don't touch me attitude. Oh yeah, she had an attitude."

Stacy grinned. "Thanks. You've been a good help. Oh, did she buy one set of cuffs or two?"

"As I remember, she bought three sets."

"Thanks, we appreciate your help." Lee gave her one of his cards. "If you think of anything else about her, give me a call. That's my cell so it's good seven-twenty four."

Back in the unmarked, both took time out to write in their notebooks. Stacy slapped Lee on the shoulder. "Partner, I think we just had a good description of our killer. You figure it would do any good to have an artist visit our friend back there and try for a sketch?"

"After two months? I wouldn't guess so. We'll ask the boss. Hey, we may have hit something good here."

Stacy drove. "Yep. You're right. A lawyer. That would make her a defense attorney since a prosecutor could get all the plastic cuffs he wanted. So, a blue eyed brunet, with shoulder length hair, expensive dresser and a defense lawyer.

Partner, I'd say we just earned our day's pay."

22

STACY WROTE the description of the suspected killer on the bulletin board. Cain stood by watching. She and Lee worked together on the points.

"She's a brunet with blue eyes.

"Probably a criminal defense lawyer.

"Hair medium long around her shoulders.

"About five feet six.

"Smooth and fast talking.

"Expensive business suit, pricy blouse, and high priced shoes.

"About twenty-seven to twenty-nine.

"Slender, good figure 'stacked' the wit said.

"Did not wear glasses.

"Prissy, don't touch attitude. Lots of attitude."

Cain looked over the list and nodded. "Too damn bad you couldn't get her name and address. We've got a hell of a lot more than we had yesterday. Now all we need is to find her. Any ideas?"

Lee shook his head.

Stacy grinned, walked around the desk, and came

back. "How about we pay this shop owner a hundred a day to take a tour of the criminal courts in session. We might get lucky and our wit will ID the lawyer. If she positively ID's her, we move in, grab her, and see what we can get on her."

"Would this store owner do it?" Cain asked.

"This time of year she probably doesn't take in fifty dollars in sales all day," Lee said. "I think she'd jump at the chance. We'll have to tell her why we're hunting the buyer."

"No sweat there," Cain said. "Bump it up to a hundred and fifty if you have to. How about an early start in the morning? Get back out there now and make her the offer. She can't more than say no."

"I think she'll go for it," Lee said. "Had the feeling she hated the bitch on sight."

A half hour later Stacy made the pitch to the shop owner. Her name was Selma Harland. She watched Stacy for a long moment and then chuckled.

"God, but that would be good to see that bitch go down. I disliked her the minute she walked in here. Then when I found out what she wanted, I knew she was a damn lawyer. Two cold assed lawyers beat me out of my half of a ten year marriage pile of cash. Hate those fucking lawyers."

"So you'll close up tomorrow and tour the courts with me?"

"Nope. But my sister will come in and run the store. I'd pay you to get something on that bitch. But I'll take the hundred clams a day. How many days to cover the criminal courts?"

"I'd say we can do it in two. Might have to go to Vista, South Bay, and maybe El Cajon, but we can do it.

Want me to pick you up at nine in the morning? Most of the courts don't get started until ten."

"Sounds good. Pick me up here." Her eyes glittered just a moment and she looked at Stacy with a strange expression. Then she stared down at Stacy's chest. "Are you seeing..." She stopped and looked away. "Oh, damn. Okay, I'll be here at eight in the morning. Fancy clothes?"

"Wear whatever you want. There's no dress code down there." Stacy headed for the door. Behind her Selma watched her go.

"Hey, thanks again for this chance. I really didn't like that bitchy lawyer."

From her unmarked, Stacy called Cain and told him they had a go on the Party Time shop owner.

"Her name is Selma Harland, and she is anxious to try to find that bitch lawyer as she called her."

"Good. Work the criminal cases. You can get a print out from the superior court of the cases. You won't need much time in any one court. Oh, you got a call from vice. You in trouble for nude lap dancing at night again?"

"Something like that. Is there a number?"

There was 1416. She put the first three city office phone numbers in front of it and called.

"Yeah, Vice. This is Young."

"You sound so damn official. This is DeFrain."

"Good. Tried to get you. How is the case going?"

"From bad to worse. What's happening?"

"Hey, I'm off tonight. Can we make this Wednesday?"

"Wednesday?"

"We were going to get together Wednesday for your special cook-in."

"That's vs a cook-out?"

"Right. Old vice trick."

Her heart did a thumping in her chest and her eyes went wide. "Hey, my plate is so full...." She paused. He didn't reply. "Okay, okay, I'm not busy tonight. I'm cooking my specialty, right?"

"That's what you said."

"How about seven o'clock?"

"How about I pick you up from the garage and follow you home. Then I can see how you cook."

"First we hit the supermarket."

"I've been there before. You off at five?"

"Better make it five thirty. Some paperwork to do and I'm still in the field. I'll see you in the lobby at five thirty."

"Done. Take care."

Stacy did a little dance sitting in the unmarked, then patted the steering wheel and gave a yelp of delight.

Wasn't that just last night they ate out? Two nights in a row? This guy must have something on his mind. She was sure she knew what it was. He was so good looking that she was thrilled. And so far he had seemed like a real nice guy. What for dinner? Some prime Angus steak, mashed potatoes, some asparagus, what else? Then an ice cream cake for dessert. Oh, they could start with a hot tomato juice cocktail and a tossed green salad. She was planning as she drove back to the garage and got up to the office.

Cain was gone and only Lee worked. She did a run down on her day for her personal cover your ass file, then a page on the computer for the file on her talk with Selma Harland.

All of a sudden it was five forty five. She turned off the computer and rushed down to the lobby. She found him reading Sports Illustrated. He looked up and grinned.

"How do you think the Yankees will do this year?" he asked.

Stacy frowned and lifted her brows. "I hear that they won both at Concord and Lexington."

He stood and roared with laughter. "You win that one. You are a little weird."

"Just a little. Come on, let's go shopping."

They stopped at an Albertsons Supermarket and she worried over the steaks. At last she took an Angus rib eye at seven dollars and ninety cents a pound.

"I finally learned never to buy the four dollar a pound or cheaper steaks. You get what you pay for. This one should melt in our mouths." She stopped. "That is should melt in one mouth at a time...." She giggled.

It took twenty minutes to finish her shopping, and he tailed along. At last she had everything she needed for dinner and they dove on to her place on Juniper.

THE DINNER WAS A SMASHING SUCCESS, with the steak seasoned just right with her combination of Mrs. Dash and some other season salts. They let the dishes sit on the counter and found the sofa.

He kissed her once, she kissed him back, and then pushed away.

"Hey, I feel all gritty. I'm going to take a shower."

She stood and took two steps away. "It's a big shower, plenty of room for two."

THE NEXT MORNING Stacy picked up Selma at her store and they hit the first San Diego Superior Court room at nine forty five. The principals were in place. Two men were consul for the defendant. They didn't wait for the judge, just moved on to the next courtroom. From there on it was a matter of checking court rooms against the list of cases set for that day. In the big building there were twenty three trials in progress. Ten of them were criminal trials. They checked six before they found a woman in the second chair. She was short and blonde.

Selma shook her head and they went to the next court. It was packed with spectators, and they squeezed into the last two public access seats. The woman at the defendant's table was brunet, but her hair was piled on her head. She had on a blue business suit with white shirt and tie and large lensed glasses with black plastic frames. Selma stared at her for a moment, then looked away.

"I don't think so. The hair isn't right and those terrible glasses." They got up to leave and a man in the aisle yelped as Selma stepped on his foot.

"Watch it," he barked. Half the court spectators and lawyers turned to look. Selma apologized and they hurried out the door.

At the defense table beside Trevor Jamison, Twyla watched the small drama and noticed the tall woman with the short blonde hair. She turned away quickly. She had no doubts. She had trained herself to recognize faces. The woman just leaving the court was the same one that Twyla had bought plastic cuff from a month or so ago. Had to be the same one. Had the police found one of the cuffs and traced it back to the woman's store? Twyla felt a chill race down her spine. She turned to look again but the two women were gone. Had she recognized the woman with her? Shorter, straight brown hair cut close. A cop cut? Could they be looking....Twyla edged down in her seat. No, no more danger today. They could have been looking for her in all of the courts, but decided that she wasn't the right one. Maybe having her hair up today had helped. They were almost forty feet away. Positive ID from that distance could be a problem. Twyla felt an urgency overwhelm her. She had to do something about this. Tonight if possible. How? The Party Time shop. The court would let out early. She could be nearby watching. The woman might go back to her shop. If she did it would be simple.

A gun. Not the .32. She had disposed of that. From some of her criminal clients she had learned a great deal. First was never to use the same gun on more than one job. Too easy to match slugs. So she had thrown the .32 pistol as far as she could off the end of the Ocean Beach pier that extended far out into the Pacific Ocean. The gun must be in fifty feet of water. She was safe there unless some lucky fisherman snagged it.

She had another gun hidden in her Lexus.

Alex Tretter poked her as he stood. The judge came in. She got to her feet just in time to sit down.

"Hey, you all right?" Tretter asked. "Looked like you were a thousand miles away. You ready to take notes on that lap top?"

"You bet, Alex. Ready and waiting. If the prosecution has anything at all of any substance."

She turned on the lap top, brought up her notes from the session before, and went to the end. She typed in the date and number of the day of the trial and waited for the testimony to begin.

STACY AND SELMA toured the last four courts before the noon break. They found three more women lawyers, but none of them was right.

"That one we saw early was the closest, but somehow she didn't seem like the one," Selma said.

"Tomorrow we'll drive up to Vista for the court up there. It's an hour or so on the road. Why don't I pick you up about eight and we'll be there in plenty of time for coffee before we start our tour."

Selma agreed and Stacy continued driving out to El Cajon for the court sessions there. They started at two o'clock and there were only three courts in session. Only one woman in any of the defense chairs and she was overweight and had black frizzy hair.

Stacy drove Selma back to her shop. It was about five o'clock.

"I'll let my sis go home and finish the day," Selma said. "I usually stay open until nine. Makes a long day, but sometimes I open late. See you here in the morning at eight."

Stacy picked up her cell as the car sat at the curb outside the Party Time shop and dialed.

"Yeah, Young in vice."

"Just wanted to check to be sure you didn't come down with food poisoning," Stacy said.

"Hey, hi. Not a chance. Best steak I've had in months. What did you put on it?"

"Stacy's secret sauce with herbs and spices."

"Hey, I really liked last night."

"Good. Me too." There was a pause. She let it go for a while. "Hey, I better run. Just wanted to check on the state of your health."

"Hale and hearty. When can I see you again?"

"Easy, easy. Let's go a little bit slow here. I really like you and I don't want to mess things up. Call me in a couple of days. I've got work to do."

"Sounds good. I've got plenty of time. You take care."

STACY GRINNED ALL the way back to the office. She found Cain staring at the bulletin board with the lists and told him the bad news.

"We'll check Vista tomorrow. Then aren't there some courts in South Bay?"

"Yeah, but don't worry about not connecting. This was a long shot finding one damn woman lawyer in a town this size. At least we tried and now we have more specs on her. We're moving ahead slowly."

"I just hope we're moving fast enough before she strikes again."

"Damnit, if we could make some connection," Lee said. "These are totally random killings. They have nothing to do with each other. Is she just grabbing up any old victim and killing him or her? Somehow I don't believe that. There has to be some kind of a connection between the three. Some common denominator. We have to figure it out. Once we find the connection we'll be half way home to nailing this broad."

TWYLA HAD LEFT the society murder trial quickly after they adjourned for the day. No chit chat with her boss. She grabbed her Lexus out of the parking lot and drove out to El Cajon just east of San Diego. She recognized the Party Time shop where she had at last found the plastic cuffs a month ago and parked across the street three stores down. The party shop was open. She waited. Just before five o'clock a Crown Victoria Ford drove up in front of the store. The car was a San Diego Police unmarked car. Half the people in San Diego knew those cars. A woman got out. She was tall, with short blonde hair and even at this distance you could tell she was a damned dyke. She was the same one Twyla had seen in court today. How could she have remembered a customer from a month ago? It didn't matter. She had and it would be the last customer she ever tried to finger for the cops.

A short time later, Twyla saw a woman leave the store. She hadn't noticed her come in. Time to move. She slid the .38 revolver into her handbag and stepped out of the car. One of her clients had schooled her on guns. He told her not to rely on an automatic. Too many things could go wrong and it could jam. A reliable, simple revolver was best. Always worked and cheaper to buy.

Twyla walked across the street and up to the Party Time store. She went by slowly, saw no customers inside. She reversed and stepped through the door quickly. The door had a night lock. She snapped it on, closed the panel, and looked around.

"Be with you in a moment," a voice said from somewhere in back.

Then Selma came through the beaded curtain. "Yes, may I help you with something?"

"Lady, you sure as hell can," Twyla said as she lifted the .38 caliber revolver and pointed it directly at Selma's chest. She fired three times.

23

SELMA GASPED and took a step backward. Twyla stared in amazement that the woman was not dead. The shots must have been high and missed her heart and lungs. Selma stumbled, hit the counter, and stopped. "What on earth? Look, I don't have much money in the till...."

"Shut up," Twyla snarled. "Keep your fucking mouth shut. Turn off the lights, you're closed."

"I really don't...."

Twyla swung the revolver and the front sight sliced down Selma's face tearing a furrow through her left cheek, staggering her backward.

"You bastard," Selma blurted. She frowned and stared at Twyla. "Yeah, sure. You're that bitch I sold the plastic cuffs to. You're the serial killer, sure as hell."

"The lights. Kill the lights."

"Yeah. Okay." Selma eased away from the counter. "Over here, in back." She took a step away and started to turn. She saw Twyla turn with her. Then in a sudden burst she whirled, her hands clasped together in one fist and slammed it into Twyla's wrist, spinning the revolver to the floor. Twyla froze for a moment and it was enough for Selma. The bigger woman lunged forward, grabbed Twyla around the throat with her strong hands, and squeezed. It took only a few seconds for Twyla to gag and be unable to breathe. Then her hands came up scratching, clawing at Selma's face. She found Selma's eyes and the larger woman twisted her head away. Again Twyla clawed at the enemy eyes, found one and jammed her thumb into the socket.

Twyla was losing it. Starved for air and the hands gripping tighter and tighter. Then when her thumb plunged into Selma's eye, the pressure eased as the woman roared in agony and disbelief. Selma's hand dropped off Twyla's throat and her hands covered her own face. Blood oozed down her cheek under her hands. Selma's long wail of pain, fury, frustration, and disbelief billowed through the small store.

Someone jangled the front door, knocked. Both women ignored it.

Selma staggered backwards, hands still covering her face. Twyla shook her head, felt her bruised throat as she kept gasping for air. It took her almost a minute to get her senses back. Then she saw Selma sagging against the counter, one hand over her face, the other stabbing for a telephone.

Twyla lunged forward and whacked the grasping hand with her fist knocking it away from the phone. She shoved the phone off the counter to the floor, then turned and looked for the gun. It had skittered six feet across the floor half hidden under a stack of cardboard cutout characters. She grabbed the revolver and looked at Selma. She still had her hand over her face covering her right eye. Her left glared at Twyla.

"You bitch. You bastard. You hurt my eye."

Twyla pushed Selma through the beaded curtain into a back store room. Had the person at the door seen enough to recognize her again, Twyla wondered? No probably not. She turned Selma, lifted the revolver and from two feet away shot Selma in her good eye. The roaring blast of the .38 revolver in the closed room blocked out Twyla's hearing. Selma had slammed backwards, bounced off a stack of boxes, and she slumped to the floor. The billowing sound of the gunshot faded slowly. Twyla stepped forward, saw the body remain motionless, and shot Selma once more in the side of her head. The sound of the shot didn't seem so loud this time. Twyla looked around, found a master switch, and turned off the lights. She groped her way to the back door she had seen earlier, found the handle, and eased the door open. It was almost dark outside. There was no one in the alley. She set the night lock on the door, eased outside, closed it, and then walked the long way down the alley to the street. Twyla watched the cross street for five minutes. Her senses were up and turned on full blast. She heard every sound, every horn honk, each dog that barked, the buzz of some insects, and the call of a bird far off. When she saw nothing unusual on the street, she walked up to Main. Again she paused and watched. No activity around the Party Store. No sirens sounded. This time she waited two or three minutes, her senses still on high alert. When nothing happened, she walked casually as she could across the street and to her Lexus. Once inside she let out a sigh of relief, started the machine, and pulled away.

Twenty minutes later she eased into her parking slot in the Mission Valley condo complex. She sat there thinking. The cop with the Party Time woman must have a description of her. The two of them must have been in court looking for her. It was luck she had on her for show reading glasses and her hair pinned up. That may have saved her life. Her breathing was still ragged. Her throat hurt. She knew she would have bruises there tomorrow. The bitch had almost strangled her. If she hadn't found that eye, she'd be a corpse by now. Luck of the Irish. Only she wasn't Irish. She'd take the luck anyway. She'd need a high necked blouse for tomorrow. Maybe a turtle neck to completely cover her neck and throat. Yes.

She thought of dinner, then shook her head. Just the idea of food right now set her stomach churning. Maybe some carbonated soft drink to settle down her stomach. She rubbed her head. Not another migraine. That she didn't need. She still had to print out her lap top notes from the trial today and then rewrite them into readable narration to give to Alex in the morning. He always read the notes from the day before just prior to the new day of trial. She had to do it. She had to keep her job. She had to impress her boss. Twyla stepped out of the Lexus and headed for her condo.

She stopped. She remembered what several of her clients had told her about guns. Never use one twice. Dispose of a kill weapon as quickly as possible. Taking it apart and spreading the parts in several places miles apart. She had to do that first. A revolver was simple. She could take the cylinder out. Then there were two screws that held the barrel onto the rest of it. She had screw drivers in her condo.

It took her a frustrating twenty minutes to get the revolver broken down into three pieces. She had resorted to a hammer as the last solution. Now where to dump them? She went back to her Lexus and drove to the far end of the condo and tossed the handle of the gun and the cylinder holder into the dumpster. Then she drove down where there was actual water in the semi dry San Diego River that ran through the valley, and tossed the cylinder in the deepest part. The barrel she worried about. The grooves in the barrel could be matched to the bullets in the simpering shop keeper. She drove around the valley more and at last found some construction work. They were putting in deep footings for a highway overpass. The hole was ten feet deep and looked ready to have concrete poured. She dropped the barrel in the hole then shoveled dirt in the side where she dropped it so it would be covered up and not attract attention.

A FEW MINUTES later in her condo, she slipped off her suit jacket and frowned. She noticed a large dark red spot on the front. She touched it. Wet. Then she realized it was blood. The big bitch dyke's blood. There was no way that she could get it all out of the cloth. Forensics would nail her in a heartbeat. It was one of her trial suits and had cost almost six hundred dollars.

Twyla shrugged. She found a pair of scissors, ripped a hole in the fabric and cut out a four inch square of the blood stain. She inspected the rest of her jacket and the skirt, but found no more blood. She went over them again and this time found one small spot on her skirt. She cut that piece out as well. Then she put the fabric swatches in one of her cooking pots, soaked them with rubbing alcohol, and dropped in a flaming match. The alcohol burst into flames, caught the fabric and burned brightly. She had to soak the fabric twice more before it had completely burned to an ash. She flushed the ash down the toilet.

Next she bundled the rest of the suit in a plastic trash bag, filled it with smelly food from her kitchen garbage can, and with some other items carried them down to the dumpster and pitched the trash inside. The pickup date for the dumpster was the next morning, so there should be no problem there.

Back in her condo, she looked at the two remaining file folders on the next victims. She destroyed the first three folders about the three dead enemies.. She knew all too well how that kind of evidence could bring a hasty guilty verdict in a criminal trial. She had two more hated persons to kill. She chose as the next one, Kimberly Roberts. Dear Kim. She had been salt in Twyla's wounds that whole senior year.

She had tangled with Kim several times the first semester. Once during a field hockey game when Kim almost broke her leg. Again in the hall when there had been a minor dispute over who would wait while the other one opened her locker. There had been a dozen other small things and they built into a pattern.

Twyla had not been the most popular girl at Hoover High their senior year, Kim had been. She had a string of boyfriends, seemingly using them and discarding them like used Kleenex. Twyla had a few dates, and tried, but boys seemed to go for the flashier blondes that year. Then Quint came along. Actually he had been there all the time. He was in her American history class, two rows back. He had a long talk with her over lunch one day. Then the next day he asked her to go to a movie. They went. Then to another. He was exactly her height but not the best looking boy in class.

He grew on her. She liked him. They studied together a few times, then went out again. The last time they went to a movie they tripped over Kim and her current boyfriend. She couldn't even remember his name now. Kim had been surprised and looked carefully at Quint.

Twyla and Quint became a couple, and went everywhere together. Then one day near spring break, Kim had shown up in history class and talked to Quint. Twyla didn't want to butt in so she waited. After class she asked him about it.

"Oh, it was nothing. She invited me to come to her eighteenth birthday party this Friday."

Twyla scowled. "You going?"

"Might. Sounds like a hoot. Going to have a live band and dancing and lots of punch. She said there would be something stronger in it."

"Don't go."

"Thinking about it. You know, just as a lark."

Turned out Quint had gone, and Kim had several special surprises for him. After the party was over and the rest of the kids had left, they sat on a chaise lounge in the dark back yard, she kissed him, opened her blouse and urged him to fondle her breasts. She told him how she liked it and said they could do it again.

That was all it took. Quint never went out with Twyla again. He'd hit the A list and went to parties with Kim and hung out with her for two months before she dumped him.

Twyla had been crushed. She was sure that Quint was her soul mate and they would spend the rest of their lives together. Quint had planned on being a lawyer. She had too. They could open a practice together. Then it all evaporated with that one party and Kim wanting what someone else had.

After graduation, Kim had gone on to San Diego State University and majored in broadcasting journalism. Two years ago she had been promoted from reporter on Channel 8 to one of the afternoon news anchors. She was doing well, was still unmarried and everyone said she had slept her way up the ladder at channel 8. Twyla had a few ideas how to bring Kim down the ladder all the way into a silent, cold, dark grave.

"Oh shit," Twyla said out loud. She threw down the file folder and gently rubbed her neck. She just realized she had not worn latex gloves at the Party Store. Her fingerprints could be on the front door knob and on the rear one and on the night lock lever. Sweat popped out on her forehead and the back of her neck. Could she risk going back to El Cajon and that little store? Someone may have found the body by now. What in hell should she do? Her prints were on file, had to give them when she passed the bar. Now what the hell? What the hell to do now? She decided in a flash.

She grabbed her keys, dark glasses, a floppy hat, and headed for the front door. She had changed into jeans and a tee shirt when she trashed her suit. Now she ran down the steps to her parking slot and backed the Lexus out. She squealed her tires getting out of the parking, then slowed at the street. She stopped and took a deep breath. Now wasn't the time to get a speeding ticket or for blowing through a stop sign. Slow and easy, out Interstate 8 to El Cajon.

TWENTY MINUTES later she slowed to a crawl as she drove past the Party Store. No lights. No cops. No crime tape. Both doors were locked. How to get in? She remembered the shop's front entrance had foot square panes of glass in the door. Smash one of them, reach in....

She was inside quickly. She had a soft kitchen towel and wiped the outside knob completely, then closed the door and wiped the inside knob. She had touched nothing else inside. As she had planned, she went to the small cash register, opened it with the towel, and scooped out all of the bills and change. She stuffed it all in her pocket and left the cash drawer open. Now it would be a robbery gone sour. She grinned. For a moment she looked down at the body, stepped over it, and went to the back door. There she polished the twist lever on the night lock, then opened the door, worked the inside knob and the outside one with the towel, snapped the night lock on again, and went out to the alley.

Twyla didn't breathe easier until she had parked her Lexus in her slot at the Condo. Then she gave a long sigh, stretched, and nodded. She had done it right this time. Now nobody could tie her to the death of the shop owner. The El Cajon Police would treat it as a robbery. Good. She was in the clear.

24

THE NEXT MORNING Stacy went past Central, left her Sentra, picked up an unmarked, and headed for El Cajon. She had no idea where Selma lived. The store pick up was convenient. They should be in Vista in plenty of time for a coffee before court opened. She hoped Selena was in her store and ready. They would cut across to Highway Fifty Two, hit Fifteen, and head north for Vista. Stacy saw the cop cars and the yellow crime scene tape when she was half a block away from the Party Store. She frowned. It couldn't be. But it was. Cops all over the Party Store. She parked and hurried up taking out her badge to get past the yellow tape and the uniform. She saw a detective just coming out the front door and grabbed him.

"Bennett, is it Selma?"

He looked at her a minute then nodded. "Oh, Stacy. It's you. Yep, afraid so. DOA a gunshot through her left eye. Till is busted, could be a robbery." He frowned. "Why are you here?"

She explained about the appointment.

"This has to tie in with the serial killer. Selma was a witness. She had seen the killer, sold her some plastic cuffs. We were trying to ID her at the courts yesterday."

"You must have triggered somebody," Bennett said. "You must have been where your killer lawyer was and she recognized you as a cop and Selma as the shop owner. Damn bad luck."

"You have any prints, any witnesses?"

"Not so far. We're working the prints now. I'll let you know if we get anything. Want to take a look inside? The ME is still there. This one isn't pretty."

Inside Stacy looked at Selma for just a second and then shifted her eyes away.

"We figure there was a fight. Selma is a big girl, strong. She might have been winning then the other person got a thumb in her eye. I've never seen an eyeball hanging down a person's cheek that way before."

Stacy shook her head then looked back. Terrible. The pain must have been horrendous. "Got to be some prints. We have to tie this into our three murders. We'll take her any way we can."

"Her?" Bennett asked.

"Right. We're sure our serial is a woman. So a woman must have done this one, too. That criminal defense lawyer. We must have looked at twenty or so yesterday."

"How many women?"

"That's what I'm going to check over again today. We might just have narrowed down a new list of suspects."

. . .

BACK IN HER UNMARKED, Stacy called Cain.

"Hey, not before I have my second cup of coffee," he said.

She told him about Selma. He groaned.

"Which means you set her off yesterday. You saw the serial killer in court. You just didn't know which woman defense attorney it was."

"But I'm going to make the same circuit today and get names of every woman defense lawyer in those eight court rooms."

"You can get those names from the Assignment Clerk over there."

"Good idea. Then I'll tour those courts again, looking for a brunet damned lawyer." Stacy slumped in her chair at her desk. "If only El Cajon PD can come up with some prints. All lawyers are printed and on file. This could be our big break."

"She probably wiped her way in and out."

"Let's hope she got so excited that she missed one small spot, just big enough for a thumb print."

Cain picked up his land line phone. "I'll call Lieutenant Jason out there. I've worked with him before. I'll explain our intense interest in this case."

"I wish our crime scene guys could do the job," Stacy said. She sat up straight and shook her shoulders. "Okay, I'm off to superior court to get me some names, one of which has got to be our serial killer bitch."

"I didn't think you liked that word."

"I don't, but if Selma called her a bitch, she must be one. See you later."

. . .

THE ASSIGNMENT CLERK was interested and helpful. In the twenty courts Stacy had visited yesterday, there were eleven women lawyers as main counsel, or in second or third chairs. Stacy wrote down all the names.

The clerk was Antoinette Henry, a small woman in her fifties, white headed with glasses, and twenty extra pounds. Her face was soft and unlined, pink cheeked, and light brown eyes that brimmed with kindness.

"Usually we don't offer names and addresses, but if nobody tells me not to, I'm giving them to you. Police business and all. We're all on the same team here."

Five minutes later, Stacy had her treasure chest of names, addressed, and current telephone numbers. She then began working the courts in the same order she had the day before.

The first case, the society woman's murder, was not in session. Two of the jurors had reported sick, the flu. Stacy worked the rest of the courts and tried to assign names to faces, but had no luck. She did eliminate three of the women. Two were blondes and one a red head. The other eight were either dark, dark brown or brunet and in the running for serial killer of the month.

She had the names according to court rooms, and could tie some names to faces, but only where there was only one woman in the chair. One stood out. A Wendy Callahan. A true brunet, about five-six, slender. She was first chair on an assault and battery case and doing a good job of defending her client. Stacy tried not to be noticed as she made her rounds. She got back about four that afternoon to the office and stopped at Cain's desk.

"So, anything from El Cajon?"

Cain grinned. "Well now, we might have something. It's a partial print, maybe half of one. She slipped up on the rear door knob. Nothing we can tie down. No way even to run it for a match. But if we get anything else, we can use it to match up and then nail her for the Selma killing as well. Progress in a rather lateral manner."

"No shoe prints in blood, or torn clothing, or matchbooks, or any damn thing we can use?"

"About it. Head shot so some sprayed blood but not much on the floor. When the heart stops beating, the blood stops pumping out. It just settles to the lowest part of the body."

"There's got to be more."

"Have a talk with Detective Bennett. Lt. Jason said you briefed him before. Call him. There might be something else we can run with."

She called. Detective Bennett sounded tired. "Yeah, Stacy. Been on this one all day. If it was just a robbery, it was piss poor. There was a small metal box under the counter with over two hundred dollars in it. In the back room a jewelry case with some good diamonds."

"Not a robbery. She didn't even make it look good. You found a print?"

"Just a washed out partial. Might not be any good at all. If you get a good set on her, this one might be enough for a collateral match. Have to wait and see."

"Anything else turn up? Any fabric, any dropped prescriptions?"

"Sorry. That damn eye still bugs me. If you find a suspect, you might look for some heavy bruises on her throat. Our guess."

"I'm hunting like crazy. Thanks. Anything else

shows up, give me a call." She told him her cell number. Cain looked up.

"Anything?"

"Not a whisper. Not a ghost of a whisper."

"Put Selma on the kill board," Cain said.

Ten minutes later, Stacy had the board set. There wasn't much to put down:

. Selma Harland.

. About 30-33.

. Owned Party Time store in El Cajon.

. Sold killer the plastic cuffs.

. Six feet tall, slender.

. Looked for killer in 20 courts.

. Killer must have recognized her.

. Described killer.

. Partial print left in store by killer.

Kevin and Fernando came in. Kevin was fuming.

"Thought for sure we had a good one," he said. "The plate was right, the Lexus black as sin and owned by a woman. When we finally tracked her down she was some big shot in a brokerage firm and we had to wait two hours to see her until the damn market closed."

Fernando laughed softly. "Man, that's why I always keep a paper back book in my pocket. All you had were financial magazines to read."

Cain snorted. "So she was a washout?"

"She was one of the vacation blanks we had. Last one. She was in Paris and had the travel stubs to show us. She was working them into an expense account."

"That's absolutely the last one of those twenty four?" Cain asked.

"That wraps it," Kevin said. "We nailed all twenty

four and all had solid alibis for the night of that first kill."

"So we're back to doing detailed biographies on our three victims. We're not considering Selma as one of the serial killer's program kills. Looks like she was a danger for the killer and she had to eliminate her. So, all we have right now to work on are those bios. Anybody done yet?"

The three shook their heads.

EARLY THAT SAME MORNING, Twyla had pinned her hair on top of her head and found some large lens glasses with darkly tinted lenses. She looked at herself in the mirror. Should do. She wore an expensive blue cashmere turtleneck sweater under a sleekly tailored blue business suit. None of the bruises that were turning black on her throat would show.

At the court she came in just as the judge should be entering the room. There were only a handful of people there and the bailiff was notifying everyone the session had been cancelled for the day. Court would resume at nine o'clock the next morning. Why? Two of the jurors had taken sick with touches of the flu. Twyla turned around and headed back to the offices of Brandon, Knox and Tretter. She wondered if the cop would come back and look at the courts she must have been at yesterday with the Party Store owner. Twyla hoped that she had time to get her hair restyled, maybe even cut to throw off the damn cop. Back at the office she would make a call and get an appointment for late today. She wondered how many women lawyers were in the various court yesterday?

She rejected the idea. That was not a good way to find a person.

At work she talked over the case with Alex. He almost had her go out and vet a new witness for their side, but he decided she would be not much help. Twyla made a hair appointment for five fifteen and relaxed a little. At the salon she told her usual stylist what she wanted. The woman stared at her hard.

"You sure, sweetie? You know that's going to change your basic look."

"Oh, god, I hope so."

"Hiding from an old flame. Yes, honey, I understand."

A half hour later Twyla had a short cut that clung close to her head and her natural brunet hair had been streaked with generous blonde swatches. She stared at it in the big mirror and grinned. "Perfect," she said. Now it would take a fucking genius to ID her in the courtroom.

25

ON HER WAY home from the hair dresser, Twyla stopped at an Applebee's Neighborhood Grill and Bar with the big sports TV screens and good steaks. She settled in at a booth and enjoyed her steak. All the time she was planning and writing notes on a napkin. By the time her apple cinnamon pot pie came she had a lot of the thinking done on how to get back at miss fancy pants Kimberly Roberts. She almost giggled as she reviewed her notes, then finished the delicious apple pie, and headed home to Mission Valley.

IN HER CONDO she looked at the napkin and memorized what she had written down. One of their clients, a truly bad guy who had killed his mother and sister, taught her straight out that it was suicide to write anything down.

"No fucking records on paper. Nothing on your computer either if you go that way. Don't write nothing down, then they got a tougher time hanging you."

He was right. But they convicted him anyway and he was currently on death row waiting out his ten year series of appeals.

She savored the whole idea. Kimberly was a semi public figure being on the tube as a news anchor five days a week. She would have to be careful. No simple snatch job. She'd have to play it close to her chest and have a totally believable story to get Kimberly in a vulnerable position. It couldn't be a straight TV story. That would involve bringing along a TV cameraman and his gear. It had to be an information only type meet, and then later they could use the camera on the culprits as they were arrested.

Twyla shivered. This was going to be so fine. She shivered again and began typing on the computer exactly what she wanted to say to Kimberly. She'd go out later, use a pay phone to call the station, and get Kimberly's voice mail so she could leave a message. Yes! She jumped up and did a little dance. That boyfriend stealer was going to get hers. Yes! She sat down and went over the message again. It had to be just right. She rewrote part of it, cut it down some, and left it with a line that she would call again. When she had it perfect, she printed it out then erased it from the screen so there would be no hard disk record of it.

She practiced it twice, then ran down to the Lexus and drove to Mission Valley Shopping Center five miles away. She found an outside phone and called channel six. As she guessed she got the voice mail. She looked around. Nobody near who could hear. There was just one phone so nobody close. She lifted her rehearsed speech and began.

"Kimberly. You don't know me, but I have what

might be the biggest, ugliest story in San Diego all year. It involves a mother and her two sons and the unthinkable things that she does with them. She says it's for their own good. But I don't agree. I can't tell you anything more now. I just want to say that this involves the mother and her sons and sex. I'll call later. I have to go." She hung up and grinned. Then walked away from the phone booth and bought two new blouses, the pure white kind that juries seemed to like. It had been a good day. She passed a mirror in the center and was startled by the woman who stared back at her. Then she laughed. Her new hairdo was fantastic. She did look like a different person. She hoped that her boss at work liked it. Just so he didn't throw her off her second chair on the hot society murder case. It was getting more fantastic every day.

THE NEXT MORNING, Stacy went to work determined to make some progress on her quest for the right female lawyer. First she checked out the criminal defense lawyer Wendy Callahan she had seen in court. Stacy hit wants and warrants and came up empty. She ran her two other data banks and found one DUI arrest two years ago. Wendy had beaten the charge in court, arguing that she had been slightly sick to her stomach and light headed from some food poisoning and had been weaving a little on her drive home. The officer who stopped her said she passed the breath test but could not walk the line. She told him about her sickness and he guessed she was on medication, which would still be DUI. She proved she wasn't and that he had arrested her purely because he found out she was a defense attorney. Case dismissed.

Another source showed that she worked for the Johnson and Johnson law firm. A six person group that handled mostly criminal cases. She was thirty four years old, solidly married, had two children, and had been with the firm for three years. Her supervisor said he had nothing but praise for her and her work ethic and family life. She also was a soccer mom, sang in the church choir and planned the family's month long camping venture each summer. Not a good prospect for a serial killer. Stacy wrote Wendy off her list of suspects.

Cain loomed over her desk. "You ever finish that complete bio on Judith, our first kill? I'm looking for one on all three of them. Drop this lawyer thing for now and finish the Judith bio. Then we'll get back on those lady lawyers. It looks good, but let's get cleaned up on this old stuff first."

For Stacy it meant one more talk with Judith's mother. She didn't relish the job, but it had to be done. She called and caught the woman at home. They met a half hour later and Mrs. Lancaster had baked oatmeal cookies and had hot chocolate ready when she came. They dug into as much about Judith as her mother could remember. There never had been any fights. None of the usual teen age rebellion or the "I hate you mother" lines from Judith. Just a hard working, happy teenager who enjoyed high school, tried a year of college, then got married, had her kids, and somehow wound up divorced and working full time.

"Any serious boyfriends her senior year?"

"Not that I remember. Surely none she brought

home, you know like she thought this might be the one. She dated, but nothing too heavy. I never had to worry about Judith having sex. We talked about it and she swore she would wait until she got married. I think she did."

"Any grudge fights with other girls? You know how teen girls can get into spats that sometimes escalate."

"Not that she mentioned at home. She just sailed through high school, and I thought she would be a teacher, but she never had a chance to finish college with the two little girls."

Stacy shook her head. "I'm afraid I'm not learning much that can help me. Oh, where did she go to high school?"

"Hoover High. It's not far from here. Oh, dear, I heard about that Hoover High teacher who was murdered. He could have been one of Judith's teachers. I don't remember her talking about him, but he was there when she was there."

"What about grade school?"

"Oh, Johnson Elementary, then Franklin Middle School before Hoover." She paused and sipped the coco. "I don't remember much about those years. They kind of slipped by, with no trouble, no problems. We were thankful that we had such a well adjusted and bright girl as our daughter. Oh after the divorce she took back her maiden name." Mrs. Lancaster touched a tissue to her eyes and shook her head.

"Sorry. I just get so lonesome sometimes. The granddaughters are close and I'm afraid I'm spoiling them."

A half hour later, Stacy gave up. She had accomplished absolutely nothing. She wished she had brought her lap top, but she had found that most people tended to close up and get self conscious when she typed on the keyboard. She thanked Mrs. Lancaster for the coco and cookies.

She scooted to the kitchen and came back with a small paper sack. "Some more cookies, for you, dear. You seemed to like them. Goodness knows I shouldn't be eating any of them at all."

Stacy thanked her and went back to the car. With any luck she could transcribe her notes onto her lap top and get the whole biography of Judith Lancaster finished that afternoon. She ate two more cookies as she drove back to the barn.

TWYLA SURPRISED her lead defense attorney at the trial that morning. He nodded.

"Not bad. Shows a little spunk. I kind of like it. Different. Where are the notes on yesterday?"

That day went quickly and she hurried home afterwards her mind racing with what she had to do. She started by tearing apart an old video tape of a movie. She didn't even look to see what it was. The tape was what interested her. Just how strong was it? She tried pulling it apart with her hands. It didn't tear easily. She reeled off twenty feet, made six loops, and taped the twelve strands together. She taped the ends together and had a loop about six feet long. She anchored the top over a kitchen chair and stepped into the bottom of the loop. Would it hold her weight? It did. She nodded and went to work with the rest of the tape. She made a twelve strand rope out of the rest. She set it up so it was twenty feet long. There was just enough tape to finish the last layer. Then she used two-inch wide Scotch tape and bound the layers together at two foot intervals.

About six o'clock she made another call to Channel six and got Kimberly's voice mail. This time she was specific.

"Kimberly. I'm giving you an exclusive on this. You get to alert the cops. This woman is having sex with her two sons, age fourteen and fifteen. She says they need to learn a bout sex sometime, why not at home? The neighbors suspect but can't prove anything. I have a home video tape one of the boys made and smuggled out to me. I can give you the tape and the name and address of the family. The woman is divorced. Don't tell the police yet. Meet me at the Starbuck's

Coffee shop in the little strip mall at Navajo Road and Lake Murray Boulevard. This is in the San Carlos Area. The Starbuck's is a half block down Navajo on the street out from LA Fitness. I'll be at an outside table wearing a Padres baseball cap. Be there at ten o'clock tonight. No cameraman. That's later. We'll drive past the widow's house. Be there at ten or I'll go to Channel 8. See you tonight at ten."

She had read her script perfectly. Twyla looked at her watch, six-thirty. Plenty of time. She needed a vehicle.

THIS TIME her hunt in Mission Valley took only a few minutes in the daylight. She didn't need a van, any car with the keys in the ignition would do. She found a three year old Buick on the second row she toured. It started easily, she drove out, back to her condo, and left it in a visitor's slot.

In her condo she put the video tape rope in a soft sided gym bag, added her last cold gun, .32 caliber revolver. She put in five rounds and left the hammer down on the empty chamber. What else? She added a set of plastic cuffs and a big pair of scissors to cut them off. She let her anger start to build. She relived that last month or so with her high school boyfriend. She remembered how Kimberly snatched him away, teased him with bare breasts, then seduced him, and at last dumped him for another. The gall of that woman! How could she do it? She was still not married, which was a sign she was still sleeping around. Probably slept her way into her anchor job.

Twyla went to the kitchen and took out a ten inch carving knife. It was the one she used on a turkey that time she had a turkey dinner for some friends. She hefted it, then a wicked smile spread over her face and she dropped the knife into her gym bag of tools. That was all she needed. She had researched the site weeks ago with the chance she could use it on one of her victims. She took the gym bag, a two foot high kitchen stool down to the Buick, then went back to her condo, and watched TV.

She left the condo in the Buick at nine o'clock, drove out Friar's Road to Mission Gorge Road, took the turnoff at Jackson up to Navajo, and turned left toward the intersection with Lake Murray Boulevard. She was early. She parked across from a sub sandwich place and waited. There were few patrons at the Starbucks that faced Navajo. Three tables out front were unoccupied. She would not get coffee, that would allow a clerk to see her and maybe remember her. She would sit at the table when it was ten minutes to ten. The woman might come early.

At 9:45 Twyla drove up to the parking slot next to one of the Starbucks outside tables and stopped. It was six feet from the table to the passenger's door of the car. She eased out of the Buick, closed the door silently, and made sure the passenger's side was unlocked. She wore the Padres brown and white baseball cap, a heavy blue sweatshirt and black sweatpants. The night was cool, but not cold. She made a bet with herself that Kim would be early. She sat on the edge of the table and waited.

She was right. At five minutes to ten a car pulled into the space next to hers. There was a momentary lull, then a door slammed and the perfectly coifed blonde Kimberly Roberts came around the back of the car and stopped. She wore brown slacks and a brown contrasting jacket over a white blouse. She looked over at the table, then went forward slowly.

"Are you the woman who called about a widow lady?"

"Right. Are you Kimberly?"

"I am. Let's sit in my car. It's a little chilly out here."

"Fine, but I'd be happier in my car. It's the Buick. Okay?"

Kimberly hesitated, then shrugged. Twyla figured she was counting her chances of having to jump out if the Buick if things went badly. At last she nodded.

"It's unlocked." Twyla grinned as Kim walked up the side of the Buick and opened the door. She waited until Twyla got into the car.. Kim got in and closed the door. The soft gym bag rested between them.

"Hey, nothing to worry about. Just get the goods on

this bitch who's fucking her sons. Means a lot to me. I hate it when something like this happens."

"You said you have a video tape, a home video. You have it with you?"

"In the gym bag." Twyla unzipped the top. "May I reach in and get it?"

"Yes. Yes of course."

Twyla reached in and came up with the short barreled .32 revolver and pushed it against Kim's side.

"Okay, don't move, don't even breathe hard. Put your wrists together, now."

Kim showed total surprise. Her eyes flared, she looked at the door, then down at the gun. Her breath caught and her voice came out low and scratchy. "What's going on? What about the story? I don't understand."

"You sure as hell don't, Kim. You never did. Now hold still." Twyla took the plastic cuff out of the gym bag and wound it around Kim's wrists, put the end in the slot and pulled it tight.

"Hurts," Kim said.

"It won't hurt for long. Put your ankles together."

"Why? I'm not running anywhere. I want that story."

Twyla laid down the revolver, bent down to put the cuff around Kim's ankles. Kim made fists out of her hands and slammed them both down on the back of Twyla's neck as she bent down to cuff the TV anchor's ankles.

Twyla bobbed up and backhanded Kim across the face. The TV anchor shrieked in pain.

"Do that again, bitch and I kill you right here with one round up your nose. You want that?"

Kim shaken by the attack shook her head.

Twyla forgot about binding her ankles. She stared the car and pushed the button locking all doors. She backed out, drove carefully to the left out Navajo to where it went under highway 125. She turned on the on ramp and took the new freeway down the hill past Grossmont College to where it merged with the freeway 52 out near Santee. She took an off ramp and up an access road, then nosed up to a fence around a broadcast tower. She wasn't sure if it were radio or TV. But it would work. The gate in the fence was not locked and she parked close by. She pulled Kim out of the car and over twenty feet to the tower. She pushed her to the ground under the eighty foot tall steel tower. Just over their heads was a steel cross beam that was ten feet off the ground.

"What on earth are you doing?" Kim asked fear spreading through her voice like spilled ice water on a kitchen floor.

"You don't remember me, do you Kim?"

"No. should I?"

"You damn well should. I'm Twyla Farnham, you old classmate from Hoover High, class of eighty seven. Remember."

"That Twyla?"

"How many Twylas have you known, you dipshit?"

No response. Fear rising in Kim's eyes, showing even in the soft moonlight from a three quarters moon.

"You stole my boyfriend our senior year, remember? You wanted him only because I had him and you knew you could do a tit show and entice him. You sure as fuck did."

"But that was a long time ago." Desperation was

creeping into her voice. It broke how and she nearly sobbed. "Surely you've forgiven...."

The knife came out then an inch from Kim's eyes. She edged back.

"I have a long memory and total recall. I remember every single time you snubbed me our senior year, every time you took my boyfriend, the whole damn thing. Now it's pay back time."

"Twyla, I have money. I can give you money. A....I can give you a hundred thousand dollars." Her eyes were frantic now, darting from side to side. Searching the desolate, dark area cleared around the tower for help. There was none.

"Poor little rich girl, begging for her worthless life."

"Two hundred thousand. I can raise it. Twyla, please. You can be rich by this time tomorrow." Her voice shook. Her bound hands coming up in a last appeal.

Twyla took the video tape rope out of the gym bag and threw one end over the steel beam. She pulled the loose end down, gripped both parts of it up high and pulled herself off her feet. The video tape rope held.

"Now comes the fun part, Kim. I'm afraid that you won't make your noon deadline tomorrow to report on it. Hell, those things happen. Any last words to say to your TV viewing audience?"

26

A BELL RANG SOMEWHERE. She thought it was a bell, maybe more like a front door chime. She was in a valley with dozens of wild orchids. She'd never seen so many different kinds and colors. Huge ones and tiny ones on long stems. Maybe she was in Hawaii or somewhere that orchids grew wild. She'd heard there were hundreds of kinds in the rain forest jungles of Mexico. That was it. Why wouldn't the damn ringing stop? Slowly the orchids faded, the ringing kept going and Stacy lost the dream. She sat up in bed rubbing her eyes.

The damn phone. The land line. She fumbled for it on the stand at the edge of the bed. She caught the glow of the clock next to it. Four-forty-five a.m. Not a fit to me...

"Yeah?" she said. "I'm not really awake. Is this some crazy dream?"

"No dream, DeFrain."

"Oh." The voice was Sergeant Cain Baker. "Yeah, give me a second to get back from that great dream. It was good. Now, I'm back on track, in focus and still sleepy. Something happen?"

Cain chuckled. "You always have been slow to wake up. Good thing you were never in combat. You'd be dead on the first night mission."

"You called me just to chat?"

"Get your pants on, DeFrain. We've got another one. Bet my suspenders it's our girl again. You'll never guess who the victim is."

"Guess, guess, guess. I guess not. So who?"

"Kimberly Roberts."

"The TV news anchor person?"

"The same one. Get your britches out to a transmission tower just off highway 52 outside of Santee."

"Yeah, I know the one. Just past Mast Boulevard."

"That's it. I'll give you twenty minutes."

"Takes me that long to wake up. Say forty minutes and I'll be there with bells on."

Stacy bounced out of bed, stripped off the oversize tee shirt she slept in and ran for the shower.

TWENTY SIX MINUTES later she pulled up behind half a dozen cop cars near the transmission tower. The crime lab guys were already there doing their work. She found Cain staring at the body, which still hung by the neck from the steel cross bar of the tower. The woman was bare to the waist. Stacy took a closer look and turned away, bile boiling up in her throat. She furiously swallowed it down and looked back.

Both of Kim's breasts had been cut off. Hacked was a better word, Stacy decided. Kimberly's chest was one mass of blood and blood had gushed down her torso darkening the brown slacks almost to her knees. On the ground lay a pristine white blouse and a brownish jacket. A tipped over kitchen stool two feet high sprawled to one side. Kimberly still wore her shoes that Stacy figured had cost her more than two hundred dollars. Her feet dangled a foot off the ground. Evidently the rope had stretched. It was looped over the steel bar and the two ends knotted around Kimberly's throat.

There were no signs of a struggle. The blood had dried to a deep coral almost black color. A half dozen flies buzzed around the bloody chest until a deputy swatted them away. The coppery smell of blood singed the area.

"My god, so much blood," Stacy said.

"That means she was cut up while she was still alive. This isn't just a murder, it's torture and then a butchering."

"We're back to the intense, furious sexual component," Stacy said. "Our girl is still working out her anger."

An ME Stacy didn't know arrived in a county marked car with his black bag. He took one look at Kim.

"For God's sakes, cut her down," he barked.

One cop used a knife to saw through the strange looking rope. Two more caught Kimberly's shoulders and gently let her down to the ground on her back.

"What kind of a rope is that?" Cain asked. They walked around the body where the rope had been dropped on the ground. Stacy picked up the cut end and frowned.

"Not a rope, it's video tape. A whole bunch of video tape fastened together to make a kind of rope." Stacy looked back at the body. "This is getting really, really sick. A TV anchor person is hung with video tape, television video tape. Our killer is sending us a message."

Cain scowled and shook his head. "The tape won't have any prints on it, for damn sure. The stool must have been used for Kim to stand on. It could be a pick up item from some used furniture store, or it might have come right out of the killer's kitchen. Make sure they dust that whole damn thing for prints."

Kevin boiled up in his Ford Focus and ran over to them.

"Jesus H. Kereist," he said looking at the body. "Has to be our girl again. Another sexual retribution?"

"Looks that way."

"Any tire tracks?" Kevin asked.

Cain pointed to the mass of cop cars in the only area where the killer could have parked.

"Not now there aren't. It would have been a stolen car anyway. She wouldn't risk using her own car for a kill like this one. Let's talk to Anderson."

Lieutenant Anderson, the top man at the crime lab, had latched on to the kitchen stool and had two men dusting it for prints.

"We might get lucky on the stool. Depending where it came from. You know how you pick up a stool like this to move it. Thumb on top and fingers underneath. If it was hers, and she didn't wear gloves out here, she might have forgotten to wipe the stool. It must have been a highly emotional situation and maybe for once she slipped up."

"I'm getting a couple of partials," one of the tech men said. "Might not be enough to match, but it could support that other partial we have."

The detectives went over to the ME. The county medical examiner grunted when he saw them come.

"I.D. on her is most likely the TV anchor, Kimberly Roberts. No purse, no paper I.D. Preliminary cause of death could have been either strangulation by that rope thing, or she might have bled out before she strangled. She was definitely cut up before she was dead. That's about all I can say now. You'll get the usual autopsy report."

An ambulance rolled up and three paramedics boiled out. Right behind them came an on location TV van with Channel 6 painted all over it. Somebody had tipped them. A serious faced male reporter and a cameraman scurried up to the edge of the cars where three policemen stopped them.

"Is it really her?" the reporter towing a cameraman with him asked the cops. "Is it Kim who got murdered?"

The cops nodded.

"Oh, God, no." The field reporter rubbed his eyes. "Let me go see. We can't do any video, but let me go look."

The cop called to a sergeant, who listened and let the reporter thought the line. He walked up to the scene and dropped to his knees sobbing.

Cain waved to his two detectives. "Nothing more we can do here. Let's get back to the office and see what we have, which is almost nothing. You guys get those bios done?"

Both said they had.

"Good, get print outs on my desk when we get back. Now we have another bio to do."

. . .

BACK AT CENTRAL STACY printed out two copies of her three page bio on Judith Lancaster. She gave one to Cain. Kevin had done the same and he and Stacy traded printouts to read.

Kevin came over to Stacy a short time later.

"We're looking for something similar, right? Something that might tie these people together. Maybe I found something."

Stacy lifted her brows. "I haven't so far, but I'm not done with your epic. Six pages? I had only three."

"Bert Showley graduated from Hoover High School in 1996," Kevin said. "Judith graduated from Hoover High...."

Stacy cut him off. "In 1996. And Mr. Ingram was a teacher at Hoover High School in 1966." They both looked at each other.

"Wow," Kevin said. "We might have a handle."

"I'm wondering where Kimberly Roberts went to high school. I'm giving Hoover High a call right now."

"First let's tell the boss," Kevin said.

Cain snorted. "You mean this could be a bunch of hatred generated during high school ten years ago? Why would she wait ten years to start her deadly vendetta?"

"She'd have college to get through and law school," Stacy said. "Then get established in a law firm. Maybe then she would have money enough to settle old grievances."

"Call Hoover High and check on Kimberly," Cain said.

Five minutes later, Stacy was back at his desk with a grin.

"I talked to the principal and asked her to check the

class roster for 1996. Yes. Kimberly Roberts not only attended Hoover, she was a mover and shaker, one of the most popular girls on campus and full of promise. I asked her about Judith Lancaster and she looked her up. She also was of the class of 1996 at Hoover."

Cain slouched lower in his chair and rubbed his left knee. After five years it still hurt where the bullet had jolted through. "So we have a commonality. Now what the hell can we do with it? Call up all of the graduates of Hoover in 1996 and warn them a killer could be after them?"

"That would be about nineteen hundred graduates," Stacy said. "I asked the principal how many."

"What we don't do is let this fact out to the press. Say half the class is still in the area. We don't want a thousand people yelling at us for protection. Call the principal back and tell her this is top secret, highly classified, and not to let it out to anyone."

Stacy made the call and the principal agreed.

"We don't even put this on the board," Cain said. "But we do make out a new listing for Kimberly. I liked to listen to her on Six. She had a good way with the news."

"So we don't need a bio on Kim," Kevin said. "We have our common fact about all four. What do we do now? How are we any better off than we were before we knew this?"

"Not much, but maybe a little," Cain said. "Stacy, hie thyself to the nunnery of Hoover High, get the yearbook for 1996, and see what you can dig out of it about Kim. Who her friends were, any predictions, anything about dates to the prom or pictures of her activities. If you can figure out who her best friends were, we might have somebody to talk to about those good old days. We're looking for girls here."

"Yes, this might produce a girl or two with a long memory of Kim, a good one who might know who really hated her that year. I'm running."

"Kevin, go over to the crime lab and baby sit them on those partials. See if they can match them to anything. Not the usual criminal data bank. Go into others that might pertain, like federal and city employees, etc. We need them to wring them out as much as possible."

ON THE WAY to Hoover High in an unmarked, Stacy's cell rang. She picked it up.

"Yes, who is calling?"

"Hal. Wondered if you were free for lunch? We could go downtown somewhere. I'm fed full of the cafeteria food."

"Would love to, but I'm going back to high school."

"What? Undercover?"

"You heard about Kimberly?"

"The TV anchor. Yeah. Damn shame. A beautiful woman."

"We're right in the middle of that."

"But high school?"

"Don't ask."

"Maybe dinner?"

"Not sure. I'm not putting you off. I just don't know where this morning's work might lead."

"Okay, understand. I've been there. You have my cell number. Give me a call sometime."

"Will do, cowboy. I better sign off. I hate to see

people using their cell phones while they're driving. I'll call."

At the school, Principal Wilforce nodded about the year book, and dug out one for Kimberly and gave her a small office to use for her research. The principal hesitated, then gave Stacy her idea.

"We have a teacher here who was a classmate of Kimberly in 1996. She talked to me this morning just after we heard the news. I think it would be helpful if you could talk to her. She's only been with us for five years, but is one of our very best. I'll see when she can come talk to you."

"That's exactly the kind of person I was hoping I could find in the yearbook. The sooner I can talk to her the better."

"Good. Her name is Piper Rowland." She paused, face showing a conflict. "Tell you what. I'll have a substitute take over her English class and get her in here right now."

"That is greatly appreciated. It could be terribly important."

27

TWENTY MINUTES later Piper and Stacy had gone over the senior section of the ten year old Hoover High School year book. It was complete and showed dozens of shots of Kimberly in her many activities.

"Hey, there I am on the yell squad," Piper said. "That was quite a year. Kim was the group's leader and got two girls booted off the squad. I never quite knew why."

"Do you remember their names?"

"Let's see." She screwed up her face, stiffened her jaw, and then lifted her brows. "Nope, don't remember either one of them. They aren't in the picture since it was taken around the first of the year."

"I understand there were quite few girls who didn't like Kimberly. Do you remember any of them and why?"

"Why. Oh yes. Kimberly made it a habit her senior year to steal other girl's boyfriends. The more serious the couple was the harder she tried to break them up and take the boy. The talk was she was having sex with them to get them away, but nobody ever proved it. Sex was big back then. Most of it was talk but a lot of screwing went on."

"Do you remember any girls who got their boyfriends stolen from them?"

"Well, let me think about that. Not me. I never had a real steady boyfriend. I was too much of a nerd and studied too much. Oh, oh. Yes. Patti Vining. She was furious. She thought for sure she and her boyfriend were going to get married right after graduation. Then along came Kim and whammo. She was out and Kim was dating him."

"Is Patti still around town?"

"Not sure. I ran into her a couple of times. I think she was at our fifth reunion. Okay, we are planning a tenth. I bet our secretary has the names and addresses of all the active grads. I'll give you her phone number. Her name is Violet. She can tell you if Patti is in the area."

"Good. Now who else? You said lots of the girls didn't like Kim. Any more good names for me?"

"Maybe Phyllis. She went steady with this guy for two years, then Kim tried to move in. we all thought there goes the guy, but evidently Phyllis held on to him with some midnight sex parties. At least by March she was so pregnant she couldn't hide it. The guy finally knew and he shot out of school like a cannon, joined the Navy and she never saw him again. You might say Phyllis might be a candidate for hate Kim club."

"Her last name back then?"

"Oh, Phyllis.....Canton. Phyllis Canton. I did see

her at our fifth reunion, so we should have her home address."

"Good I'll ask Violet."

"Oh, you need Violet's phone number. I can get it for you from the office. Let me use the phone."

Two minutes later Stacy had the name and number in her notebook. Violet Johnson with an 858 number.

"Now, I've got two names. You said there were several. Can you come up with any more for me?"

Piper closed her eyes. "That's a long time ago. Wait a minute. The cheer leader, what was her name...... Terri. Yes, Terri Warnick. Right. She was so upset when Kim took away her boyfriend she was out of school for a week. She got into two cat fights with Kim. I remember that. Hair pulling, scratching and some good punches. Both wound up suspended for a day and had to do a week after school time. Yes, Terri is another one. Tell you what. Let me take this year book home and do some hard thinking and I should be able to figure out two or three more names of girls who got dirt thrown in their faces by Kimberly. I'm sorry to see her end up this way. Murdered. I figured something might happen to her before now. Then she got on the TV as a reporter and now a big time news anchor." Piper shuddered. "Murdered and cut up. Damn. You think somebody from our class did this to her?"

"That's one of the leads were trying to follow. Let me see what I can find out from the three names I have. Is there a number where I can contact you?"

"Yes, at home. I don't have a cell phone." She gave her number and Stacy gave her a card.

"That's my cell so it's on seven twenty four. Call me anytime. And thanks for your help."

Stacy stopped by Mrs. Wilforce's office and thanked her, said they might be making some progress, then hurried back to San Diego Central Police headquarters and briefed Cain on what she had.

Next came the telephone call. She tried Violet's number. She probably was at work.

"Hello, this is the Johnson residence."

"Hello. This is Detective DeFrain from the San Diego Police Department. Do you have a minute to talk?"

"Police. Oh, God. Did something bad happen to my husband or children?"

"No, nothing like that. Nothing serious and you're not in any trouble, so relax. I understand that you're the secretary of the alumni group from Hoover High class of 1996. Piper Roland gave me your number."

"Oh, yes, that's right. Haven't seen Piper for a while."

"I'm hunting three of your classmates. Piper said you might have their current last names and phone numbers."

"I might. We have only about three hundred names out of the almost two thousand who graduated. Still it's a big list. Who were you interested in?"

"Patti Vining for one."

"Patti. I remember her from school. But no, she isn't on our list and didn't come to the five year reunion. I remember because I used to be good friends with her. Last I heard from her she was moving to Los Angeles. That was about two years ago."

"What about Phyllis Canton?"

"Let me get out the list. Just a minute."

The phone clicked as if it were laid on a hard

surface. It took two minutes before Violet came back on the line.

"Yes, I have the list and Phyllis is here. We alphabetize the people by their last names in school, then a married name for the girls. Here she is Phyllis Canton Gerhard. She lives here in town. You want her phone and address?"

"That would be most helpful."

She's at 619-464-5847 and the address is 8181 Beaver Lake Drive, San Diego, 92119."

"Perfect, Violet. Piper is trying to remember some more names for me. How well did you know Kimberly Roberts?"

"Oh, that poor woman. I heard about it on the news. Just terrible. Is that what this is about?"

"Partly. We're trying to find friends of hers so we might get some angle on who might have killed her. Did you go around with Kimberly at school?"

"Oh, my no. She was one of the popular ones. I did good just to keep my grades up and go to the football games. I didn't know her at all."

"I have one more name: Terri Warnick."

"That one I know. We were good friends. She's still in town and married to...Tom Warnick. They came to the reunion and she's working with me on the ten year. Her phone number is 858-455-6531. I remember she had a big fight with Kim. Both were suspended."

"That's what I heard. Do you know of any other girls who were really furious with Kim back then?"

"Not that I can think of. It has been ten years. I'll see what I can remember."

"If you think of any more names, give me a call." She gave her the cell number. "I might be calling you again with another name or two. Would that be all right?"

"Of course. Anything I can do."

They said goodbye and Stacy hung up. She hesitated a moment, then called the 619 number for Phyllis. It rang twice then a computer voice came on. "We're sorry but this number does not take unsolicited calls. If you wish to call this number, hang up, dial star eight two, then the phone number."

One of those, Stacy thought. She did as the computer voice instructed. The phone rang four times, then another voice came on. "Sorry, we can't come to the phone right now. Please leave your name and number and we'll call you back just as soon as possible."

"Hi, this is Stacy DeFrain. Would you please call me at my cell, six one nine, two two three, three two three two. I need to get in touch with you today if possible. I'm not selling anything. This is important. Thanks."

Stacy growled and hung up. She'd had little luck in getting people to call her back. Now she never said she was from the police. That seemed to spook half the people she tried to get to call her back.

Beaver Lake Drive. She thought she knew where it was, but got out the Thomas Guide to San Diego County and looked it up. Yes, out in the San Carlos area. A fifty year old development of medium priced homes. Now probably selling for about $400,000. Kind of upper middle class. Could be a nice spot for a serial killer to live. Outside of that, maybe Phyllis might know somebody else who had hated Kim with a passion back in high school.

Kevin came back from the crime lab. He looked frustrated.

"Damn, I thought we had a match. One of the partials was close to some guy who worked for the post office. Then we lined up the second partial and it was absolutely wrong for any of the set of ten. Three hours of work right down the drain. They have gone over every computer bank of prints that they can access, including the FBI, the military and the California Penal System. We're dead in the water on the partials. Anderson said something might turn up later if we can nail some better prints."

"Lots of luck," Stacy said. "Those partials would get thrown out of court so fast Anderson's scalp would tingle." She looked at Kevin again. "Hey, you miss lunch? I sure did. Let's go down to the Crestwood and get a sandwich or something."

"You buying?"

"When you take up skydiving without a chute."

Stacy had minestrone soup and half a ham and cheese sandwich. She was starved. Kevin had a half pound hamburger and fries. It was a cop hangout and Stacy recognized ten or twelve officers there in and out of uniform.

"Hey, how's your love life?" Kevin asked.

"Fine, how's yours?"

"Glad you asked. There's this little secretary for one of the assistant chiefs who is really hot. I think she likes me. All I have to do is get up nerve enough to ask her out."

"You sound like you're sixteen, still in high school, and need a date for the prom."

"Hey, I'm not big on dating."

"If you think she likes you, she's probably tearing her hair out waiting for your call. So call her this afternoon. Don't be a nerd. Call her today."

"Yeah, maybe."

"No maybe. Call her. Promise?" She pointed her fork at him.

"Yeah, okay. Today for sure."

"Let me know what happens."

They finished eating and worked on the second cup of coffee.

"Hoover High, who would have thought of it," Kevin said. "Some little lady is slaughtering classmates and a teacher and we can't get a line on her."

"If one of these girls I'm contacting gives us a name that's on our defense lawyer's list, we may be damned near home," Stacy said.

"Yeah, another if."

"So, it's better than what we have so far. Hoover High has to be the tie. Now we have to make it work for us."

"How?" Kevin asked.

"Not sure. If I can find three or four girls who remember Kimberly and remember girls she fucked over that senior year, we should come up with a matching name."

"To the criminal defense lawyer list. How many names?"

"I've got nine possibles and one of them has got to be the killer."

"Why don't we just start interviewing the nine?" Kevin asked.

"No, we thought of that. Cain agrees. That could spook the killer and she'd be on the next plane to Iowa or Mississippi never to be heard from again. Cain says we don't touch any of them until we have enough hard evidence to get an arrest warrant."

"But we don't have any hard evidence," Kevin said.

"That's what's bugging me. Some circumstantial, like the four LOY partial plate near the murder scene. And the two eye witnesses there. That's damn thin."

"The partial prints could work, if we get something from her that matches to ten points," Kevin suggested.

"She's been too careful for a really good print."

"Ballistics," Kevin said.

"No good. The .32 we got from Showley didn't match the .38 slugs they took out of Selma. She either has a whole bunch of cold guns, or is smart enough not to use the same one more than once. She might have learned that from her criminal type clients."

"Does the small shoe prints at the Ingram kill do anything for us," Kevin asked.

"Points to a woman, and half a million suspects."

"So we're down to sexual rage. It surely shows with Kim getting cut up that way. And the penisectomy on Showley. But we need a motive."

"Which we don't have. Say she was one of the girls in the senior class at Hoover who got her boyfriend stolen. Would that hold up after ten years?" Stacy asked.

"Could if she figured the boy was her future husband. Some kids get married right out of high school."

"Is there any way that we could find the boys involved who Kim seduced?" Stacy asked.

They stared at each other a minute and shrugged.

Then they had another sip of coffee and walked the four blocks back to work.

When they stepped into the office, Cain waved a paper at Stacy. “You had a call from somebody named Phyllis. She said she’d be home for two hours if you wanted to call her.”

“Oh, yeah, I do, I do,” Stacy said and reached for the team’s land line.

28

TWYLA LISTENED to the next witness on the stand for the prosecution in the trial of the State of California vs Trevor Jamison, the charge: murder in the first degree. She was taking notes on her lap top as she had been doing for a week now. The flow of the trial fascinated her as it always did. The witnesses saying exactly what the prosecution wanted them to say. Her fingers danced on the laptop.

Prosecutor: "Now, Miss Varner, you say that you have dated Mr. Jamison in the past?"

Varner: "Yes, that's right."

Prosecutor: "About how long was that?"

Varner: "For almost four months."

Prosecutor: "Did he entertain you in his condo?"

Varner: "Well, sure."

Prosecutor: "Were you an overnight guest several times?"

Varner: "We lived together there for three months."

Prosecutor: "Why did you leave?"

Varner: "Because he enjoyed beating me."

"Your honor I object," Tretter said. "The prosecution is showing no direct evidence of any beatings or misconduct."

Prosecutor: "Your honor the prosecution wishes to submit into evidence the following photos, numbered prosecutions thirty two through thirty nine." He brought them to the defense table. They were color photos of a mostly nude woman showing deep blue, brown, and black bruises on her arms, legs and back.

"No objection, your honor."

He took them to the judge, who looked at them a moment and nodded. Then he took them to the witness.

Prosecutor: "Now, Miss Varner. How did you receive these bruises?"

Varner: "Oh, when Trevor hit me."

"Object your honor. There is no evidence tying these bruises to the defendant. This is he said she said and in no way is credible proof."

"Looks highly credible to me. Objection denied. Proceed."

The morning continued with one witness after another painting Trevor Jamison as an abusive, often violent, hard drinking, man who seemingly enjoyed hurting his lovers. At the noon break Alex Tretter, Twyla and Jamison had sandwiches in the prisoner holding room and had a conference.

"Why didn't you tell us you beat up so many women?" Alex roared.

"Hell, you didn't ask. You're supposed to be the fucking expert on the law."

Alex threw up his hands and walked around the

room. "Trevor, you talk like that in court and the judge will throw you right out the door."

"Hell, I know that. What I want to know is can you get me a second degree plea."

Twyla dropped her sandwich. "You told us last week you never would accept plea bargaining."

"Yeah, I know. That was before I heard how hard the DA is trying for the death penalty. He's got me fucked good."

"The DA hasn't even brought up the subject of a plea," Twyla said.

"That's because that's our job," Alex said. "We go to them and try for a second with fifteen to twenty."

"Years?" Trevor exploded.

"It's a first degree murder charge, Trevor. You surely didn't expect us to get you probation?"

The usually confident, even swaggering, Trevor Jamison melted down a notch or two. He shook his head. "Christ, I was thinking three to five. Five I could do. Fifteen...."

"They will start out with a twenty five to life," Alex said. "Our job is to work them down to fifteen." He dropped the rest of his sandwich and gulped the coffee. "I know where the DA usually has lunch. I'll see if I can catch him and make our pitch."

"Come?" Twyla asked.

"No. finish your food. I'll see you back in court."

Twyla stared at Trevor when the door closed behind Alex. She'd never been alone with him before. She frowned and stared at their client.

"Rough sex. You just went too far this time. I've never understood what men get out of beating up on a woman while they're having sex."

"Hey, we've got time. I'll show you." He grinned and stood up. She didn't know if he was kidding or not.

She stepped to the door and knocked three times. It came open at once. She walked out and watched the guard close the door and heard it lock behind her. It was the most satisfying sound she had heard in months.

THAT NIGHT AT HOME, Twyla thought over the plea bargaining that Alex had done. He said the DA laughed at him at first, then they talked some more. The best the DA could offer was second degree and seventeen to twenty five. He left it on the table, but Trevor had turned it down.

Twyla mentally disconnected from the murder trial and thought about her own situation. She had learned to do that early in her career as a defense lawyer. To get too emotionally involved in a case could burn you out quickly. Another thing she had learned from her times with hardened criminals was never to keep any mementos of a robbery or any kind of crime. Nothing. She had seen some men convicted because they kept a blouse from a little girl they raped and murdered, or a robber who kept the driver's licenses from each of the people he robbed at gun point. They both went down hard.

She looked around her condo. Did she have anything that would in any way connect her with any of her three dead classmates and one teacher? She certainly had no mementos, no bits or piece of anything the dearly departed had owned. She did still have that cold gun. She learned about cold guns from the cops. Some of the officers would get an unregistered gun that had no history of any crime and keep it for their personal use. Say they were in a shooting and they thought that the perp had a gun but they couldn't find it. The cold gun could be planted and later found as proof that the guy had a gun and had fired at them. She would get rid of the .38 revolver. Break it into pieces and scatter it around.

What else? She still had two sets of the plastic riot cuffs. They had been invaluable in her revenge episodes with her classmates. She would cut them up with scissors and toss them tonight into the dumpster where dozens of people threw out trash. Yes. She found the white plastic cuffs. First she washed them off with hot soap and water. Then she wiped them dry and with plastic gloves on used large scissors to cut them into inch lengths, put them in a plastic grocery sack, and scattered them in the dumpster down at the end of the complex. No way the plastic could be traced to her.

Hard drive in her computer. She turned on the box and looked at the file listing. There were over a hundred files. She went through them one at a time. If she didn't recognize the file name, she brought it up and checked it. She found herself deleting many files she didn't need or want to keep not associated with her revenge. She found only two where she had used the computer to get her thoughts in motion. One was about Judith. She wiped it out. Farther along she found something about the teacher and it fell to the delete button as well. By the time she was through with the files it was after one in the morning. She had cleaned up her hard drive and cut out more than twenty files.

As she got ready for bed she tried to think of anything else that could implicate her. Oh damn. Those last two file folders. She still had them on Zack and Kim. She took them out of her desk and ran them twice through her shredder. She took the hundreds of thin strips of paper and put them in two different dumpsters. She had learned that lesson well from her convict clients. No notebooks, scrapbooks. Nothing but the yearbook.

"Oh, damn!" She found it in a shelf on the coffee table. She remembered that she had circled the faces of the four students and the teacher when she began planning her vengeance two years ago. There they were. She ripped the pages out and burned them in the kitchen sink, then ground the ashes down the disposer. The rest of the year book she would throw in the trash in the morning.

Yes, she felt cleansed. Now there was nothing in her condo or her clothes or her car that could in any way implicate her in any of the four pay backs fatalities.

THE NEXT MORNING, Stacy tried to call Phyllis Canton Gerhard again. She had tried the afternoon before but there had been no answer. This time someone picked up on the second ring.

“”"Yes?"

"Is this Phyllis Gerhard?"

"Yes, who is calling?"

"I'm Detective Stacy DeFrain with the San Diego Police Department. You haven't done anything wrong and are not in trouble. I just want to talk with you a minute."

"Oh, good. That's a relief. What do we talk about?"

"Do you remember Kim Roberts from your high school class at Hoover High?"

"You mean the Channel Six anchor who just got herself murdered? Oh, yes, I remember Kim."

"Were you friends with her back then?"

"On and off, depending who she was trying to date. She was a little weird, always trying to steal somebody's boyfriend."

"That's what I wanted to talk about. Do you remember any girls who she stole boyfriends from?"

"How many do you want? I could name three or four right off the top of my head, and with some time and looking over my year book I could get you a couple three more."

"Great. Give me the names and I can get local addresses on them from Violet Johnson."

"Oh, the one who's running the reunion."

"Right, what are the girls' names?

"One I remember is Irene Parker. She almost quit school when Kim ripped off her boyfriend. Then there was Ellen Olson. She wasn't upset at all and had a new steady a week later for the senior dance. Let's see. Who else? Oh, yes, I remember another situation but not the names. This was a two year going steady deal. Everyone figured they would get married right after graduation and we all wondered if she was pregnant. She wasn't showing. After Kim teased her guy and stole him, this gal cut classes for two days, and when she came back she burned Kim every chance she got. Kim just laughed it off. I guess that's all for now. I'll check the yearbook. I should remember that girl's name pretty soon. Can I call you?"

Stacy thanked her, gave her the cell number and said call anytime with any more names. Then she spent four calls trying to get Violet Johnson. No luck.

Kevin came in and she asked him if he'd called the secretary yet for a date.

"Nope, been too busy."

"Kevin, you promised."

He gave a long sigh, stared at the ceiling for a minute and then nodded. "Hell, I'll do it right now, but you go out in the hall and don't listen. She has a name, she's Ginny."

Stacy grinned and walked into the hall.

When she saw Kevin hang up the phone, she went back in. Kevin was beaming.

"Hey, she said yes. Dinner out and then a movie."

"Sounds promising. Now don't you wish you'd done that a month ago?"

"I hadn't even noticed her a month ago. But, yeah, it would have been good."

"When you going out?"

"Tonight."

"Wow, you do work fast."

Cain came in not quite blowing smoke out his ears but almost. He looked ready to go ballistic. His face was red, his limp was obvious, and his hands rubbed his face.

"What the fuck does the lieutenant want me to do, manufacture a suspect? So the captain is riding his tail raw, that don't help me no how." He looked up at Kevin and Stacy, and then at Lee and Fernando who had just walked in.

"So what the hell are you four highly paid detectives doing? Looks like you're sitting on your asses waiting for somebody to give you a golden suspect on a silver tray. Get the fuck to work."

He dropped into his chair and rubbed his knee. "Let's dig out that list of defense lawyers and start touching them somehow. Work out some sly way to talk to them or contact them so it won't completely spook them. We've got to do something before all five of us are on third watch guarding the dump out at Miramar."

"What if the perp catches on and takes the next plane out of Lindbergh field for Podunk, Iowa?" Stacy asked.

"There's always that. So be clever. Dig up some survey or something so they won't suspect. Even if the perp does 0074 and take a ride out of town that will stop her killings here and will take some pressure off."

Kevin sat at his desk and took out a pad of paper. He picked up his pen and looked at the other three. "Okay people. Let's get clever and creative here. How can we contact these nine suspect women without tipping them off they are suspects?"

They worked the rest of the morning trying to come up with something. Every idea got shot down in a rush. They had ten suggestions, and they all were so transparent that an idiot could know what was happening.

Stacy got a wrapped tuna fish sandwich to go at the cafeteria and hurried back to the office. She had a strange urge to look over the list of clues and facts on the big board. Somewhere on there was something they had missed. Something that could break the case wide open. All she had to do was figure out what it was. The little wheels kept turning in her head as she read through the clues.

She had taken only two bites of the sandwich when she let out a yell. She might just have an idea that would produce some results maybe tie down the killer.

29

STACY STARED at the DMV note and the twenty four 4-Lot license plates. That had to be it. A year ago, she had done a DMV search and found nothing. Then later she had wailed and moaned to another cop from the stolen car team. He told her something she had forgotten.

"The DMV has a separate category for fleet cars and trucks. They treat them differently. Many times they issue license plates in groups of ten or fifteen or fifty to the same company in numerical order. It's a different routine and goes through a different computer program."

That had to be it. The DMV probably didn't check the fleet computer license plate hard drive because no one asked them to. She ignored the rest of the tuna sandwich and grabbed the phone. It took her five minutes on the phone to get through to a supervisor in Sacramento.

"Yes, we do work differently with fleets of cars and trucks. Have them on a separate listing. When you request a check for license plates and want the fleet list, you have to ask for it."

"Great. Now I'm asking. Will you have someone check the fleet list for the number Four LOT. It's a partial and all we have. What we need is any listings for Four LOT for new Lexus models in San Diego County. Can you do that?"

"Detective you know we can. Where can I email the list?"

She gave him her email address there in the office, thanked the man and hung up. Now she grabbed the sandwich, went for a Coke out of the machine down the hall and ate the sandwich, her mind racing about the possibilities. This had to be it. This search had to show some more listings of new Lexus in the county with that partial plate.

If it didn't she would die.

Well, maybe not really, but she would want to. At least she hadn't told anyone else about her wild idea. Just in case it bombed. She paced the room, walked up and down the hall but close enough that she could see her computer. She wished computers had a little bell on them that rang whenever an email came in, like the fax machines did. Or did they just set up a strange noise?

She waited ten minutes, then checked her computer.

No emails.

The can of Coke was empty. She ran down to the machine and got two more and brought them to her desk. Kevin came in from his lunch and watched her.

"What's got into you, Stacy? You're as jumpy as a new bride."

"Nothing. Not a single thing. Just waiting for an email. I get jumpy when I wait for emails."

He frowned. "You're up to something. Who is the email coming from?"

"Can't say. Just a wild idea. If it's wrong, you'll laugh at me. I'm not in the mood to be laughed at. So we wait." Instead she checked her email file. Nothing. What was taking them so long? Usually it took only five minutes to get a report from the DMV on a plate check.

To fill in the time she called Phyllis Gerhard, the girl from Hoover High. The phone rang three times, then was picked up.

"Yes?"

"Phyllis, this is Stacy. Have you remembered any more names?"

"Hi. I've been wracking what's left of my brain. The only new one I have is Joyce Nelson. She had a real big fight with Kim over something. But it seems to me that they made up our senior year."

"What about the other one with the stolen boyfriend but you couldn't remember her name?"

"Still working on that one. And I'll try to remember some more. Kim had a lot of fur flying that senior year. She thought she was God's gift to the senior class boys."

"Thanks, let's keep in touch."

Stacy put down the phone and walked around the room, then surged back to her computer and kicked up the Internet. She had one message, from the DMV. She hit the read button and the message came up. There were four plates with the first four number/letters 4LOY. All were registered to a law firm Branston, Knox & Tretter. She yelped in delight and printed out the email four times and took one copy over to Kevin.

"We might want to check into this," she said.

He read the email and bellowed in delight.

"Might want to? So that was your secret. But why didn't we get these plates before?"

She told him about the fleet car/truck deal. He nodded.

"Yeah, now I remember hearing something about that, but since I never had a fleet car to worry about, I never paid it any attention."

"Hey, this firm listed is one of the law firms that I have that had defense lawyers in court that morning before Selma was murdered."

"There were two women defense lawyers working that morning from that same law firm," Kevin said. "So our girl is one of the two. Where is your list of names?"

Stacy had already pulled the list from her file folder.

"The names, the names," Kevin said.

She checked down the page, found the law firm and the two names.

"Pricilla Donovan and Twyla Farnham."

"No use to run them for wants and warrants if they're both lawyers," Kevin said.

Cain bristled in the door and stared at their faces.

"What got into you two? Have a good lunch?"

Stacy told him about the fleet computer check with the DMV.

"Fuck me, I should have thought of that. So we have four plates all at this one law firm?"

"Right."

"Company cars, I'll be damned. So, tonight, we put six of us at the outside of their parking area or garage, and we follow all four of those Lexus to their homes.

We check to see if any of those cars goes to the two addresses we have on the two defense lawyers on your list."

"Then we've got our killer," Kevin said.

"No," Cain said. "Think about it. So we know who she is and where she works and lives and the car she drives. We still don't have enough hard evidence to go and even get a search warrant for her place, let alone get an arrest warrant from the DA. We need more."

"So how do we get it?" Stacy asked.

"Once we've established for sure which one is our killer, we check her prints with that partial we have. That could be a help. Then we put a box around her, and shadow her day and night seven twenty four. I can get six more men to help. We'll have two on her around the clock. We'll know when she comes to work, where she has lunch, what court room she's in, who she sleeps with, and for damn sure know if she's getting ready to kill anyone else."

"What if she's done her last killing?" Stacy asked.

"Then we might just be shit out of luck. We need to catch her in preparation for or the actual carrying out of a plot to kill someone. Then we get the hard evidence we need to arrest and convict her of the five killings and the attempted murder of the sixth."

"I'll go check to see if one of them is still in court," Stacy said.

Cain shook his head. "No way. She must have seen you with Selma. We'll send Kevin into the court room. Stacy, you find out where she parks. Kevin might have to tell you that when he follows her out of court after it recesses for the day. She would park around the court house somewhere. Then you pick up her Four LOY plate."

"Couldn't we just go to the firm and ask them which plate is assigned to which person?" Kevin asked.

"Not a chance," Cain said. "We would spook the one we want for damn sure. She would be on the first plane out of Lindbergh for your Podunk, Iowa farm."

Lee and Fernando walked in.

"You guys have a late lunch?" Cain said. He filled them in where the case was.

"We need to have two people on the firm's parking lot or building, whatever they heave. Lee you and Fernando take two cars and check that out now and let me know how many Four LOY plates are in house. If one, you have two cars to tail the plate when it leaves. If two or three, I'll send two cars for each one. We might get lucky and find three there and one down at the court building. Lawyers don't spend all their time in court. Go, Kevin to court. Keep in touch with your cell. Lee and Fernando get over to that law firm."

"Stacy will be prowling the parking area around the court building where lawyers usually park and try to find a Four LOY plate. If she can't, she'll be close by when you tail the lawyer to her car. Tell Stacy, and then the two of you do a two car tail until you spot where she lives. And let's all pray that she goes straight home. When you have her address nailed down, we check it against our two girl list. If we're lucky her address will be on it and we'll have our suspect. Keep in touch here with your cells."

"If we need them I'll have six more detectives on standby to help us with tailing those Lexus rigs. Everybody cool?"

Stacy grabbed her list of four plates and headed down to get an unmarked. Parking was always tight around the criminal court building. Lawyers needed all day parking, so they used the lots. Stacy cruised four lots, didn't see any black Lexus with the right plate. She parked by a fire plug, flipped down the SDPD Logo on the visor and checked the two closest lots on foot looking at every car. No hits.

She got back in her unmarked and called Kevin who would have his cell on buzz rather than ring. She got a call back from him two minutes later.

"They're just about ready to call it quits today. Some flap about evidence pictures. I've got the brunet in the second chair, but she must have cut her hair. It's short and streaked with blonde."

"Figures, she could be our girl. Why else change her hair so drastically?"

"Never can tell. I had a girl once who changed her hair style and color every six weeks. I never knew what to expect. Okay, the judge just took off and people are coming out. I'm on this brunet like a cream pie in a comedian's face."

"Let me know if you get her in a black Lexus with the right plate, and tell me which way you're headed. I'll stay three cars behind you. What color is your unmarked?"

He told her blue, then signed off and hurried after the lawyer.

Stacy tried to relax as she waited. It took five minutes before her phone came on again.

"Okay, I've got her. She's in a black Lexus with the right plate. We're heading up Fourth Street, now turning on Ash that flows right into Highway Fifteen that goes through Balboa Park. From there she could go either direction on Interstate Eight, keep on north on Fifteen or go any which way. Can you catch us?"

"I'm on it. I'll get on A Street as quick as I can, but with the rush hour traffic, it's going to be a hassle. Not even sure I can spot your blue unmarked."

"You said you were in a gray, I'll watch. Yes, we're on Fifteen heading north. I'm five cars behind her. Can't close up, traffic almost at a standstill and no shoulder lane here to cheat up on. That would be a give away."

FIVE MINUTES LATER, Stacy knew she'd missed them both. She was at Interstate Eight and Kevin had not responded in two or three minutes.

"Okay, that does it," her cell chirped. "I've lost her. I think she went across Eight and then she might have turned on Friars Road, or continued up Fifteen. No way to tell. That's a wrap on this one. Any clues on the other guys?"

Stacy called Cain and reported their problem. They went back to the office. It was just before five o'clock.

"Tomorrow we'll know where she's headed and be able to pick her up closer and get both cars on her," Kevin said. "We won't let her get away tomorrow."

Lee at the four story building the law firm owned had better luck, Cain told them.

"He found two more black Four LOY new Lexus in their underground garage. We have two cars on each of them. Both are still in the garage. As soon as they come out we'll track them. Maybe we'll get lucky with both of them."

Kevin went out for pizza and Coke. It could be a long evening. He got back just as one team reported they had a driver. It was a woman and she was heading north on Interstate Eight.

"Hey, Sarge. She could be heading to Del Mar or all the way up to Carlsbad. We'll stay with her. We're rotating behind her three cars every five miles or so. I'd say we have a live one here."

"Keep on her tail. We lost one. We need this one."

"That's a Roger. We're on it."

The other team on the Tretter Building was still in place.

"We're still here. That last Lexus 4LOY137 is still in the parking slot. Somebody is working late, or it's a spare car not assigned to anyone. We'll hang out here as long as we need to."

"We'll keep it covered until midnight. If its still there, we'll send out a new team to relieve you."

A HALF HOUR LATER, Lee called in.

"Hey, Boss. We have landed. Our black Lexus 4LOY 135 is parked at a condo at 1345 Orchid Lane in Del Mar. Is that a hot address?"

Cain checked a copy of the eight lawyers. "Negative, Lee. That is not one of our criminal lawyer suspects. You can cut and come back to the barn. Take the rest of the night off. We lost one, one isn't in the parking garage, and another one might be a supernumerary. Good work."

Stacy dropped in her chair. "One down, three to go. What are our odds, boss?"

"I'd say three to one, Stacy. Trying to tail somebody

in rush hour traffic is a chancy thing. We were probably lucky that we nailed one of the two. Tomorrow is another day."

Stacy checked her watch. Just a little after seven o'clock. She picked up her cell and dialed. It rang four times and she was ready to leave a message when somebody picked up.

"Yeah?"

"Is this Vice?"

"Not this time of day. I'm off tonight. Stacy?"

"Yeah." She lowered her voice. "Tough day, Hal. You had dinner yet?"

"No, just got home."

"Can you find your way to my place?"

"Be there in half an hour. What's for dinner?"

"Beans and franks. Still interested?"

"What's for desert?"

"You'll have to wait and see. A half hour." Stacy waved at Cain and headed out the door. She had a new smile breaking out and was glad Cain hadn't seen it.

30

TWYLA PARKED in her reserved spot in the garage and climbed up to her condo. She was glad it was on the second floor. It gave her an added sense of security. She felt grimy. It had been warm in the court room, and absolutely nothing new came up, so she had few notes. The prosecution kept hammering at Trevor's rough style with his women. They were laying the ground work for their circumstantial case.

She pulled off her clothes in the bedroom and stepped into the shower. Just what she needed. As the hot water streamed over her she thought about her next project: Zack Hunt. It was coming at a good time. Zack was an actor, had been since grade school. He'd had several shots on TV series, done a movie or two but always came back to the Old Globe Theatre where he got his professional start. The director there pleaded with him from time to time to come back to take certain leading roles.

Twyla remembered the Hoover High senior class play. She had been in it and had several scenes with

Zack, who even then was doing commercials and bit parts in local plays. They had one scene on stage in this play where he was supposed to grab her and rip off part of her blouse. It was cut and stitched lightly so it would tear away, but leave her adequately covered with two more layers of clothing. She always said he did it deliberately. They only did three performances of the play and the last night when he grabbed her blouse, he hooked under all three layers and yanked so hard that she staggered across the stage and to her horror, her entire blouse and bra ripped off exposing her all the way from chin to waist. She was stunned and couldn't move for a moment. Then she put her arms over her chest and rushed off the stage tears streaming down her face as the audience hooted and clapped.

Zack had covered himself with some ad lib remarks about how they didn't make clothes like they used to, and continued with the rest of the play.

Twila had been so shaken that she couldn't do the last scene with Zack. He had ad-libbed through the scene and finished the last act.

When Zack came off stage Twyla had rushed at him, knocked him down, scratched his face, pounded on him with her fists, screaming and crying and kicking him. Two boys had to pull her off. They said they were afraid she was going to kill him.

Now she was.

She had only four more days. The play Zack was in at the Old Globe Theater would end Saturday night. She had briefed out some ideas how to eliminate him months ago, but had no solid plan. Now she sat down with a pen and a pad of paper and began getting ideas.

She first thought of killing him on stage in front of

the audience, but that would be playing right into his hand. How could he ask for a better exit scene? It would have to be in costume. He was Shakespeare's Henry the Eighth with the authentic old English costumes as only the Old Globe could do them. Good, he would be in character.

When would she take him? After the performance? Which day? Not the last, there could be a cast party. Then do it on Friday nigh. Yes. Now it was coming together. But how to take him?

She still had one cold revolver. It was remarkable the way most people feared guns. Good. Could she go see him backstage after the play in some disguise, then when most others cast members had left, she would let visitors out of his room, lock the door and hold him with the gun. Turn out the lights so they would think he had gone, but first bind his wrists together with cuffs. No, she cut them up. She would use duct tape. She would gag him early on. Yes. Now what?

After the place had been locked down and closed up for the night, she would have the whole stage to herself. She could use one small work light, take him to the stage in his costume. How should he die? Dramatically. In character. How? By a sword? No, too hard. By a spear? Yes, a shake spear. She chuckled at the play on words. They would have spears on the set. But with plastic tips. She would break off the tip and replace it with a foot long butcher knife bound on tightly with duct tape. Then in center stage, what ho, Horatio? She would ram the spear through his heart and he would die as the others had. What else? Perhaps put the theatrical mask of sadness on him. What were the two drama masks, one of joy one of terror and pain? Yes. At a costume shop. Again a disguise at the shop for her. Maybe a long blonde wig, big sunglasses, casual to sloppy clothes. Now she was rolling.

This was Wednesday. It had to be Friday night. She had two days to get ready.

HAL YOUNG and Stacy were up early the next morning so Hal could go to his apartment and get a change of clothes. They had a quick shower together wound up on the bed and then back in the shower before Hal dressed and rushed down the steps to his car in the visitors section.

Stacy had a wide smile as she fixed breakfast. They were so good together. It might not last but she was gong to play it for all she could for as long as she could.

Over a second coffee she thought about the day to come. They would shadow the three cars again, this time she hoped with better results. It had to be one of the three. They had the names of the two defense lawyers and their addresses. Now all they needed was for them to track one of them back to one of those two addresses. The chances were the third Lexus driver might not be one of the two names they had. Stacy would take either one, just so they could tie it down for certain and put her in a box, a surveillance night and day, until they nailed down some hard evidence that she was the killer.

KEVIN AND CAIN had their heads together when she got to work carrying a cup of coffee.

"What's happening?" she asked.

"Figuring the odds," Kevin said. "Our killer is one of the two defense lawyers from the Tretter law offices. One is Twyla Farnham; the other name off your list of eight is Darci Templeton. So far the betting is fifty-fifty."

"I've got Lee watching the Tretter garage. Only one Lexus is there, the same plate, one thirty seven, as was parked there yesterday. We think it's a spare."

Cain's cell beeped.

"This is Lee, we've got one more candidate. The same Lexus we tracked to Del Mar last night just drove in that's the one thirty five plate. Maybe the other two drove to court."

"We're covering that. Let me know if any more of them show up there."

Cain put down his cell and waved at Fernando. "Do a check around the parking lots next to the court building and see if you can find either of the Four LOY plates we need. The last three numbers are one thirty six and one thirty four. If you spot either of them give me a call."

Stacy watched Fernando leave and then caught Cain's eye.

"We have anybody watching the other lawyer, Darci?

I can find out from the clerk which court she's in and sit in. She hasn't seen me so she won't be bugged."

"You got it. Kevin is taking Twyla as soon as court opens at nine. You two better get over there. Keep me informed about what's going on. Follow them to their cars and we'll have unmarked in place ready to tail them. Maybe court will be over quicker today and we'll miss the rush hour traffic."

. . .

STACY GOT the number of the court that Darci was working in that morning. It was the finish of the trial and the judge dismissed the charges. Everybody on the plaintiff's side hugged and then left. Darci had been described by the clerk as about forty, short and stout, with straight dark hair and almost always a blue suit. Stacy spotted her quickly and when she left, Stacy was six paces behind her. She went to the parking lot three blocks over and got into her car. It was a two year old Buick.

She called Cain. "Hey boss, you can scratch Darci as a suspect. She's driving a two year old light green Buick."

"We're down to one. We'll have four cars on Ash tonight when Twyla heads home. She's got to be our pigeon. Unless something happens with that one thirty seven plate. Good work."

Lee chimed in on the cell. "Hey, Boss. You can scratch four loy one thirty six. It just wheeled into the garage and an oversize man got out. Doubt if he's our girl."

"Roger that, Lee. You can come on home. We have it narrowed down to one thirty four and we think we know who is driving it. All we need to do is watch her walk into the address we have for her and we've got a lock."

"Good. I'm half way there."

Cain dialed his cell. "I just hope that Kevin has his cell on vibrate if he's in the courtroom."

A second later Kevin came on.

"Hey, I'm moving out of the court to the hall. I've

got this one in a lock. Twyla, I think she is. Anyway, court's moving and it could be a short session. Some flap about something. The lawyers are in conference with the judge."

"Good. We've eliminated the others. Twyla is our girl. Tell us the minute she leaves the court. Track her to her car and tell us when she leaves. Follow if you can. We're going to have four cars waiting on Ash Street when she heads home we'll spot her and follow."

"Got you. Okay, we're back in session. Looks like we're here until lunch and then some this afternoon. We'll be back in the rush hour traffic. But with four cars we should tail her. I'm out."

Cain told them what he'd heard.

"So, we sit tight and wait for Kevin to give us the go," Stacy said. She lifted her brows. "Hey, we have a complete set of prints on Twyla in the banks. I'm going over to the crime lab and bring up her prints and see if that partial can in any way make a partial match."

Cain nodded. "Go," he said. "I'm going to battle with the lieutenant so we can get some more bodies. Want to put two men on her around the clock. Even with eight hour shifts, that's going to take six bodies. We can show four. I'll try to get four more. No telling how long we'll need to watch her."

AT THE CRIME LAB, Stacy talked to Lt. Anderson. He grinned when she told him their progress.

"You guys do good work," he said.

She explained what she wanted.

"Hey, no problem. Lawyers all have to be printed.

We can dig out her prints in about ten minutes. Hang around."

IT TOOK FIFTEEN MINUTES, then Anderson put the prints on the machine and the partial on a matching screen and they worked from one finger to another. When they came to the right hand first finger, Anderson chuckled.

"Hey, hey, hey. Look what we have here." He showed her the prints overlaid one on the other. The partial was a perfect match as far as it went. About half of the print showed.

"Is that enough to show to a jury?" Stacy asked.

"Depends on the judge. Most of the time a partial that good, that follows line for line in at least half of the print, the judge will permit into evidence. It's not much, but it's a good solid piece of hard evidence. I'll do print outs on these individuals and the match and give you four copies. Just hope this helps stop the slaughter."

BACK IN THE OFFICE, Stacy gave the printouts to Cain who thundered his approval.

"Yes, we at last have some hard evidence. This ties her to the Selma killing. And that ties her to the cuffs which is part of the other three killings. Great work. Most judges should allow this kind of evidence. Now, if we can just verify her damn address."

Stacy tried to think what else she could do on the case. They mostly waited for the court to close. By three thirty Stacy was on her second Coke. She'd given up on coffee as she did about once a month. Her cell beeped.

"Yes, this is Stacy DeFrain."

"Stacy, this is Phyllis the Hoover High grad. I thought of the name I was fishing for. The girl who had the big fight and got suspended for a while all over a boyfriend."

"Right, you have a name?"

"Yes. I'm sure of it now. I checked the year book and everything. Her name is Twyla Farnham."

"Good. Thank you Phyllis. We may ask you to testify to that in court if it comes to that. Could you do that?"

"Oh, I'd be glad to. I heard somewhere that Twyla is some kind of hot shot criminal lawyer. Be good to see her get what she deserves."

"Thanks, Phyllis. You have just made my day."

Stacy told Cain. He grinned. "The noose is tightening. When is that damn court going to adjourn for the day?"

Five minutes after four, Kevin called. "Hey, team. I'm out of the court heading for a parking lot. It's about three blocks from the building. Twyla with the short black hair with blonde streaks is walking fast like she's in a rush. Get your cars out there on Ash Street."

"We've had four cars out there since two o'clock. I'll alert them. Black new Lexus, plate four one one thirty four. Let us know the minute she drives out."

Four minutes later Kevin called again. "She's moving. My car is two blocks away. I'll never find her. Looks like she's moving up Fourth Street heading for Ash. We have people ready?"

"I have four cars waiting. They are spaced about a block apart. The first one to spot her alerts the other four and they move out, one in front and three trailers."

"Good. I'm off the air."

Cain used his cell again. "Okay, she left the parking lot, should be there within two or three minutes. Nail this one guys, we really need it."

He made the same call to the other three chase cars, then leaned back in his chair.

"Now we wait and see what happens."

31

THE DETECTIVES in the four cars on the chase all had cell phones with speed dials directly to Cain. Within minutes his phone buzzed.

"Sarge, got her coming off Fourth and onto Ash. She's in the left hand lane, so probably is going out on highway Fifteen through the park. I'm right behind her, third car."

Another call. "Yeah, we have her Lexus and an unmarked, will stay three cars behind the unmarked."

Shortly all four of the cars were trailing her.

"We should have one car ahead of her, but in that traffic there isn't a prayer," Cain said.

"Okay, we're on Fifteen through Balboa Park."

Later they were told she was going over Interstate Eight and keeping north on Fifteen.

Less than two minutes later the three detectives heard the lead car come on the cell.

"She's taking Friars Road to the east. Yes, I'm with her, four cars back. She's on Friars and heading up Mission Valley."

"Isn't one of your addresses in Mission Valley?" Cain asked Stacy.

"Right. The one for Twyla. This has got to be her."

The cell chirped again. "Okay, Sarge, she's taking a right on Gill Village Way, lots of condos down there. Now we take a quick left on Rio San Diego Drive. Okay, she's heading into a complex called Mission Terrace Condos. The numbers go from 4356 to 4465. I'm heading on past. Probably underground parking in there. Is this close enough?"

"Right. We've got her. She is our suspect. I want two of you to stay on the job. One headed each way outside the driveway. Is there only one way in and out?"

"I'll check. Take me a minute. Talk to the other guys, they are piling up out here."

Cain talked to the other three, sent two of them back to the barn and kept the two on a stake out.

Cain's phone burped again. "Right, only this one in and out. We're planted one car heading each way on Rio San Diego Drive. We're on each side of the drive fifty feet down. There is curb parking along here so we won't look out of place."

"Roger that. Keep us up to date. If she moves, keep up the tail. We want to know everything she does."

Cain heaved out of his chair and headed for the door.

"Now I'm going after four more men and cars to put our girl in a box she can't get out of. We'll know everything she does outside of her condo."

An hour later, just as it was getting dark, Cain's phone chirped.

"Will here. She's moving. Just came out under the entrance lights. She has on a brown shoulder length wig and big glasses. She's heading Joe's way, so he's in first car. I'll track him."

Cain, who had come back from his talk with the lieutenant, grinned. "Keep tabs on her. Everything. We want to know if she even spits on the sidewalk."

IT HAD BEEN a frustrating day for Twyla. She threw her purse on the couch and stormed into the bedroom. The trial was a joke today, nothing of note, nothing to respond to when it was their turn. She wanted to get away, but Alex said she had to stay. Something might happen. It never did.

She had shopping to do. The drama masks. Probably have to buy them both. Where? That big costume shop should still be open. She took out the .38 revolver from a box deep in her closet. Yes, still there and with a box of rounds. She loaded the cylinders, five of them, and put the hammer down on the empty. Check. She put it on the night stand beside her bed. She wouldn't even need to steal a car this time. She could drive her own. The parking lot around the Old Globe would be filled. Actually one lot was across the street and another one behind the Organ Pavilion. That might be the best spot to leave her car. Yes.

Duct tape. She knew she didn't have any. Where to buy it? At a small hardware store, or a big Home Depot type place? She didn't want to drive all the way out to El Cajon. There must be a store in the Mission Valley Shopping Center where they sold duct tape. She'd take a look, then go to the costume shop. Was that all she needed? Yes, he would be wearing his Shakespeare Henry the Eighth costume. Duct tape for his hands and the mask. She looked in her kitchen and found a butcher knife with a ten inch blade nicely pointed and with a strong handle. Yes.

She looked in her closet at the box of wigs. She took out one with long brown hair and tried it on. Perfect. Three bobby pins and it was in place. She picked out a pair of large black rimmed glasses that had almost no correction. The mirror smiled back at her and she hardly recognized the face. Great!

FIVE MINUTES later she drove out of the garage, through the entrance, onto the street heading for Friar's Road, and the Mission Valley Shopping Center only five miles away. She made a left on Camino Del Este and turned on Camino de la Reina that ran along the back side of the center. A half hour of walking around the complex at last produced a store that sold duct tape. She bought a twenty foot roll, and headed back to her car.

She went out to Highway Eight and to Fifteen and downtown. The costume shop was on G Street north of Ash. She found it easily. It was open. She told a young clerk with acne what she wanted and he showed her four different sizes and prices. She took the middle ones, with masks about a foot high with rubber bands on them to stretch around the head. Perfect. She went back out, drove down to Fifth Avenue into the historic Gas Lamp District that had been restored and now held some of the best restaurants and clubs in town. She selected one she liked that specialized in lobster and steak and parked. The steak and lobster were delicious. She paid with plastic and went back to her car. It was dark out and she hesitated when she saw a man standing beside a car six spaces beyond her. He didn't move as she got in her Lexus quickly and drove away. Was he watching her? Watching her car? No. No reason to be watching her. He didn't look like the masher/rapist type. She shrugged and drove back to Mission Valley and parked in her slot under the condos.

JOE CAME on Cain's phone.

"Okay, she may be tucked in for the night. We took her into Mission Valley Shopping Center and she ran us crazy. She finally bought something. I checked with the clerk of this small store. She bought duct tape. Then we followed her out of the center and downtown to a costume shop on G Street. She was in and out fast and we couldn't find out what she bought there. We tailed her into the Gas Lamp District where she ate dinner and then went home. She's inside now. We're still at the exit one pointed each way. Oh, there's more than one way out of this street. San Diego Rio Drive joins with Qualcom Way and to Eight. Just in case we have to cover both ends."

Cain thanked him. "Hang on there until eleven o'clock and we'll have two new cars out there to relieve you. Report back here to Central by ten tomorrow morning."

"Good, I can use the overtime."

"Damn, I never checked. I'm sure we're authorized for overtime now that we're this close. See you tomorrow."

He pointed at Stacy and Kevin. "You two are on relief of Joe and his buddy. You know the spot. Take unmarked and be there by ten forty five. You'll get relieved at seven in the morning. Better take lots of coffee and sandwiches."

THURSDAY MORNING AT WORK, Stacy had two calls waiting for her. One was from Phyllis Gerhard who had given them a positive ID on Twyla in the boyfriend stealing high school flap. Stacy called her first.

"Phyllis, this is Stacy DeFrain."

"Yes, Stacy. You got me thinking back to high school again. There was something edging around my memory but I couldn't quite nail it down. I went through the year book again and it hit me. I was looking at the senior play pictures and there was Twyla. She was in it and the last performance of the play triggered the biggest fight of the year."

"Fight? Twila got into a fight?"

"Oh, did she. She was in the play and it was the last night of a three show run. I had a minor part so I saw the whole thing. The leading man was supposed to pull at Twyla's blouse and tear off a part of it that had been stitched on loosely, and was supposed to come off. Something happened, whether on purpose or accidental, but when this guy yanked at her blouse that last show, he tore the whole blouse and her bra ripped off leaving Twyla exposed from chin to belly button for the six hundred people in the audience to see. Twila froze for a moment, then began sobbing, and rushed off stage.

"Well, when the guy came off Twyla slammed into him, knocking him down. She fell on him screaming and scratching at his eyes and face. Then she jumped up and began kicking him with her hard toed shoes. Two boys had to drag her away. The kid wound up with two broken ribs."

"How does this affect our situation now with Twyla?" Stacy asked.

"Well the boy actor was one who has become quite famous. He's our local boy made good as an actor. He's had some TV series, and a movie or two but he comes back to the Old Globe now and then to take parts. His name is Zack Hunt, you may have heard of him. He's in town now at the Old Globe staring in a Shakespeare play."

"And you think Twila might have her deadly sights set on this actor?"

"It's a possibility. Anyway, I just wanted to tell you. If I hadn't mentioned it and something happened to Zack, I would be a total wipeout."

"Thanks, Phyllis. We'll keep an eye on Zack. You've been a good help."

"Anything else I can do?"

"Oh, one thing. If you know Zack well enough to call him, don't mention anything about Twila. All right? We want everything to be as normal as possible."

"Oh, absolutely. And, no, I don't know Zack that well."

They hung up and Stacy told Cain about it.

"That actor. Yeah, I saw him do something here last year. He's good."

"Should we warn him? Maybe put a man on him around the clock for protection?"

"If we did that, and he is her next victim, she'd spot it a mile away." Cain rubbed his right knee without realizing it and groaned softly. "Damn knee." He doodled on a pad on his desk. Stacy watched him letting him work it out.

"Maybe I should have a talk with Zack Hunt. Tell him about Twyla. He might remember her. He certainly would remember getting beaten up after the play." He thought about it again. "Naw. We'd just bug him and he'd take off for Broadway or Hollywood. He'd cut and run. Actors are notorious for being wimps."

"So what should we do?"

"Almost nothing. For now. If she makes any moves toward the Old Globe, then we set up something. For now we just cool it and keep her under our twenty-four hour watch."

32

FOR THE NEXT two days they tailed Twyla wherever she went. Sometimes she had brown hair, sometimes blonde. Once she was a red head. But the new black Lexus with the plate, 4LOY134, remained a constant. She went to work Wednesday and Thursday. She stayed home both nights and Cain was starting to get flack from his lieutenant.

STACY HAD Friday night off from surveillance and Hal Long had called. They went to a movie, then back to his apartment. She hadn't been there before.

"So how is the watch on your killer going?"

"Slow. Three days now, two days and a night. So far she hasn't done anything illegal – if you don't count the terrible wigs that she wears."

"Wigs, when she goes out on her own?"

"Yes, not in court. Why?"

"Maybe she's buying something to use in her next kill and doesn't want to be remembered."

"We figured that, but so far she hasn't bought anything lethal. Some duct tape, groceries, pills at a drug store, and something at a costume shop that the clerk couldn't remember."

"Why duct tape?"

"Because she used to use plastic cinch cuffs. We found out where she bought them, and she killed the lady who sold the cuffs to her."

"You're sure?"

"We have half a print that matches a hundred percent and the crime lab says it's so good most judges will allow it as evidence."

"Without the ten points?"

"Yes."

"More coffee?" he asked.

She shook her head. He trailed one finger down her cheek to her lips and kissed her.

"Now that is lots better than coffee," she said holding his face close to hers. "Just one problem. I'm getting used to this. It fits. It's comfortable. It's also exciting and sexy and.....and just great."

He watched her for a minute. "I'm feeling the same way. Never anything this good before."

She stood from the couch. "Hey, feel like taking a run?"

"A run?"

"Yeah, I'll race you into the bedroom."

They both ran and decided that it was a tie.

FRIDAY MORNING, the stake out men reported that Twyla slept in. Evidently no court today. She went for a jog along the dry San Diego River, and then out to lunch in Mission Valley Center. Lee and Fernando were with her all the way. They had a quick snack as she ate, then followed her as she drove into town and cruised through Balboa Park, over the tall bridge from Sixth Street, past the Old Globe Theatre, and down to the Museum of Fine Art where the street is blocked off and you have to turn right past the Organ Pavilion. She made the trip twice and Lee called it in.

Cain was waiting in Central.

"Through the park twice? You see her checking out anything in particular? Did she stop and look at the Old Globe? You know about Zack Hunt."

"Yes, we know about him. But she cruised right on by twice. She may have been looking at the Globe, we couldn't tell. But she didn't stop or even slow down. Just telling you what the old recorder sees. She left the park and looks like she's headed back to Mission Valley."

Cain thanked Lee and hung up. He called Stacy and Kevin over and told them about the run past the Old Globe.

"My money is on Zack as her next victim," Stacy said.

"Sounds like a good bet," Cain said.

"So what do we do now, warn Zack?" Kevin asked.

"No, we can't risk it. He'd run and with him would go our chance to catch her with some incriminating evidence, maybe even catch her almost ready to kill. How the hell do we work it?" Cain rubbed his knee.

"We can have people inside the theatre," Stacy said.

"That's easy enough," Cain said. "When would she kill him? Surely not on stage. Not a Lincolnesque hit. Probably not on stage during the show. Maybe after the show."

"Late at night when nobody else is there," Kevin said.

"So how does she keep him there when everyone else leaves?" Stacy asked.

"After a play, the actors go back to their dressing rooms. Zack is the star, so he must have one to himself," Cain said. "Friends and other actors always go into the star's dressing room after a show to congratulate him."

"We need to have somebody in his dressing room," Kevin said.

"And in the lobby and outside," Cain said. "Can't be Stacy, she knows you."

"How do we do this without spooking him?" Stacy asked.

"We go in after the show, with the admirers. And we stay. Then we can warn him. Too late for him to run."

"Okay, we keep tailing Twyla. The minute she heads for the Old Globe, if she does, we set our trap. Kevin, you'll be in the lobby as the last curtain falls. Get back to his dressing room. Find out where it is. Be a fan. Watch for her to come in. Don't let on you know her. She has to take him in the dressing room after the rest of his fans leave."

"Where will the rest of us be?" Stacy asked.

"We go in as soon as the play is over, three of us in the lobby watching for her and back up for Kevin."

Stacy shook her head. "Boss, I don't like it. She can spot a cop a mile away. She proved that in the court room that day. We've got to be outside, close by and wait for a call from Kevin. If they start to close up the place and Kevin hasn't hit us with his cell, then we go in and find him."

Cain nodded. "Yeah, you're right. So Kevin stays in the dressing room after all the other fans leave. When Twyla scoots in at the last minute, we've got her."

"Maybe not," Stacy said. "She's just a fan so far. No threat to Zack, no overt try to harm him."

"Kevin, go down to the Old Globe and brief the top dog there, quietly. Ask to see Zack's dressing room, and see if there's some place you can hide. Then all the rest leave, he's alone and she jumps in and pistol whips him or something, ties him up and starts to kill him. Then you pop out and take her."

"Best Idea I've heard so far," Kevin said. "You guys will be close by for back up."

"Right in your hip pocket," Stacy said.

KEVIN CHECKED out the Old Globe dressing room. He made the excuse that he was writing a mystery about a killing at the Old Globe and he wanted to get his locations right. The manager bought it. Kevin toured the dressing room. Zack wasn't there yet. He found a closet on one side stuffed with Shakespearian type costumes. On the other side was a smaller closet where the star could put his personal clothes.

Kevin decided he'd hide in the larger one with the sliding door open a crack. Yes, he could do it. He reported it to Cain on his cell and went back to the office. If it was tonight, they had a few more preparations to make.

TWYLA STAYED in her condo the rest of the afternoon. Lee and Fernando stayed on their watch on

Twyla. By eight thirty she was still in her condo and Lee was getting worried.

"You guys still think it's tonight and it's the Old Globe?" Lee asked. "She sure hasn't moved a muscle for the past six hours."

"We think it's tonight," Cain said. "She doesn't have to be there until the play is almost over around eleven."

IT WAS JUST after ten that evening when Twyla came out the condo's driveway. Lee had the right direction and followed Twyla's Lexus out of Mission Valley and toward town.

"Okay, boss, she's on the move, heading for the Fifteen, so probably to the park. We'll stay on her."

"We're in Balboa Park down from the Old Globe waiting," Cain said on the cell. "Let us know when she hits Fifth and then comes over the bridge. Kevin is hiding in Zack's dressing room waiting for her."

"Wilco," Lee said. He'd heard the WW II term meaning will comply and loved using it. Lee followed Twyla up Fifteen, turned off on Sixth Street and then across the high bridge into Balboa Park. Lee kept up a running commentary on her progress.

Cain, Twyla, and Constantine, a detective from Team Two, were near the Fine Arts Gallery and saw Twyla's Lexus go by.

"Okay, so far, she's turning past the Organ Pavilion and now taking the turn into the parking lot behind it," Lee said. "I'll park away and keep tabs."

A few minutes later, Lee came on the cell again. "Now I've got her walking toward the Organ Pavilion. She's wearing a rather large blonde wig and big horned rimmed glasses. I'm about twenty feet behind her. A dozen or so people on the sidewalk moving the same way. Now she made a left turn toward the Fine Arts Gallery, on the Old Globe side and is moving down the walk headed for the playhouse. She's carrying a large purse but nothing else. Dressed for the theatre, looks like a blue business type pants suit."

Cain and his two detectives had spaced themselves out around the courtyard of the Old Globe where there were booths selling trinkets and various books and refreshments. Cain saw that the time was ten forty five. One of the plays had just let out. There were two plays on tonight on two of the three stages.

Twyla didn't seem to be in a rush. She stopped at one of the booths and looked at the items, bought something and talked with the volunteer behind the counter.

Stacy and the other detectives mingled with the play goers. Some tarried shopping at the little booths. The theater complex had been explicitly built to resemble William Shakespeare's Old Globe Theatre in old time London. The detectives kept track of Twyla. Stacy hung back since Twyla had seen her at the court that day.

As the after show crowd thinned, Twyla concentrated on the booths. She was stalling and Stacy didn't know why. Maybe she was early on her kill schedule. Stacy was positive now that Zack Hunt would be the target. They had word a half hour ago that Kevin had hidden in a closet in Zack's dressing room. So the trap was set.

Then the main stage play ended and two hundred people streamed out the doors into the courtyard. For a moment Stacy lost Twyla who was swallowed up in the throng. She had her in the blonde wig one minute. Another group of people walked past and when they were gone, so was Twyla.

Stacy put on a search and soon found Cain and Constatine on the same mission.

"Where is she?"

"Don't know," Stacy said. "Last I saw her she had on the blonde wig."

"I saw her after that," Cain said. "She had dumped it and put on a black wig, shorter, still with the big glasses. Where the hell is she and what is she doing?"

33

WHEN HE HAD BEEN THERE that afternoon, Kevin took special note where Zack's dressing room was and how to get there quickly. As soon as the curtain dropped and the curtain calls were finished, he hurried back to the dressing room and was one of the first three there waiting for the star to come. He came with a swagger and wearing his Elizabethan costume, said hello to them, and welcomed them inside this dressing room.

Moments later eight or ten more people crowded into the room and Kevin saw his chance and slipped into the closet when no one else was watching him. He tucked in behind some heavy costumes and made sure his shoes didn't show, then leaned against the back of the closet wall and got as comfortable as he could. Every three or four minutes he'd peek out and watch for Twyla in any one of her three wigs. He'd seen them all by that time.

Slowly the well wishers faded out of the room. When Kevin looked again there was only one woman left talking to Zack Hunt. He couldn't hear what they were saying. Then before he realized what happened, Zack had been backed up against the closet and the door jerked open.

A revolver muzzle pushed out beside Zack's side and the voice came strident and hash.

"Okay you in the closet. Let's see both of your hands right now or I put three rounds right through your gut. Move your hands out, now."

Kevin wanted to surge out after her, maybe take a costume with him and smother her. It had to be Twyla talking, and she had her gun out and trained on him. Slowly he realized he had to do what she said. He should have had his gun out as he waited. He pushed his hands past a fancy ruffled shirt.

"Good, now ease out of there. Zack, come back a step with me and I might not blow your guts out. Get out of there whoever you are."

Kevin came out of the closet slowly.

"Hey, a closet fan," Zack said "Never knew I had any closet fans."

"Shut up, asshole. Zack, get down on your belly on the floor, right now. Move. Do it."

Zack shook his head in dismay. "I really don't know what you're trying to prove, miss."

"Shut the fuck up and drop." She had watched Kevin all the time she yelled at Zack. Now she motioned to him with her gun.

"You too, down beside him. Now."

When both were on the floor, she felt around Kevin's waist, found the holster and took out the Glock pistol.

"Yeah, what I figured, a fucking cop. Both of you

put your hands behind your backs. Now, or I start shooting."

They did. She bound Kevin's wrists together with pre cut strips of the duct tape, then did Zack's. She went back to Kevin and bound his ankles together. Then she did the same to Zack.

She leaned back on her knees and stared at Kevin. "Zack, you got to learn about cops. They're like rattlesnakes. Usually travel in twos. When you find one, there's usually another one close by. So I better move fast. How long will they wait for his signal? No telling. "Zack, do you remember me?"

He turned his head and stared at her. "No."

"The senior play at Hoover High, remember that?"

"Oh, yes. One of the girl's got exposed that last show."

"Yes, you bastard, that was me. Twyla. You ripped my blouse and bra off on purpose while I was at center stage."

"Oh, yeah. I told you it was an accident."

"Bullshit. On purpose." She went to her large black handbag and took out a butcher knife. "I wanted to do this on center stage out there, but no chance now. Do it with a spear. See the irony? But the old fashioned way will have to do." She rolled Zack over on his back, knelt with her knees around his waist and raised the butcher knife.

Kevin had been waiting. He curled his legs up, shifted on his side and drove his pinned together feet at Twyla. They hit her in the side, slammed her off Zack, and she rolled on the floor. She screeched then got back on her knees and waved the knife at Kevin. "You are the second man I kill tonight, asshole," she shouted, then lifted the knife again.

The door rattled. "Zack, let me in. Everyone else has gone just like we planned. Let me in."

It was a woman's voice.

"Sweetheart, you're too late. I've already got Zack naked and panting on his couch," Twyla said. "Go away and let Zack have his fun."

"No, I want to talk to Zack."

"Get the hell out of here, girl, or I'll come out there and kick the shit out of you. You want that. Now beat it."

Twyla watched the door a minute, then lifted the blade again and brought it down. The heavy blade sliced through Zack's costume near his shoulder. Zack screamed.

The locked, thin door, blasted open and Stacy stood there with her Glock out. Twyla dove to the side as soon as she sensed the door blasting inward. She caught up her revolver and fired two shots at the door from where she lay on the floor. One of the slugs hit Stacy in the right shoulder, staggered her backward and spun the heavy Glock from her hand.

Without a wasted motion, Twyla came to her feet running and jolted past Stacy who had scrambled after her gun. Then Twyla was gone.

Cain came from one way and Detective Constantine came from the other way. Stacy sat on the floor and looked at them, her Glock at last in hand.

"You're hit," Cain said. "Your shoulder. Had to be Twyla. Which way did she go?"

Stacy sat there looking at her bleeding shoulder.

Cain asked her again. Stacy pointed down the hallway that angled toward the back of the theatre.

"Where's Kevin?" Cain asked. Stacy pointed into the floor behind her. Cain ran in and cut Kevin free, then called an ambulance for Zack and Stacy.

Outside the dressing room, Stacy headed down the hall. Constantine ran ahead of her and opened a door.

"Nothing back here but a bunch of trees and some brush," he said. "Looks like there's a canyon right down there."

Cain called Lee on his cell and told him to get back to Twyla's car and stop her from driving anywhere. "Shoot her if you have to. We've got the evidence we need."

Stacy and Constantine went around the side of the theatre to the courtyard. It was deserted. They checked the booths, but they were closed.

"Down toward her car," Stacy said and the two detectives ran that way.

Stacy's cell chirped. It was Cain.

"I'll stay with Zack until the ambulance comes. You guys head for her car. Lee should be there watching it. How's the arm?"

"I haven't looked. Forget it. I'm not getting in that ambulance."

They jogged a few steps and Stacy stopped.

Constantine looked at her arm. Her jacket sleeve was dark with blood.

"Walk, we'll walk," Stacy said. "Just a scratch, I can move my right arm and everything."

. . .

IN THE PARKING area behind the Organ Pavilion, Lee slid against a Pontiac thirty feet from the black Lexus with the 4LOY134 license plate and waited. There weren't more than a dozen cars in the huge lot. He saw a shadow dart from the sidewalk into the lot and pause beside a car. Then the shadow moved heading for the Lexus.

Lee lifted his Glock. She was fifty feet away. Too far. He kept against the car and out of sight. The shadow came closer, paused beside a canvas topped jeep and waited. Then it moved again and he could see it had to be Twyla. No handbag, but she seemed to have something in each hand.

When she was twenty feet from her car and thirty feet from him. He called out.

"Hold it, stop right there. Police. Lift both hands over your head."

Her response was immediate with her right hand coming up and blasting three rounds from the Glock. Then as Lee shifted around the Pontiac, she darted to her Lexus and jumped inside. Lee put four rounds toward her driver's side front tire. Thought the got a hit then put two more rounds through the driver's side window.

To his surprise the Lexus started and laid a strip of black rubber on the blacktop as it screamed away from him heading for the exit.

He went to his cell and pushed Cain's auto button.

"She got away in her car. Mine is fifty yards away. She's probably heading for the exit and then south on Park Boulevard so she can get on I-Eight or the Fifteen freeways. Get some help from Dispatch."

Cain called Dispatch and told them the problem.

"We've got a chopper in the air on a burglary up in Kensington, couple of miles from you. Where is she headed?"

"My guess is she'll hit the park exit, go right and get on the freeway, probably go out toward I-8."

"A black Lexus, right?"

"Yes, should have some bullet holes in driver's side window, maybe the door. She won't be driving slow. Send out an APB so all the black and whites will watch for her. The license is four LOT one thirty four."

LEE WAS first out of the lot and headed south on Park Boulevard, then took the ramp for Fifteen. It was the logical choice. It would take her into her neighborhood that she must know better than the rest of town. He found out the chopper was on a search. Couldn't hurt. He got on Fifteen and soon heard the whupping sound of a chopper overhead. It soared down Fifteen headed toward I-8. He couldn't hear the chopper talking on the radio with Dispatch. A short time later he could see the chopper's intense stream light probing the freeway from a hundred feet overhead.

Lee used the car's radio to Dispatch.

"Okay, we've got one suspect car on Fifteen, going well under the speed limit. Probably not our girl."

There was some dead air, then Dispatch came back. "Now we have something. The chopper says he has a Lexus with damage to the driver side window. It's racing down Fifteen, Okay, she's over Eight and turning off on Friars Road east. Short run and now she's taking a right on Mission Center Road." There was dead air time, and then the Dispatcher came back on.

"Okay, now she's doing a right going west on Camino De La Reina. It goes along the back side of Mission Valley Center. Now she's on some side dirt trail that heads toward the river. There are a lot of trees, brush, and water along there."

More dead airtime. Then Dispatch came back on.

"Now she's driven into some trees and the chopper can't spot her, but she hasn't come out. He's doing a small circle of the area, but so far, she's still in there."

Lee was one of the first police cars on the scene. He parked beside the Lexus, noted the bullet holes in the safety glass driver's side window. He drew his Glock and approached the car from a blind spot and made sure no one was inside. Then he began a slow search of the area, pausing to listen.

Three minutes later police cars began arriving. By the time Constantine and Stacy got there, there were a dozen black and whites parked near the trees. They had the Lexus, but Twyla wasn't there. Men with three cell Mag Lites probed into the thick brush that led into a swampy section fifty yards across. The water extended half a block either way. During the winter rains this would be flooded with a torrent of runoff, but now it was sluggish and mostly stagnant.

Sergeant Cain came boiling up a few minutes later.

"Who the hell's in charge here," he bellowed. A uniform told him he was.

"Let's get organized. Anyway to track her from the driver's side of the rig?" the cops said no way, not in the dark.

"So, let's spread out and do a sweep each way along the edge of the water. She's got to be in here somewhere. I want two men at both ends of the water. We don't want her slipping out of here. We've got her penned in. Let's see that she doesn't escape. She's got a issue Glock and another hand gun, so be cautious. Shoot if you have to. Let's move."

Stacy sat in the passenger's side of the unmarked she had come in. Constantine had got her to take her jacket off and looked at the wound. The round had sliced a hole through an inch of her upper arm, missed the bone and exited. He tied it up to stop the bleeding. Stacy thanked him and put her jacket back on.

She moved out with the string of cops heading west along the edge of the water. They were four feet apart and probed every spot where anyone could hide.

Stacy went fifty feet and then stumbled and dropped to the ground. Her head felt a mile wide, and fuzzy. She waved at Constatine and he went on with the search. Stacy sat there ten feet from the water and took deep breaths. She wouldn't pass out. Damnit to God damned hell! she absolutely wouldn't pass out like some weak kneed woman. Her vision cleared and her head felt better even if a little fuzzy and light. She knew she had to sit a while longer.

She heard a sound, like a splash. It was ten feet out in the water. In the faint moonlight a series of small ripples expanded toward her.

Stacy lifted her Glock and studied the area. Would Twyla go into the water to get away from the searchers?

34

STACY STUDIED the ripples and the surface of the stagnate water. She shone her three cell flashlight beam on the area and watched it again. Was there movement under the water? More ripples? No splashes but definitely more ripples. Could it be night feeding fish? Fish in this swamp? Highly unlikely.

She could hear the men searching up and downstream. She had no idea how deep the water out there was. If it were three feet deep it would be enough to hide a body, a person swimming or crawling along the bottom heading for the far side.

Then she saw it, the momentary surfacing of something, a head, the side of a face. She shone the light on it and it vanished.

It had to be Twyla crossing the water. She punched up Cain's number on her cell phone as she took off her jacket and kicked out of her shoes.

"Cain, she's back here near the car. She's going across the water to the far side. I saw her surface, just her face I think it was. I'm going in the water. Get some men back here and some on the far side of the swampy area."

"Stacy, wait for some backup. Don't go in the water alone." She looped her cell around her neck by a cord, dropped her purse on the ground under her jacket and shoes, and stepped into the water. Cold. She took several steps and found the water only up to her knees. When she was ten feet from the shore line she had to struggle over a sunken log, then some brush that managed to survive the drought and surplus of water. Soon the water came up to her waist. She held her Glock out of the water in one hand and her Mag Lite in the other and walked forward, trudging slowly through the water, but probably as fast as Twyla was going. She worked hard at it, puffing and swearing under her breath.

A sharp stone bruised her left foot. She let out a small cry and moved ahead. A voice shouted from behind her.

"Stacy, damnit. I told you to wait." Then she heard splashing behind as Cain moved into the water. Half way across she felt the bottom coming up, and the water getting shallower. She stared ahead, her left hand on the heavy Mag Lite.

There. A form broke the surface, a back, and then a head. It turned and stared behind. The shot came as a surprise. The sound of a .38 revolver jolted into the quiet. Stacy returned two rounds with her Glock. She didn't know if the Glock Twila had would work after being underwater that long. They could be finicky. She fired three more times, not sure if she made a hit. Then the form came upright and splashed through foot deep water in a slow run. Stacy fired again, saw the woman stumble, go down flat in the water, then lift up and yell something before she surged ahead out of the water, into thick brush, and out of sight.

Stacy drove ahead as fast as she could. She heard Cain behind in the water gaining on her.

Suddenly the water was only a foot deep and she could run. She didn't go into the brush where she had seen Twyla enter. The killer could be waiting for her just out of sight. She went in twenty feet downstream and paused listening.

Sounds came from the west, someone crashing brush and moving fast. Stacy went back to the edge of the water where there was no brush, sprinted downstream for twenty yards, then stopped and listened. More brush crashing from downstream, but closer now. She charged ahead thirty yards and stopped.

She heard nothing.

Either Twyla had left the brush or she had stopped. Stacy considered the possibilities. There should be two cops at the end of the water. They would hear Twyla if she crashed out of the brush there. She could have worked out of the brush and toward the solid ground on the far side that led to the roadway behind Mission Valley Center shopping mall. As she considered it, Cain puffed up beside her.

"Wait, damnit. I'm not twenty two anymore. Where the hell is she?"

Stacy told him the options.

"You go down along the water and listen for her. I'll go through the brush and see if I can spot her on the other side. Take it easy and don't get yourself shot again."

He charged into the brush.

Stacy ran ahead along the water. There were only thirty yards now until the water dried up to a trickle and the brush took over. At that point she stopped and listened.

Yes, more brush crashing. She told Cain on the cell and inched her way into the brush. There should be some cops down here somewhere. She didn't want to get nailed by friendly fire.

She listened again. More movement, slightly ahead and downstream. She worked that way silently, never touching her stockinged feet to the ground until she was sure she wouldn't break a twig or make noise. Twenty feet into the brush and she heard another cautious movement ahead. She froze, staring into the darkness. She could see only a dozen feet in front of her.

A shadow moved. A large willow tree loomed out of the darkness just ahead. The shadow had melted into the darkness of the two foot wide trunk. Then the shadow moved again. Was it Twyla or some homeless person who made his home down in this brush?

She had to be certain before she fired.

The figure bent and held its right leg a moment, then stood and looked around. The shadowy form was twenty feet away.

"Twyla," Stacy bellowed.

The figure dropped to the ground and started around the tree trunk. Stacy's two handed shot blasted into the night silence of the swamp. Twyla screamed, and then vanished around the tree trunk. A moment later the .38 fired from the other side of the tree, but was six feet wide of its target.

"Give it up, Twyla. Live to have your day in court. You can even defend yourself."

Three rounds from the Glock came in rapid order. Stacy hit the dirt and edged behind a four inch tree. She hit Cain's cell button. He came on at once.

"Hey boss, Got her twenty feet away behind a large willow tree at the downstream end of the water. You must have heard her Glock. It works fine after its bath in the swamp."

"Hold it right there. Be quiet so if she moves you'll know. Don't get yourself killed. That's an order. I'm moving in from this side of the brush. A big willow tree? Yeah. I can see one sticking out of the tops of the brush. I'm about forty yards away and moving that direction. I'll call Kevin and have him tell the cops down at that end to hold their fire."

Stacy waited. There was no movement that she could hear behind the tree. As she watched, the shadows seemed to darken. She squirmed noiselessly behind a six inch tree and aimed her Mag Lite around the side pointing it at the willow and turned it on. She could see nothing on either side of the tree trunk.

"Give it up, Twyla. There are fifteen or twenty cops out here who would just love to put a round through your head. Live and take your chances with a jury."

"Fuck off you dumb cop. I'm going to vanish into this brush, right past the cops like a ghost. You'll never spot me again."

Stacy frowned. Big talk. But she noticed a catch in the woman's voice. Maybe she was in pain. She should have two rounds in her. One a leg, where was the other one?"

Stacy left the Mag Lite shining on the tree and crawled three feet away from it. It was a calculated move. She was surprised Twyla hadn't tried to kill the light before now.

Two shots jolted into the brush. One slammed through the lens of the Mag Lite blasting it way into the darkness and killing the beam.

Stacy put one round on each side of the willow tree, but heard no response. Nine, she told herself. She'd fired her Glock nine times and had eight rounds left.

Twyla must be moving. Stacy listened and heard some brush crashing some distance away. Could be Cain coming in to get at her from the other side.

The swampy brush returned to soft moonlight quiet.

Then Stacy heard sounds of movement near the willow tree. Twyla's Glock should have nine more rounds in the magazine. Stacy took a deep breath. She knew she had to risk it. Nothing ventured. She got to her knees, to her feet, eased around the tree, then forward, making no noise whatsoever. The ground was damp here, the sticks and small branches not brittle. She stepped cautiously heading directly for the willow. Half way there she stopped and listened. Ahead to the left she heard a branch swish back after it had been bent forward when someone passed. She hurried to the willow and looked around it. Nothing. She should have saved the Mag Lite, although it seemed like a good idea at the time.

She punched up Cain on the cell. "She's left the Willow. I'm here now, so don't shoot. We're both heading downstream."

Stacy heard voices. Male sounds coming from the brush far downstream. It must be the screen of cops beyond the water extending into the brush. Kevin must have positioned them. Twyla would hear them too.

Stacy moved forward cautiously. Twyla would stay in the middle of the brush line. Stacy had no sign or trail just instinct and an occasional sound from the fugitive. What would Twyla do? She knew someone was close behind her. She could hear the men downstream. She must have heard Cain crashing brush on the far side. Where could she go? She was surrounded. A sobering thought came to Stacy. In this situation a woman with Twyla's bent to violence might just decide she wasn't going to be taken alive, and that she would kill as many of her chasers as she could. Stacy didn't want any cops to die that night. She set her jaw, beat down the pain in her arm, and moved forward again.

Twenty feet farther downstream, Stacy saw a gully that the torrent of runoff had carved in the soft river bed soil. It began only a few inches deep but soon went down two and then three feet. The brush had thinned here and there was enough moonlight she could make out the cut. It was a perfect hiding place and cover for Twyla. She couldn't miss it if she were anywhere in this area.

Stacy considered it a moment. She could see how the wash went straight for thirty of forty feet, and then made a sharp turn to the right. If Twila was in there she would be somewhere beyond that turn to give herself maximum protection. But if Stacy tried to walk down the gully, Twyla would be able to see her. She got down on her hands and knees and crawled over to the depression then went downstream. Soon the dirt bank beside her was three feet high and she could walk in a crouch.

Another twenty feet and she came to the turn.

Stacy dropped to her stomach and crawled up to it slowly, then poked her head around for a look and jerked it right back.

She saw Twila in the fading moonlight kneeling in the dirt with the Glock in her right hand resting on the top of the bank and aimed upstream where she expected Stacy to come.

Stacy sat down trying to think it through. She'd heard men in military combat say in the heat of a battle there was no time to think. You reacted with your training taking over and you did the right thing. But now she did have time to think.

She could lean around the corner and pump six or eight rounds into Twyla without warning. She could warn her and if she turned to shoot, then fire. She could wait for the brush beaters downstream to work up closer and spook Twyla.

She could hope that Cain was closing in.

She called him. He came on at once. She explained her situation.

"I'm still just outside the brush, but I don't know how far downstream you two are. I could create a diversion by crashing into the brush on this side. Spook her maybe."

"I think she's hit twice and has decided not to be taken alive," Stacy said. "She probably wants to kill as many cops as she can."

"Don't let that happen."

"Cuts down my options."

"Do what you have to do," Cain said.

Stacy leaned around the corner again and watched Twyla for a moment then eased back. She had to give her a warning. Then whatever happened, happened. It was by the book.

She leaned out around the corner with her Glock aimed at Twyla twenty feet away and called sharply: "Twyla, I have you in my sights. I'm in the gully too. Don't move or I'll shoot."

Twyla jumped, surprised by the voice so close and in the wrong place. Then her face took on a fury and she brought her right hand down from the bank and aimed the Glock down the gully at Stacy.

35

STACY DIDN'T HESITATE a fraction of a second. She squeezed the Glock trigger and saw the round hit under Twyla's right arm. Almost at the same time she felt the impact of Twyla's round jolting into her upper chest. She slumped back for a moment, then edged around the corner of the bank again and saw Twyla leaning against the ledge, the Glock she held still pointed at Stacy. Stacy fired four times. The rounds hit Twyla and jolted her sideways into the dirt. In the faint light Stacy couldn't see for sure, but she didn't think that Twyla moved. She sat down hard in the dirt and caught her cell on the cord around her neck. It rang before she could hit the automatic dial to Cain.

"Yes," she said softly.

"Stacy, are you all right?"

"I don't think so. But Twyla is down and probably dead. I took a round. My chest, up high. Hurts like hell. You better find me. Don't think I...." She coughed and spit up something. "Don't think I can walk. Head's getting all light and fuzzy and my eyes are kind of misty. I can fire a round so you'll know where I am."

"No, don't fire again. I've got you pretty well spotted. I'm coming through the brush. Let me call an ambulance. Hang on there, girl. Hang on."

Stacy knew she should go down twenty feet and look at Twyla. She could hear the men from the south moving up. Then the sound faded and she blinked. She coughed again. Something came up. She didn't have the strength to lean out to spit it. It dribbled out of her moth on her blouse. Red. It was red. What was it? She couldn't remember. Everything so damn fuzzy and getting darker. It wasn't this dark just a few minutes ago. For a moment she thought she was back in her parent's home growing up. She loved the old house, and the furniture, and the books. It was a good place to grow up. Something stabbed into her heart and she shivered, then she couldn't stop shaking. She reached out and held the wall of dirt and slowly the shaking went away.

Her cell phone buzzed. Where did she put it? Where? Oh, yeah, still in her hand. She lifted it up.

"Yes?"

"Stacy, Cain. You hang on there. We're coming in. Some guys from the south may be closer than I am. Don't move. Just take it easy. Keep talking to me."

"What we talk....talk about? Getting darker out. Thought we had a little....little moonlight." She shivered and a knife drove into her chest. "Oh, God, but that hurts. Hurts, Cain. Never been shot before and now twice within an hour. Damn that hurts. Maybe I should lie down and go to sleep. Yes, go to sleep sounds good. No more worries. Go to sleep and dream and then...." She stopped as the pain drilled through her again. It hurt worse than anything she had ever known. A deep, throbbing, numbing kind of pain that you never knew for sure where it came from and then you knew it came from every part of your body.

"You wait for me, DeFrain, and that's an order. You put Twyla down. That's good. Now we take care of you. Ambulance should be here in about five more minutes. You just wait."

"Stacy?" somebody asked. She hadn't heard the uniform come up. He knelt beside her, Looked at her chest, and then carefully lay her down in the trench. He put his jacket under her head.

"Stacy. I'm Wolford. You just rest and the medics will be here damn soon. I'll be back in a minute. Want to check on Twyla."

"You'll be back?" she asked, barely able to hear her own voice.

"Absolutely. Just take me a minute."

She wasn't sure if she saw him go. The pain came again and she cried out in alarm. Wolford rushed back beside her and held her hand.

"Hey, detective, just hang on here. Twyla is stone cold dead. We've got the paramedics coming. I can hear a siren off to the left somewhere."

Cain knelt down beside Stacy and caught her other hand. "Okay, DeFrain, you're relieved of duty for tonight. You get some rest and report back when you feel like it. You hear me? Our team can't function without you. I left two uniforms back by the road to direct the ambulance in here. They can drive almost up to the brush. Have you out of here in no time. You just hang with us for a few minutes."

Stacy tried to stifle it, but another jolt of pain

brought a gasp and a screech from her. The pain slanted down her torso all the way to her toes and felt like a hot poker dragging over her skin then boring a hole through her flesh. Sweat beaded her forehead. Cain had put a jacket over her but still she shivered.

"Coming through," a new voice said. Cain and Wolford backed away as the three paramedics moved into the scene.

FOUR HOURS LATER, Cain and the three other detectives in his team paced the waiting room at UCSD Hospital Emergency Room. A dozen more cops waited in the hall to see what would happen to Stacy. Most of them had been on the hunt for Twyla. Cain pretended to read a magazine. Lee paced the length of the room and then came back. Kevin sat with his head thrown back but his eyes were wide open. Fernando worked furiously on a cross word puzzle book he had been using on the stakeouts.

"What's a four letter word meaning the end of an era?" he asked. Cain waved it off. Kevin shrugged. Lee frowned trying to think of the answer, at last shook his head.

A cell phone buzzed. Cain looked at his, then dug Stacy's out of his pocket.

"If you're calling Stacy, she's tied up right now."

"I heard. This is Detective Hal Young. How's she doing? What did the doctor's say?"

"A nurse told us Stacy took the bullet in the upper part of her lung and it collapsed. They got that reinflated and now they're working on finding the bullet fragments. It hit a bone and shattered. The nurse said they treated the arm wound and there's no problem there. She said Stacy has a good chance."

"That the best they can say?"

"So far. She's been in surgery for almost three hours. We should know something soon."

He gave Cain his cell number. "I'd appreciate whatever you can tell me. Give me a call. I'm on a stakeout otherwise I'd be there. Let me know."

THE NEXT AFTERNOON Cain sat in the critical care room and watched Stacy breathe. The doctor had come by and looked at her chart, checked three monitors hooked up to her, then tested her pulse, and listened to her breathe.

He smiled. "Oh, yes, this little lady is doing fine. I think we found all of the shards of lead. We closed up the tear in her lung but that won't completely heal for two months. She's over the hump now. All she needs is time."

Later Stacy woke up just long enough to look at Cain and try to work up a smile, but before it bloomed, her eyes drifted closed and she slept again. As Cain settled back in his chair, Hal Young came into the room.

"My turn on watch," he said. "I had to lie like a lieutenant to get here, but I made it. She doing better?"

Cain told him what the doctor had said. "you have my cell number. Anything happens, you let me know pronto." Cain stood, stretched. "Now I have one hell of a big after action report to do, so I better get with it. Then I talk to the DA and we show her the evidence on the five kills and give her the school mates and we should clear all of those homicides. Thanks to Stacy."

"She'll be riding a desk for a while?"

"When she gets out and is fit for duty. Then they'll have the shooting board, but nobody is going to even think of voting against her." Cain nodded, lifted his right leg, and stretched the knee.

"Hey, Young. You be damned good to our lady here. She's a mighty important part of our team."

Young smiled. "Sergeant, I intend to do just that."

THANK YOU

Thank you for taking the time to read *Scream Vengeance*. If you enjoyed it, please consider telling your friends or posting a short review. Word of mouth is an author's best friend and much appreciated.

Thank you.
Chet Cunningham

ABOUT THE AUTHOR

Cunningham was born in Nebraska, grew up in Oregon, worked in Michigan, and went to college in New York City. He graduated from Pacific University in Forest Grove, Oregon with a BA in journalism, and after his hitch in the Army he received his MS degree from the Columbia University Graduated School in Journalism in New York City in 1954.

Cunningham made his home in San Diego, California and was a prolific writer of both novels and nonfiction books right up until his passing.

www.ingramcontent.com/pod-product-compliance
Lightning Source LLC
La Vergne TN
LVHW100515110826
845146LV00002B/645